The Sara Chronicles

Book 6

Into Darkness

We Go

Up Above and Down

Below

Laura Hughes

Chapter One

All was quiet on the surface of the worlds, as the very last living, non-evil life-form landed gingerly on the ground. The small brown bird was breathing heavily, thoroughly exhausted from evading the large dark mutant versions of its species, the ones that had eaten all the real birds weeks ago. Having had no trees to land on, the winged creature had been flying almost non-stop for days now. The small areas of brush it had hidden under from time to time were gone and it sensed that death was near. No food, no safe places, and no other animals visible for weeks, it was only a matter of time before it too was gone.

Pecking at the surface in a vain search for any form of food, the tiny animal looked nervously around the barren field, fearing attack from any direction. Too weak to attempt to take flight again, the bird glanced from side to side anxiously as it tried to find something to give it strength, a chance to survive. Scratching halfheartedly at the broken and pitted earth yielded absolutely nothing for the animal's efforts; the dry rotten soil held nothing worth eating. All living nutrients had retreated far beyond the surface, well out of the creature's reach, and the dirt it had managed to break through with its beak tasted foul. The earth beneath the sparrow's thin legs trembled beneath the weight of something very large moving a few miles distant. It stood still, small heart beating rapidly, waiting for whatever was heading toward it.

The scent of death and decay covered the earth and this one natural winged creature's clean soul would surely attract a destructive evil entity soon. The presence of anything that wasn't like the bad things seemed to attract them pretty fast, they liked to kill and could smell a pure object from miles away. As if to confirm its greatest fear, a flash of lightning appeared in the sky just a few feet from the animal, followed by a movement in the dark clouds above, indicating that it had been discovered and something was rapidly approaching to claim it. As fast as it moved, something else moved faster still. Before the darkness could approach, a shifting in the air sent a gentle breeze to ruffle the bird's feathers and a shimmering white light settled over the frail form, bringing a total change in the bird's behavior. The tiny little brain housed in its skull was thinking very non-bird-like thoughts, while another presence settled inside its small frame, changing the manner in which it surveyed its surroundings.

With interest, the winged creature watched the large hulking structures now standing in place of the beautiful mountain ranges that had been here for thousands of years. The massive stone landmarks had all been crushed beneath the constant enemy assault. They had been replaced by buildings composed of crushed human and animal remains bonded together to form dull grey blocks piled hundreds of stories high. Instead of those blocks, however, the sparrow saw the shapes of all the dead things used to make them. It could identify each and every one of the lost lives, man, woman, and animal within the square clumps that formed the structures. The names of the victims were all burned in the animal's memory as clearly as the day they were created because the entity inside the bird had known them personally.

The lumpy, misshapen buildings towered over the barren land around it, casting eerie shadows on the ground. Gaping holes appeared in random spots in the front of the structures, some large, some small; they might serve as either windows or doors, but their location did not make sense. There was no rhyme or reason to the builder's technique. In fact, it was a miracle that these hulking masses were standing at all. The base of some of the buildings looked far too narrow to support the top half and yet they stood solidly in place, not moving in the slightest when the ground beneath them shook constantly.

Hideous shadows moved back and forth in the dull green light shining from the building's windows. The shapes standing inside and looking outward were twisted and unnatural to any living thing. Nothing down here was really alive anyway; they were all just poor animated imitations of Iam's creations that had managed to defy logic and exist in a place they should not.

Pin-sized eyes beaded up with moisture, in a show of emotion that wasn't natural for the animal. It all looked so different. This place was very familiar to the spirit inside the bird; it had been one of the first places created when the worlds were made. It now bore no resemblance to the original design. The destruction had looked bad from a distance, but up close, the feel of the injured planet really hit home. Gone was the fresh air and the clean, life-sustaining soil was laced liberally with decay. All the water had either dried up or been replaced with oily goo not fit to drink. The beautiful golden sun that had been one of Iam's greatest gifts to the planet was covered up by dark clouds and the bloated bodies of mutated flying creatures. Even though it had been understood that this was inevitable, it was still heartbreaking to see the results of the change in power.

Closer inspection of the battered landscape was interrupted by a shimmering wave of powerful energy moving through the air. Whatever traveled overhead was going fast. The force it generated was visible against the sky as a silver wave pushed at the black clouds, allowing the sun to highlight the darkened sky with a brief flash of yellow. That small amount of light was just bright enough to reveal a red object streaking through the sky in the middle of the silvery gust of air. The red thing looked large, even from this distance, and it raced across the sky like it had been shot from a cannon. The unidentified projectile landed about a mile away from the sparrow who had received enough strength from the spirit occupying its body to leave the ground. Renewed and full of energy, the bird took flight with no fear of attack from anything above or below. Nothing was going to touch this winged creature, for now it had an unearthly light about it that every beastly, evil thing in the area shied away from.

A swiftly moving wind carried the small body closer to the thing that had hit the ground with a heavy thump. Dirt split and flew into the sky from the force of the impact, causing the winged beast to dodge the flying debris. A few fancy evasive maneuvers later, it swooped down to circle over the item, studying it with interest. The pure creature had no fear, just a sense of satisfaction as a shrill scream sounded from the object below it. The situation in the worlds was still bad, but this one event made the occupying spirit quite happy. The tiny sparrow's eyes blinked, and if a beak could have formed a smile, it certainly would have.

After one last pass over the object on the ground, the clean, living animal was rewarded with a way out of this nightmare place. As a thank you for the use of its body and the desire of the spirit to save this true living thing, a shining white doorway opened in the sky immediately in front of the bird. The animal quickly flew through it to safety, narrowly avoiding a stream of flame sent from the ground. The bird's escape was accompanied by another scream of anger from the creature below as it disappeared into the portal.

Chapter Two

Finola moved restlessly around the cramped dark space she and Eric had been hiding in for days, keeping busy by tending to her plants and talking to Eric through their mental connection. She had to have things to do or she would soon go crazy. Even though Eric had shared his excellent night vision with her, allowing her to see everything around her clearly, she still hated the dark. Years of abuse endured at the hands of foster families had created this fear of darkness. Finola hated how those bad memories could make her weak and tremble in fear of the crawling things that were hidden here. It was a shame the fear couldn't have disappeared when she found out who she really was.

Ever since she learned that she was a Keeper, wonderful memories of a time before she had occupied this body had started coming to her. She and Eric had been part of a large and loving family of spirits. They had been formed from the intense joy and loving bonds that existed between Iam's original creations. The first Keepers had been given the honor of creating something special of their own; it was a gift from Iam for the years they had been faithful and loyal guardians of his worlds. They became parents by combining parts of themselves to form a soul that was totally unique and blessed by Iam.

She remembered that she had been drawn to Eric from the beginning, long before they had been given human forms. They had spent many lifetimes moving around as objects of pure light, watching the most wonderful developments in the worlds below. They watched the originals leave the heavens when they were called to care for the living things on the surface, but the children hadn't come down until much later. When they did, they had been separated, and the memories were gone for a while.

The skies above the earth had been their playground and while she was in paradise, she had been aware that things were a bit different below them. From high above, they had witnessed changes in the beings their parents cared for, while the scenes beneath them shifted over time and life got uglier. While she didn't remember everything, there was a lot she did, and the knowledge she carried was wreaking havoc with her current form because the two didn't go together.

She was so much wiser and stronger than a fourteen-year-old girl, now that her history as a special soul was known, but still had memories of a time when she had been at the mercy of stronger, older humans. It made her ashamed to think that for someone who had been given so much power, who had lived so long in places that defied explanation to the ordinary mind, could still let the actions of mere mortal beings affect her so strongly. Her memories of greatness should have erased the weakest moments of her youth in this immature, vulnerable body.

Finola's early human life had been spent at the mercy of cruel, heartless people who locked her in dark places with rats and bugs as punishment for being different; a burden they were forced to endure because of the money they received for keeping her. She had this in common with Sara, mistreatment by those who were supposed to be caring for her and keeping her safe from Braccus's ever-searching eye. Thanks to Rianna's goodness, she and Sara had both been given a brief glimpse of family life, and how a parent's love should feel. After that, four all too brief years of somewhat normal living, her life had changed so dramatically, she could hardly believe it ever happened.

Sara and Rianna were both gone now; Sara died to continue a quest for some stupid object that was important to Braccus, and Rianna, well, she may as well be dead. The last time she had seen Rianna, she was little more than a mindless puppet used by Braccus to try and kill Finola and her companions. There was nothing left of the woman she had known and loved, Braccus had taken over, pushing her soul out and leaving her empty body as a painful reminder that he had won again. The remaining Keepers, including herself, were all very new at their jobs, now totally separated, and with no mental connection to each other at the moment; they were supposed to save all the people left in the worlds. She and Eric were part of the rescue efforts, but they had failed; she had failed.

Lost in thoughts that only served to depress her further, Finola felt a gentle nudge at her mind as Eric tried to get her attention once again. Latching on to their invisible bond, he sent a soft kiss to her cheek from a few yards away, ensuring she was distracted from her depressing thoughts. He was using their mental connection to show her his love, and for a second it worked wonderfully. As scared as she was, Finola couldn't help but smile, he was the only reason she wasn't running back into the central cavern and letting all those horrible people have an outbreak of poison ivy in their beds or covering them with prickly stickers. She couldn't believe that they had torn up the wonderful living things she had made for them; it made her sick to her stomach to know that her plants had been destroyed so needlessly.

Her urge to help these people had been so strong that she had accidentally made all the plants grow down here while she was asleep one night, and that's what started this mess. When the refugees had walked out to find healthy growing things where before it had been just moist, cold rocks, they had freaked out and listened to that horrid man named Rodney. Rodney had been the one who set them into action, urging them to kill all the things she had created. He had called what she made for them evil! She had done them a favor, and they had repaid her with destruction and hatred.

Finola had felt so much pain when the roots were torn from the ground and stomped beneath the villager's heavy feet. Worse than that, the look on Eric's face as he rushed to her side made her feel so guilty. She had blown their cover; they had been supposed to lay low and gain the people's trust by letting certain special people introduce them into their society.

These gifted people would know what Keepers were and would have the ability to convince terrified citizens who had been forced underground

12

by hordes of hideous monsters that killed their friends, neighbors, and family members, that it was safe to trust these strangers with their survival. They hadn't met any gifted people before she had made everyone want to hang her and Eric from one of her newly made trees. They were hated and feared now and may never get the chance to get through to the panicked survivors they had been sent here to help.

Eric listened to Finola mentally berate herself again and he couldn't take it anymore. While it was wonderful to be with her, sharing precious memories of a time before they walked the worlds, it was also awful to relive those moments that had created this fear in her. He stopped her by reminding her of who they were and what they needed to do. "I promise that we will get out of here," Eric said softly. He noticed that the calls for them to come out and turn themselves over to those in the area beyond the thorny bushes had stopped a few hours ago. It was quiet now, too quiet.

Eric had silenced the shouted threats the scared group was making so that Finola could not hear them. But he had continued to listen for the first day or two as they tried to break through her barrier of prickly plants. Many failed attempts to get to them were accompanied by screams of pain and frustration until they finally gave up. Yet, even after they stopped trying to come in, Eric still heard voices raised in anger and a few quieter ones that seemed to make the louder ones stop altogether. For the first time since he had been aware of his gift, he could not hear what the softer voices were saying. This was unusual, and he didn't know quite what to make of it. As a result, he had lost the ability to eavesdrop on the refugees and was clueless as to what was going on in the other area. It might be necessary to wander into the larger cavern to find out what they were doing out there, which would be dangerous. Eric didn't want to stir up trouble, but, while they were doing quite well, the displaced villagers might not be.

Unlike the refugees in the main cavern, he and Finola had plenty of food. The love of his life had kept busy by cramming this small space with every type of edible plant she could think of, ensuring that they never went hungry. Everything growing down here thrived despite the lack of sunlight and fresh air. It was like whatever they needed to survive was coming from this one young girl. The walls around them were covered with grapevines that hung down like large curtains dripping with plump purple fruit. They each had comfortable sleeping areas covered in thick layers of moss with blankets made from another kind of fluffy soft plant that kept the chill away at night.

Their sleeping areas, located at the base of a thick apple tree, were a few steps away from a garden full of lettuce, carrots, cucumbers, corn, and peas. Any area that didn't contain some kind of food plant was covered in a soft Bermuda grass, so wherever they went it was like walking on carpet. A few feet from the garden, down the narrow corridor that joined their little hideaway to the main cavern, were rows of thick thorny hedges. The hedges went five rows deep making it impossible for any ordinary human to pass through. Eric and Finola were safe from the refugees but unable to move from their hiding-place.

Safety was nice, but this had to end soon; there was too much to do. They hadn't spoken to the other Keepers in days and there were other worlds they had to visit. Out of the seven worlds Iam had made, the groups of Keepers had only made it to three, leaving the rest with only the bare minimum protection of Alice's shields over the portal openings. All these places would need to be provided with food, supplies, and given instruction in protecting themselves from the enemy. There were only a few Keepers to go around and he didn't see how they would all get to the other worlds if they were all occupied like this.

In order to get control of a situation that had obviously gone totally wrong, Eric was thinking that they might have to do something they had been hoping to avoid. He and Finola were going to have to go back into the other cave area and reason with the people in there. Of course, she was listening in to his thoughts and answered right away.

"I can't," Finola said, looking at him with the aid of his excellent night vision. "I'm just a fourteen-year-old girl that they didn't think twice about attacking even though I made the impossible happen. They found out that I could make plants appear from nothing and it didn't intimidate them in the least bit. They tore up my plants with no fear that we would be able to stop them. We have taken on larger and meaner enemies than them, but only because we used our powers. We can't do that with these people, so how are we going to get through to them now?"

Eric saw the stricken look on Finola's face and wished with all his heart that he could make it all go away. "We need to check on them, make sure they're alright. You know we have to," he said. Even as these words came out of his mouth, Eric knew she was aware of this too. It wasn't that she didn't want to help; it was that she wanted to be in control of this situation somehow. This small form that she occupied hardly represented what she was capable of, and she didn't like it. She wanted them to think twice before approaching her as easily as they had before, ready to do harm to someone they felt they could easily overpower.

Eric's mind went back over all that they had shared over the past couple of days, trapped in here, he didn't like the fact that they were hiding any better than she did. It started him thinking about what they were actually capable of, all the gifts that Iam had given them and the limits that were currently placed on them by the forms they now occupied. While they stood looking at each other in the blackness of their surroundings, they silently appraised the things they had been able to do as free roaming spirits. Brown eyes met yellow, knowing that a decision had to be reached. They were trapped in a tiny corner with the clock ticking against them. Evil was gaining ground with every second they didn't act. But they weren't sure what to do.

The silence dragged on for a few minutes while they went over the possibilities of their next actions. The thread that bound them together hung in the air,

16

appearing as swirls of gold, red, and blue, each one a memory of a time long ago. Their time as spirits had been free of restriction, but these frail living forms had their limits and it was very frustrating to have to play by the rules imposed upon them.

At first, the idea came to them as a wild, combined thought, springing into being and growing as they stared wide-eyed at each other. What if they could draw on their connection from a time before life began and will these mortal forms to be what they wanted them to be? In order to do what they had in mind, they would have to try something they hadn't considered was even possible for these human bodies to accomplish. Teenagers were not as impressive as older adults, so maybe it was time to change that part of themselves. The plan was risky and terrifying, but they were desperate enough to try anyway.

Nodding at each other solemnly, both young Keepers reached out and held hands before a bright light encompassed them both. Flashes of electricity arced through the air followed by a fine mist while they both reached for the power they had held in check. Finola and Eric tried to use their desire for change to accomplish the one thing they felt would give them an edge when going back to face the people that had driven them into hiding.

I hope this works, was Eric's last thought as they melted into the light.

Chapter Three

Elsewhere, trapped in her own little nightmare, Alice looked at the two young men sitting across from her. These men had just appeared, and she had been less than friendly at first. She regretted that now; she had scared the one named Ray pretty badly. In her defense, Ray had tried to capture her, and she wasn't going to let that happen. She had sent him some place very unpleasant. He had seen the evil things that hung out there and were never meant to be seen by the ordinary person. When she had come to her senses, she felt badly enough about it to take the worst of the visions from his mind, leaving just enough to make him think twice about approaching her like that again.

The situation then calmed down enough for the three of them to sit together in a tense kind of peace treaty. The two large men were sitting wide eyed, every move made cautiously so as to not startle the slender young woman in front of them. It was truly a strange sight. They were a little bit afraid of her, Ray more than Steven, but then his experience with her was quite different then his friend's. Steven saw a powerful girl pushed to her limit and, while he had a certain necessary fear about dealing with her, he found himself liking her quite a bit. He didn't have the insight his brother Jacob had, but he knew a good person when he saw one. He had seen plenty of the other kind in the past couple of years roaming around as a peacekeeper with his brother.

In the darkness of the cave system she had traveled to with Randall, Alice tried not to show her new companions that she was both exhausted and terrified. As far as these guys knew she was an all-powerful Keeper sent here to save their people, even if she felt like anything but that. How impressive she must look sitting on the cold stone floor with droopy eyes, messy hair, and a tear-stained face. She was miserably alone without her precious Randall, and without a clue as to where he had gone. Yet she was still responsible for taking care of, not only these two men, but everyone else in the underground refuges. The burden of it all was getting so hard to carry. Her heart ached for her boyfriend and all they had gone through in the past few weeks. She was terrified that nothing would be okay for her again or the people she wanted to save. Starting out on this journey to the land of Yalder with Randall, she had remained invisible while he bonded with the refugees. It had seemed a good idea at the time, as the Yalderites were all tall, fair, redheaded people, much like Randall, and she was shorter with brown hair. She didn't want to startle anyone with the difference in her appearance. After all, they were trying to blend in, so she let him mingle while she watched and waited.

Randall had tried to find the special people who would help make a smooth transition from suspicious strangers to trusted allies. Obviously, that had not happened, and everything went wrong. Now Randall was gone, abducted by an angry old woman and the small mob that hung on every word she uttered, and it had all happened while Alice was asleep.

When she woke up, Randall was missing, and she had been running around frantically trying to find him ever since. He wasn't dead, that's the only thing she knew for certain. She didn't feel a void, like he had been permanently lost, but she definitely felt that something was blocking their connection. Under any other circumstances she would have been able to find him anywhere, but the dead things were interfering. She was afraid she would have to go into the shadowy in-between place where they dwelled and make them stop.

She had hesitated in taking this action, knowing that it was dangerous to seek out the dead things, but it had to be done. She had done it once before. Having been toe-to-toe with one of Braccus's shadowy followers had not been pleasant. These things were ugly, filthy feeling, and able to crawl into a living or non-living body and take over. The only thing that seemed to make sense was to call these things "its" because they had never been a someone; they existed but had never been alive. She remembered "it" saying that its kind required bodies to get through the portals that she was protecting with her shields.

One of the "its" had actually taken over Randall for a short time before she had mustered the strength to get the better of it. Something inside her head told her that she could actually touch the horrid, half-formed figure with the yellow eyes and pull out its essence. So now she knew it was possible to get rid of them, but that didn't mean it had been easy, or that she was eager to repeat the experience. Swallowing hard to keep the bile from rising in her throat, Alice made sure that the two young men with her were safe, wrapping them in a protective bubble before she phased out of her body to wander into the place she dreaded to go. Leaving Steve and Ray to stare in dismay at her hollow body, Alice entered the darkened hole she had created in front of her.

As soon as she slipped through the opening, she felt sick, senses bombarded with the worst sensations she had ever experienced. Extreme sadness, frustration, shame, and rage. It was as if every bad feeling that could have been imagined was hanging out here in the inky black space she had moved to. She was the brightest thing around, appearing like a candle flame that, of course, attracted bad spirits like moths to the light. They were drawn to her out of anger at her presence where they felt she didn't belong.

The emotions here were so overwhelming that she momentarily staggered beneath the force of them. The distressed look on her face was enough to raise an amused snicker from somewhere to her right. Alice froze, settling her face in a neutral expression, waiting for the hidden things to attack, expecting that she would have to fight her way through at any second.

But those inner voices were there again, the ones that had spoken to her the first time she fought with the dead. The clean-feeling presence in her head urged her on, reminding her of what she had already accomplished and what she could still do. The added support had the desired effect, making her feel so much stronger. Alice straightened her slumping shoulders and, after a few more steps into

the darkness, she stood still and raised her hands, uttering a two-word command. "Come here."
She said these words with authority, not giving the bad-feeling entities a chance to latch on to her fear. She had the ability to make them do what she wanted and that's all she was going to concentrate on. Hissing and screaming answered her call to action. There was also a loud scraping noise as if something heavy were being dragged along a stony surface. The things that only had substance in this place were approaching as they were told, fighting every step of the way.
"Be quiet, and come here," she quietly repeated, refusing to raise her voice above the spirits dramatic sound effects. The voices in the back of her head kept saying, *you can do it, you are a Keeper. They must obey you.*
As if to confirm what she was beginning to realize was true, she saw at least ten of the shadowy forms reluctantly dragging themselves to the edge of her light. The blue-black swimming forms were highlighted by her brightness, and she felt rage radiating from them as they were forced to follow her direction.
"Whatever you are doing to interfere with my connection to Randall, you will stop it right now." Alice tried not to let the many sets of yellow eyes glaring at her throw her in the least bit. The shifting shadows wavered at the edge of her light; swirling around and around until they merged into a very large form that hovered above her in one last attempt to intimidate the Keeper that they had no choice but to obey.

Going with the voices inside her head, she chose to trust her instincts; she raised her arm, shining a light directly at the swirling black cloud, forcing it to break apart. The thin black puffs of evil feelings and thoughts flew around Alice as she stood her ground. "I command you to stop and tell me how you're keeping me from connecting with Randall."
One of the "its" stopped moving and hung directly in front of Alice. A soft child-like voice came to her from inside the cloud. It sounded like the voice attached to the first entity she had encountered days before. "We are not keeping you from talking to that boy!" The last word referring to Randall was spoken with contempt, spat from its lips as she made it stay put and talk to her.
"Well, not us exactly," It giggled like it was telling a very funny joke; amused at only relaying part of what she needed to know. The laughter was cut off abruptly when she aimed a ray of light at the thing across from her. "It is the ones that took the bodies," the thing said reluctantly, spitting, and hissing at her through a half-formed mouth visible through the blackness as a red and brown tangle of tissue. It was powerless to resist answering her, but that didn't mean it wasn't going to try and mislead her if it could. So it paused, stuttered, trying to keep the truth from slipping through its lips, trying to find another way to avoid giving her the answer she wanted. Yellow eyes flashed at random intervals while the shadows struggled to become solid, fizzling out again when they failed to do so.
"What do you mean? The ones that took the bodies," Alice asked, every hair on the back of her

neck suddenly rising up as if she were standing in a foot of snow dressed only in a pair of shorts and a T-shirt. Shaking off her dread, she pushed on, determined to get the results she wanted. That horrid half-formed goon was going to answer her, even if what it said was not going to make her happy.

"We are not able to get through your barrier without some kind of form, you know that," it spoke teasingly, drawing out each word as it struggled to find a way to evade her questions again. She sent out wave after wave of energy, forcing the truth out in to the open. Gurgling sounds filled the air around the Keeper as she choked each word out of the shadows; forcing it to continue when it would have stopped speaking to her altogether.

"Your kind crossed through the doorway?" This was a question she didn't have to ask because she knew that it could not lie to her and it had pretty much admitted that there were a few of them sharing the underground spaces with the survivors.

"We passed through with those that weren't even aware they were dying. Distracted as they were about their injuries, they left themselves wide open to us. We finished what the armies started, they were pretty badly hurt, we healed their bodies, but stopped their hearts and slipped inside. The strange thing is though, their spirits seemed to be hanging out in there too, convinced that they are still alive and in control. When they escaped down here, they brought us along. We are having so much fun making them do exactly what we want, things they

25

would be ashamed to know they had done. And guess what else?"

The air was filled with the sound of a childish giggle. "They have your friend, and I'll bet you wish you could find them."

"Isobel and her followers are dead?" Alice raised her voice, effectively drowning out the giggles that floated around her. A twist of her hand turned the laughter into screams of frustration and anger as she waited for the answer.

"Most of them are; a few are not. The living ones are having a hard time figuring out what's going on and, for the time being they are allowed to live. Things will change soon. Do you think you can find them before we let the rest of our kind in?"

"I can now," Alice answered with a small smile on her face. "Because you are going to lead me directly to them." This she knew with certainty as her eyes focused on what ordinary people and even most Keepers never got to see: the misshapen forms lurking in the hidden places. Even when the darkness was visible to the living, it only showed itself as black clouds, but she saw them clearly. She saw faces pitted with deep holes that worms occasionally squirmed out of, slithering down bony cheeks into torn lips lined with pointy teeth so impossibly twisted that they would never be good for anything but ripping and tearing its own flesh, or whatever you called that stuff that covered it. It had substance only to her, and that's how she was able to kill what had never been alive.

"We are not, we cannot," they screamed in protest, despite the fact that they knew they would have to do what she told them. "We have been promised the rest of the bodies when they have moved back into the cave with the others. Your boyfriend has to be disposed of before we get what we were promised and that means you cannot interfere, we will not let you!"

Even as it was said, they knew it was useless to try and resist. But one shadow made a concentrated effort to change the inevitable result anyway. Rushing toward the light, as if it would be able to get close; the blackness tried to get into the Keeper's body and make her stop controlling them. The swirly threads of darkness were highlighted by her brightness when they made contact with it. Two arm-like appendages reached for her, disappearing when they got too close to the light and reappearing on her other side as it looked for a way in. Snapping sounds accompanied each pass of the entity. Whenever it tried to touch the light, it was forced back with bursts of color that rivaled the most impressive fireworks displays Alice had ever seen. Stupid determination had it approaching again and again until the Keeper got fed up and reached her hand out to grab hold of it. She took control, tying it to her with what amounted to a leash of light.

The string that bound them together was another extension of her and caused the dark thing a lot of pain. It howled and begged to be set free, promising to do what she asked one minute and threatening to kill her as soon as it found a body it could use the next. Squeezing the string until all it could do was whimper; Alice turned her thoughts to returning to her body, trying not to show this thing she was stretching her powers so thin that she felt dizzy. Her body, where she left it, was drenched in sweat. Then, despite its pain, the creature she controlled began to laugh loudly, its companions joining in until the in-between space vibrated with unpleasant sound. A strong sense of danger filled Alice's head. Her inner senses were screaming that she wouldn't have to go far to seek out the enemy, it was coming back here where she was vulnerable, and her two human companions would be at the mercy of them if her shields fell. With a sharp pull on the string that bound her to the "it", Alice abandoned the murky place she'd slipped into and let herself fall back into her body. Crawling back to the two young men who had been watching her shimmer in and out of sight for twenty minutes now, Alice did her best to place herself between them and the oncoming trouble.

Chapter Four

Two figures tumbled backward into the nothingness that was the in-between place. Loud screams vibrated through the air while globs of red material went flying around them. Slowly drifting in defiance of gravity, the spray of wet stuff narrowly missed the pair, falling instead on several areas of white puffy clouds which it quickly ate through to fall like rain, dissolving in a small explosive puff further down in the atmosphere.

Strong arms tightened on his companion, joining together just beyond the slender body that fell on top of him. Sheer terror and rage were making the man's breath come out in gasps while he struggled with the form he clung to so tightly. He had won. For the first time in a long time, he accomplished just what he had set out to do and felt very good about it.

All those times when he had promised himself that he would not let her down but had done so anyway, ran through his head, and he cried tears of relief at not having to deal with that type of failure again. Thomas helped Sara into a seated position while shaking the goo from Braccus's body off his hand. His girlfriend called a small cloud over to clean the destructive mess off his skin; which was already bubbling. A fact that amazed him, because he knew this wasn't real. Both he and the red stuff were things that didn't exist anymore. In fact, this whole place was an illusion created by powerful beings to simulate life.

Originally the good souls had manipulated the elements here, making it a wonderful place full of dreams and wishes fulfilled, but this part had been taken over by very bad things. This section of the Afterworld was just another cheap and warped version of Iam's creations, corrupted by a being that was so jealous of his creator that he took every opportunity to change what came from him or his people. Once Braccus started to meddle with things, the evil had a ripple effect, spreading wider, wreaking devastation with the things he produced. In this cursed place, Thomas had watched as the most important person in his life had, once again, voluntarily thrown herself into the thick of danger. She had blended with an evil entity intent on dragging both her and the thing they had originally come here to get back into the worlds he had ruined. He had only just been able to reach into that very distasteful meat chunk form that Braccus had made of himself and pull the very reason for his life and death back out into his arms.

Reaching into Braccus's body to retrieve Sara's filmy soul had been very difficult. The darkness he had encountered once again was all too familiar to him. For just a second, he could have sworn he felt pain from the body he had just torn into. A sharp ripping sensation traveled through him at the very same moment he'd plunged his fist into the chest cavity that carried its precious cargo. Once he had recovered her soul though, the pain was gone, passing through the portal into the living lands along with the very solid form he had attacked. Considering his past encounters with Braccus, this

30

was both surprising and disturbing; he wasn't going to fall back into this trap. It seemed that both alive and dead, he still had some kind of freaky bond with Braccus; a bond he was going to have to constantly guard against.

Burying his head against her cinnamon-scented hair, Thomas promised himself that the darkness in him would never again be the cause of her problems. He was going to be smarter, stronger, and more resourceful from now on. Whatever it took to keep his self-control, he would perfect it for her. She deserved to have a partner she could count on to be stronger than the things they sought to destroy. He couldn't be so weak that she would have to rescue him from Braccus every time he flew into a rage at the foul creature's actions.

Thomas knew there was much waiting inside of Sara to burst forth when it was called for, and he knew it would be called for in a very big way someday. He knew without a doubt that he would be part of it all with her because they were basically one. James was an important part of this too as he made the Circle complete. But it was different now. They had all changed on so many levels. All three of them were interconnected tightly, but Thomas shared this twisted, unwanted bond with Braccus with Sara. They were both going to have to continually fight it; it might never go away. But they could use it to their advantage. Here in this place where everything had been going so badly for them, each step they took had been dogged by the worst things imaginable, yet they had still come out together. Okay, they were still dead, but together

31

nonetheless, and that was more important than anything else right now.

This area was technically just a collection of dead things, things that were the total opposite from the deceased Keepers who had started it all. The difference being that this place housed evil things that only existed because Braccus's bad thoughts leaked out into the atmosphere and hung there wanting desperately to be alive. The thoughts wanted to experience life so badly that they were willing to settle for whatever form Braccus might send their way; which explained all the rotting corpses currently running around in the impossibly solid foundation beneath the nearby clouds. It was highly unusual to have anything here that came from the other side. It was just another sign of the unnatural state of the dimensions at this time. Braccus had corrupted yet another section of the universe while he spread himself around like a poison.

There was a still a small area of the Afterworld that the original Keepers held power over, Thomas and his companions had left that area behind to search out the precious item Braccus wanted to keep out of Sara's hands. The moment they entered this wretched section it was apparent that there were many things to be afraid of even after death. They had been pursued by Braccus and his foul thoughts. It was here that Thomas had finally discovered why Braccus was so drawn to Sara. The attraction was due to Shalsar's presence in her. It explained a lot, especially when he felt Shalsar there more then he would have expected. He was more than a little puzzled as to why she had not left when the other original Keepers had left. Initially, Sara had been sure she was gone too but she had become more and more detectable as time went by. It was almost as if she had rooted herself deep inside Sara's mind, waiting for something to happen. In fact, it had been Shalsar's memories that had led their little group toward Braccus's prized possession, pushing both he and Sara to the point of losing their souls to the things they fought. They had been too occupied with the need implanted inside them to find this all-important secret thing of Braccus's that they neglected to protect themselves against the evil things that were after them.

Thomas was so scared when he realized what had almost happened. If it hadn't been for James, he and Sara would have been dead in spirit as well as body, and he was so grateful to have at least one member of their Circle who had been in control at such a critical time. They had been so caught up in Shalsar's urgent summons to reach the well-hidden prize, they had dropped their guard. But they had gotten it together thanks to James and Diandra. When Braccus had swooped in and grabbed the object, he was forced toward the exit having met more resistance from him, Sara and James then he ever would have expected in a place he'd created himself. Sara had thrown her soul into his skinless form to try and retrieve the thing they had died to obtain. As determined as Braccus was to get away with his prized possession, she was even more determined to stop him and, in turn, Thomas was very sure that he was not going to get away with her trapped inside him.

With a new knowledge of his weakness, Thomas had flipped a switch inside of him and let the cooler, more logical part of his anger take control. He turned the anger into a steely determination that he used to pursue Braccus and his precious cargo. Running all the possibilities through his head, Thomas moved in a way that he had never been able move when he was alive, his body zoomed along as a ray of cool blue light close behind the red streak that was Braccus.

Moving faster than ever, Braccus raced to the doorway, fully prepared to take Sara with him; he had the object he wanted to keep hidden and he had Sara, too. Things didn't get any better than this. He was so close to winning it all. Focusing only on the doorway, Braccus stepped forward, thinking only of passing through the opening and closing it permanently afterwards. He had almost done so entirely when he felt something pop; Sara's spirit was jerked back into the shadowy Afterworld and the small object he held in his hand went with her. It was as if there was an invisible string joining her spirit to the thing he wanted desperately to keep from her.

Braccus tried to return to the dead dimension but couldn't seem to get back to the place he had just left. The door then shut with a sharp snap, effectively closing the great beyond from the living world, a door he couldn't get to open at his command. Rage built within the evil leader. His command should have been unquestionably obeyed.

34

This place was his and he should have his way! It had to be Iam, that interfering fool was making a last attempt to prevent him from having all he was entitled to. Despite the closed portal, Braccus's screams could be heard in both the living and dead worlds. It was a satisfying sound to the two souls now holding each other close in the dead lands.

Chapter Five

Having heard the screams too, Vincent and Franklin were trying to decide what to do next. Days of hearing absolutely nothing had Franklin convinced that all the Keepers' plans had gone seriously wrong. If they hadn't, he would have at least been able to communicate with his Circle members. But he wasn't even able to get through to Alice and Finola, and that troubled him a lot. Franklin felt their presence almost always. Only on a few occasions had he not been able to do so. This was largely due to interference by Braccus, but they had been learning to overcome that with Alice's help. His teammate's connection with the Shadowlands of the dead was helping her to learn how the evil things worked and how to get past the blocks they put up with their leader's help. Obviously, she had not perfected this yet because they had not heard anything for weeks.

Communication between the Keepers had worked well when they first started their separate journeys but began to fall off shortly after they had crossed through the portals into the different dimensions. Alice was spread so thin at this time, power-wise, the strain was getting to be a bit much. Franklin felt bad that so much was being asked of her; but there hadn't been much choice in the matter. She had been required to fill the gap in protection provided by Sara when she died. Worse still, it had been a task acquired rather quickly and without time for her to figure out how to do it properly.

Franklin and Finola had tried to offer what support they could to keep Alice from fizzling out the way she often did when overwhelmed, but it hadn't seemed to be quite enough as she moved further away from them and into yet another area she had to protect. Hers was a very handy power to have. Didn't everyone want to be invisible at times? But it was the hardest to maintain. It took a lot of Alice's strength to keep up the shields that afforded her and those around her protection.

One minute they were sharing thoughts, in separate areas but together still, and the next, sentences were cut off in mid-conversation and he heard no more from his Circle or any of the others. Alice had sounded so tired just before it happened, and he was afraid what that might mean for all of them. The silence was terrifying, especially after all that horrible screaming they had been treated to earlier in the day. He was making himself tired, running over the possible reasons for the screams, wondering if any of the Keepers had been hurt. This was their first big mission without the direct help of their mentors, most of whom were now dead. Robert, the only original Keeper left, and Maryann, his wife, a gifted woman but not a Keeper, were the only two living guiding forces behind them now, and that connection too had been lost for the time being. Each team had to make their own decisions based on what they encountered in the underground refuges, a somewhat new experience for them all because their mentors had always been right behind them, ready to swoop in and act when things got out of hand.

Being self-sufficient was a new thing for Franklin. At the very least, he had always known his Circle would be with him, and when they suddenly weren't, it was truly terrifying. Vincent was used to being on his own and he envied him just a little bit for that, but at least he knew how to act on his own and survive.

From a distance, Iam quietly watched them but made no immediate attempt to help. Franklin felt his presence hanging in the air like a parent monitoring his offspring with expectant interest. The Keepers knew that they were representing Iam in a world occupied by evil things that did not acknowledge his existence; it was their job to remind them who the true ruling force was. It was not proving as easy to complete this task as it had sounded in the beginning, just because they had power didn't automatically make them stronger than those they fought. This took effort and continual sacrifice, but they couldn't stop. Too much depended on them winning.

Franklin and his companions were going to take back all that had been stolen from their creator, but they had to get a little bit better at being Keepers before that could happen. Unlike the originals, who had been with the worlds from the beginning but had never been human, the new Keepers had been born into this world. Therefore they had more in common with those they were charged with helping. Unfortunately, even though they had these incredible gifts to protect themselves with, their humanity also made them vulnerable to all kinds of mortal problems. The new Keepers could be injured, both physically and mentally, and had to be careful to protect themselves from attack on several levels. They couldn't just walk into a difficult situation and automatically have it go their way. The gifted young ones had to be careful, keeping themselves safe to fight for Iam's people. They had to be tactful and earn the trust of their charges. This had all been explained to him and his companions before their journey had begun. But mere knowledge was nothing until accompanied by experience and their experiences had been far from pleasant or extensive.

Franklin sat and thought about everything that had happened up to this point in time, hoping to come up with a new strategy, a way to pull this whole situation out of the garbage. The protection placed on the doorways was still intact but would not stay that way forever. The new Keepers were working hard to help prepare the hidden people for what was coming next. He knew for certain that as bad as things were right now, they were going to get even worse before they got any better. He was just glad he had Vincent to help him through this.

Now that he understood what Vincent had been through and what he really stood for, they had become close friends. Vincent had changed so much since their first meeting. Even though he couldn't make direct contact with another person, his social skills had improved significantly. His friend had managed to reach out to people in many different ways, offering the Marrikans the benefit of his experience with the enemy. The young Keeper, because of his unique gift, had noticed things about his adversaries that others had not. He had gotten closer than most. Vincent had let loose on these things, it was the only time he said he had been glad to kill. Whatever Braccus had done to give his creatures life was quickly reversed with his touch. Vincent knew what the various mutated beings felt like, their skin, their arms, legs and even eyes and ears because he'd touched them. He outlined the flaws in Braccus's creations, highlighting the weaknesses that could be used to bring them down. This useful information gave the people here more of a chance to plan protective measures. His heart totally involved with these people, he taught them defensive moves and worked tirelessly to reinforce fortifications at the portals in preparation for the time when the shields went down. Neither Vincent or Franklin wanted to alarm the refugees, but they knew this to be more of a possibility than a "what if" situation.

When they had first arrived, Vincent had relied on Franklin to relay all the necessary information shared by the other Keepers since his own ability to get through to them was practically non-existent. He had also counted on him to act as initial spokesperson for both of them with the Marrikans. Franklin was surprised, however, that when Vincent actually started to interact with these people they seemed to really respect him. When he talked, they listened and followed his direction, responding with gratitude as he offered them something they could use to survive.

It was a good experience for him to be looked at with something other than fear by people who were aware of what he could do. Still they did have enough sense not to take it too far; the friendly, hardworking Marrikans did keep a healthy distance as they learned from him.

Out of all the Keepers that set out to help the refugees of the worlds, this unlikely pair had accomplished so much. Before all contact was cut off, they learned this was the only place that the occupants had been expecting the help of the Keepers. The Marrikans had the good fortune to have been found first by a Surren named Charlie, a powerful being who had arrived here before them and told the refugees all about Franklin and Vincent.

As a result, Vincent and Franklin had walked into a really comfortable situation. They hadn't had to seek out the special ones to gain the refugees trust; it had all been set up for them. The next few days would have been great if it hadn't been for the fact that they could go no further than they currently had without the help of the other Keepers. By reaching out and connecting with them they should be able to use each other's gifts to make the underground places fit to live in. Without them, food, water, light, and fresh air would run out and survival be impossible.

If it hadn't been for the people hiding here because evil had taken over the surface, this place would have been practically perfect. The buildings in this underground place were absolutely beautiful, each structure carved into the cave walls with such skill it was hard to believe that these people had done it in a matter of weeks. Five stories high and set up

42

like an apartment building, each housing unit had four separate living areas with four to five rooms and a wide balcony. Thick stone columns elaborately decorated with images of the sun, plants, animals and even rain clouds, provided support at the end of the balconies. Sturdy stone steps were carved down the length of the supports affording access to each level, ultimately leading to the floor of the cave.

Each separate living area was furnished with beds made of salvaged wood, cloth, and other objects found conveniently lying near the swirling doors of light that had allowed them access here. In addition to these comforts, there was even heat running from vents dug deeper into the cave and an artificial light source provided by Charlie that lit up the caves very well. There was very little food or water left, but other than that it would have been a great substitute living place for the surface worlds.

All-in-all, this would have been a fairly good experience for both he and Vincent, had it not been for the fact that they had been separated from the people they needed help from while the surface was being ripped apart by an enemy eager to find its way down here. They were all safe, for now, and Franklin was sure they would find a way to connect with the others soon. They had been separated before, but the Keepers had always been able to find a way back to each other. Franklin might even have relaxed a little bit more if it he hadn't also started to have a slightly uneasy feeling when he looked at a few of the big-headed people that dwelled here.

For some reason, a few Marrikans hanging at the edge of the crowd made the hair stand up on the back of his neck. When he first began to have that "funny feeling" about some of them, he really hoped that it was just his imagination. Maybe he was wrong, his mind working overtime from the stress of all they had been through. There had to be an explanation for what he thought he was seeing. It wasn't anything in particular he could put his finger on. The people he'd focused on acted just like the others down here; quite industrious, going about the same duties of construction and maintenance as their companions. But there was just something about them that wasn't quite right, a difference in the way they moved, a slight shuffling gait that became more pronounced as the days went by. Eyes dull and flat, the subjects of his stare had skin that seemed just a shade lighter than those around them. They hadn't been hiding underground long enough to have become as pale as the two men he was looking at now. All interaction with their fellow refugees seemed forced and distant as if they knew how they were supposed to act with them but were unused to doing it. Stiff smiles, reactions just a second or two slower than the situation called for were evident in the few he had zoned in on.

He watched one of the men in question drop a tool on the floor and stared it at it for a minute before bending down like a stick figure to grasp at the object in hands that he didn't seem to know how to make work. Fumbling around with thick fingers, the "man" finally managed to grab the hammer and curl his digits around it to get it off the ground.

44

Franklin's mind was going through all the possibilities as he continued to look through the crowd; trying to see exactly how many Marrikans were acting or looking like the males he was studying. In addition to the two he had been watching, there were two more on the opposite side of the room moving about with a slightly confused look on their faces, standing next to men and women that appeared perfectly normal. He had watched them for days after he first got the feeling they were different. The odd-acting Marrikans continued to mingle though their jerking movements became more pronounced with each day that passed. At first, their actions were greeted with tender concern by their companions. Commenting on how hard this whole experience had been on all, the people here did what they always had, worked harder to fill in for their strange acting companions until they were better.

But the differences were becoming more noticeable and it was causing a bit of discomfort to those trying to help them. A slight grimace when they spoke to them, hesitant suggestions that they might want to go to Charlie for some healing for whatever had begun to ail them. But still they were secure in the fact that whatever was going on could be fixed. The people in question, as if sensing they were becoming more noticeable, would then move toward a different section of the caves and attempt to mix in with another group. With each move, they adapted their behavior just a bit to blend with the others. They were aping their actions to fit in.

Franklin glanced at Vincent, who was staring at the same men with a troubled look on his face, nodding in his direction to indicate he had seen the odd behavior too. Both men then looked toward Charlie for confirmation that something was amiss. The little purple-haired guy frowned as if something was going on that he didn't quite understand, and this made Franklin very uncomfortable because in the short time that he had known Charlie, the Surren, knower of all mysterious things, didn't "not know" much about what was happening around him. It was apparent by the suddenly sick look on the Surren's face that he was seeing the subtle things that Franklin and Vincent had been noticing, and the significance of it had begun to sink in.

Slowly and carefully, so as to not attract attention, the little man moved toward the two Keepers and motioned them to a dark section of the caves where they began to speak in hushed tones about this unexpected turn of events. Safety and comfort was suddenly an illusion that had been intruded upon once again by the reality of evil's presence in this sanctuary.

Chapter Six

Randall shook his head to clear it; after that last blow to his noggin he was having a hard time getting his bearings. The only thing that was clear was that this whole situation had gone too far. Obviously, Isobel and her devoted followers were not going to listen to him and he couldn't wait any longer for the special ones to find them and fix this mess. All he could do at this point was get out of here and go back to Alice, who was not answering his calls at the moment.

It was strange that he had been reaching out to her earlier and she had answered him, but when he would have expected to see her, he didn't. In fact, when he freed himself by creating a wall of electricity between him and the four people in front of him, he raced around the bend in the path, sure that it was the only thing separating them, but she was not there. This scared him more than being threatened with death. They had been talking, she had moved through barriers of thin air to get to him; zipping in and out of an entire dimension, and yet she had not been where he felt she would be. How could he have been so mistaken about where she was?

Things had been a little bit different since she had used her connection with the dead things, a little more scattered then before. His beautiful, bright girlfriend had been pushing herself too hard, and it was weakening her defenses; it was almost as if she wasn't totally with him anymore. Alice seemed slightly out of focus and he had put it all down to the fact that she had not slept in several days. He worried about her so much that he had insisted she get some sleep and when she did as he asked, Isobel and her men had made their move.

Dragging him away from the startled refugees with no explanation why, they had intended to throw him out of the portal. But for some reason, both she and the three men that listened to her so intently had been unable to approach the glowing doorway. Failing to evict him themselves, they had tried to talk the two other men into doing it, but they would not. Apparently, these men still had a conscience and had not yet become like those with them. These two didn't seem to be bothered by the light and were able to stand quite close to the doorway. Shaking their heads and moving away from their companions, the men in question refused to listen to the convincing, almost threatening tones of their fellow followers. The two men stood to the side with confused looks on their faces, seeing their companions in a whole different light, and not liking what they saw.

While the group argued over what was to be done with him, Randall acted. With a quick flick of his hands, he made sure the two that seemed less sure of their allegiance to Isobel were outside the wall of electricity he sent out. It was the least he could do for them as he left their companions behind screaming foul curses upon him while they covered their eyes and crawled away from the brightness. He wondered how this could have happened when he was sure that they had passed through the lit portals at least once before or they wouldn't have been down here at all.

The two men he set free watched in shock as he broke away, distancing himself from his captors. The shaken looks on their faces told him they were glad to be away from the others. But instead of following him as he wished they would, they ran away, and he was too worried about Alice to go after them.

Randall left Isobel and her cronies where he trapped them; they were far enough away from the general population now and he was sure he could keep them captive. They could not pass through his electrical barrier and so were safely contained. He would get Alice and bring her back; together they would solve the mystery of this strange behavior and get these people under control. Running as fast as he could in the narrow caves without slamming head first into solid rock, Randall felt sweat dripping into cuts received from multiple blows to his head but ignored the stinging pain. He had to get back to his girlfriend and find out why he couldn't hear her in his head. Sending sharp snaps of electricity ahead of him, lighting up the dark cramped corridors that branched out in several directions, he made his way back toward where he thought the main cavern was located. This was the last place he had seen Alice. It would have been easier if he could just latch on to her all familiar connection to him, but he couldn't see it clearly. The only thing he could see, when he really focused on her, was a faint pink trail that seemed to drift randomly around in the air, changing direction frequently as if she were not settled in one place. He was terrified of what that might mean for Alice. She just had to be where he left her, sleeping peacefully through all this craziness until he arrived to wake her up. But a part of him was very much afraid that she was not.

He had been in love with Alice since she first appeared out of thin air to help free him from life as a sideshow exhibit for the Relgars. This dark-haired girl with incredible green eyes had pulled him out of a prison and back into a life of usefulness at a time when he had been convinced he would never see the outside worlds again.

Her gifts were remarkable, and like the other Keepers were gradually changing to include more abilities but they were still inexact and very raw. When the Keepers powers expanded to include things other than what they were already aware they could do, it was often an unexpected thing, happening suddenly with no manual to tell them how to manage them. The powers, especially the newly discovered parts of them, were unpredictable and sometimes wildly out of control.

Randall remembered the first time Alice had tried to use her connection with the dead to get them to the underground doorway. The entity that she had interacted with had taken over his body. Eventually she had defeated it, but he was still worried about her having to do that again. Before any of this happened, she had been aware of the in-between places where the dead were. Alice had sometimes shared what she saw with him, and what she saw was ugly and horrifying. Going to the dead places had made her distant and exhausted. He worried even then about her losing herself to her expanding talents. For everything she had let him see, there was a lot she had not, and it was what he had not seen that scared him most of all. As if this was not enough to deal with, she had been stretched even further by the need to fill in the gap in security left by Sara's death.

When Sara died, Alice had taken her role as protector of all the underground places. She was able to divide herself up, providing protection for the doorways that gave access to the dimensions in the worlds, but it still didn't mean that she was in control of it all. In fact, it was this division of herself that made her more vulnerable to the forces on the other side. Randall had to get to her and make sure what he feared might happen to her, didn't. The sneaky evil things from beyond these worlds would do anything to trap her in the shadowy places with them. A sick feeling inside was telling him that Alice was in more danger from the dead than the living right now and he had to be with her to keep her safe.

It was during his headlong run to find the way to the large central area of the cavern, that Randall almost ran face first into the cave wall. Gritting his teeth in frustration, the young Keeper lashed out at the stone with several snapping lines of electricity. Sparks flew from the dark rock, popping and cracking as he unleashed his anger on the inanimate objects. Randall's body hummed with energy, fine red hair sticking up in the air with static electricity; arcing bolts of energy shot out of every pore of his skin. He stood popping like a cord with a short in it, power building and building with his frustration. Again, and again, he lashed out at the stone, frustrated at this useless show of his abilities; they certainly weren't making him un-lost.

Three gaping holes in the rock were revealed by the light show Randall was putting on. Wasn't that just great! Now there was more than one possible way to travel further into the caves, he had choice of three different routes he could take to continue to get lost in this stupid maze of tunnels.

He didn't have time for this! One of these corridors was going to lead him to Alice. But which one? There had to be a way to choose. If he started down the wrong path, it would be yet another delay in reaching her. In order to make a choice, he needed to see more. But when he leaned towards the center opening, he noticed three figures standing there watching him intently. Scolding himself for having been too distracted to realize he was not alone, Randall gathered his wits about him, preparing for an attack of some kind. The air hummed with energy as he put out more power, his body so electrically charged as to make it very uncomfortable for any being to approach him while he determined to get a better look at his company. A flick of his wrist sent another whip-like stream of electricity to a spot directly above the rough round doorway; it hung there to form a tightly coiled globe of wavering light. The globe resembled a primitive light bulb that was nothing like Franklin's fireballs but provided enough illumination for Randall to see the three men staring at him. They looked at him calmly as if his presence here was expected, and what he was doing with his gift was normal as far as they were concerned. There was no sign of shock or surprise at seeing the light show in front of them.

All three men were about his height, with similar facial structure to his own. After hanging out here for a few days, he could see that it was possible that he might have come from this place originally. His resemblance to these people was one of the reasons he was able to blend in so well when he first arrived. He had the feeling that this was the place that Iam had chosen to send his spirit to be born into. Like the other Keepers, he was uncertain about the details of the first part of his life; how a body was chosen to house his spirit and where he spent his youngest years, but that hardly mattered in the long-run. It was where they had wound up eventually that had shaped their lives.

His mind went past the innocence of early childhood to a time when they were placed in situations that made them aware of just how rotten some people could be. Knowing what each Keeper had gone through to get to the point where they were all putting their lives on the line to save Iam's people made him want to reach out to them even more. He longed to connect with his Circle again, to share the fear and frustration he was feeling, needing some kind of support in these uncertain times. There was still only empty silence where there should be the sounds of at least five other people sharing their experiences; he couldn't count Vincent at this time because he didn't know him like he knew the others. Yet he would have gladly answered Vincent now if he had been able to get through whatever block was keeping them from speaking, that's how lonely he now felt.

His mind was racing as he stared back at the three men in front of him, two of them raising their hands as if for protection, while the man in the center of the group moved toward him with a hand extended. It was fortunate for this man that a small inner voice urged him to hold himself in check, to wait to see what came of this encounter. Small blue arcs of energy hovered above his hands ready to be let loose if the voice even hinted that it was a bad idea to trust this guy.

"Hello, Randall, my name is Jacob. I have been expecting you." The tall man with the noble face stared at him solemnly and Randall knew he had just met the man he was supposed to meet, the one who was to have introduced him and Alice to the people here. Lowering his hands with a small sigh of relief, he moved forward to begin a conversation he had been waiting weeks to initiate. He just hoped this man would lead him to Alice, the sooner the better.

Chapter Seven

Thomas reached down and helped Sara up from the filmy ground before turning to face James and Diandra who were running to meet them. It had been a horrifying few minutes for their third as he watched his two close companions race toward the portal, one trapped in Braccus's grotesquely displayed skinless body, the other in hot pursuit. James stayed with them in spirit every agonizing second of the frantic race for the exit to the Land of the Dead. He had thrown out stabbing waves of sound aimed directly at Braccus's brain in an attempt to slow him down and give Thomas a chance to reach him. Unfortunately, it had absolutely no effect on the monster and he was horrified to see Braccus pass through the glowing doorway that separated the shadowy in-between places from the solid dimension and the Land of the Living.

James had grabbed Diandra's hand and ran for the exit, terrified that his Circle members had been taken away from him. This could not be happening! It wasn't enough that they had sacrificed their lives to do what they had been assured was necessary to destroy Iam's greatest enemy, but to lose to him shortly after they had begun to win was a cruel fate. For some strange and inexplicable reason, they had Braccus on the run in his own territory. He and his fellow Keepers were winning after what had been a huge struggle with the entities that slithered and slunk around this portion of the Afterworld. They had forced back evil things that had taken over dead bodies and dragged them back here to use as a substitute for the sensation of being alive.

What dwelled here had never been alive, having been formed from Braccus's hate and anger. All the emotions that he had unleashed here, in the privacy of this small section of the nothingness he had shaped to suit his need for privacy and total control of his surroundings, had become something solid and real. Braccus had pretended to be Iam's perfect follower, when he felt he should have been so much more, and it was here that he had let his truth have free reign. What it gave birth to was vicious and ugly. James paused to catch his breath as he recalled all they had learned recently about this foul area of the Afterworld.

This place had been unknown to anyone else for hundreds of years, starting from a time when Braccus was still known to be a truly good soul by most of those around him, or so he thought. Iam had never been fooled and knew it was only a matter of time before what was destined to happen did. It was, after all, his design. Iam felt confident enough in his creations to give them choices and the strength to follow their convictions. Iam had loved Braccus with all his heart but he knew that the special being he made was too proud and too stubborn to let himself be led in the right direction, so things went just the way he thought they would. What followed was a constant struggle between the two of them for control of the worlds he created. It was understood that choices had to be made, sides had to be taken but unlike Braccus, the Keepers were aware that Iam would only tolerate this game for so long. This ongoing test of loyalty exhibited by his creations against the warped beings made by his formerly prized child had to end at some time. James had paid attention in classes given by the older Keepers so the stories and reasons behind them were well known to him.

James had been fascinated by the history of the worlds as taught by Olie, Ferd and Maggie on his frequent trips to the Land of the Keepers; he had learned so much more about what the worlds were really about than in his ordinary earthly school. He was amazed at the things that the "normal" people had never known about the struggle for their souls taking place every day right under their noses. Before this last great disaster that had all the worlds losing the surface areas to the evil things, very few of Iam's creations had the privilege of knowing the Keepers at all. He re-ran all the lessons in his head once again, trying to understand what might come next.

The times that evil came up the winner, were times that shaped people's character, for it brought out the best in those that already had it hidden beneath the surface. Tough times made heroes of ordinary men and brought them closer to the miraculous beings Iam had sent to watch over them. Sometimes the Artregeans allowed themselves to be seen and felt, but that was a rare thing and usually only to make them aware of Iam's more accessible surface dwelling saviors: the Keepers. People who had previously been unaware of the Keepers suddenly discovered their existence and the partnership yielded wonderful results time after time, eventually leading to another shifting in the balance of power. Back and forth it had gone for thousands of years, but this was the worst it had ever gotten. Iam had never allowed the destruction to go this far before. His planet was bleeding and broken, his worlds in distress and he asked for the greatest sacrifice to make it right. That, of course, was why they were in this ugly, evil place.

When James and Thomas had followed Sara here and faced Braccus, it had almost ended in his favor. Sara had only escaped being trapped inside Braccus by a last-second intervention by Thomas, who had gathered every ounce of strength his spirit had left and pulled her out. If she had passed back into the living dimension inside that beast, she would have been trapped within him and under his control forever.

After his initial panic, James was so relieved to feel Thomas and Sara close by as he neared the glowing portal to the living dimension. When he saw them holding each other closely, he felt a tremendous burden lifted from his heart. Eyes welling up with relief, he moved on legs rubbery and unsteady as if he were a walking Gummy Bear, James reached his Circle-mates. The four good souls stood side by side, shaken by their close-call. For a few minutes, they stayed together, merging their thoughts to gather courage for their next move.

But even as they stood together in the quiet tense atmosphere with the faint shrieks of the dead things sounding behind them and the echoes of Braccus's earsplitting cry still vibrating in the air, they felt optimistic. Even though they knew the enemy would come at them again and Braccus had made it back to a place they really wanted to be but could not go, they suddenly felt like smiling, because when they looked down into Sara's cupped hands, they saw a small silver box; the same silver box that Braccus had clutched so tightly in his own hand as he sped for the exit. It was theirs now, whatever it meant to him; and it must have meant a lot for him to come racing back here to keep it from Sara. Thomas took the small thick box out of Sara's hand. It was surprisingly heavy for its size, causing his hand to dip downward for second before he steadied it. Curious and excited, they studied the prized object they had fought so hard to obtain. The box, made entirely out of silver, was carved with ornate images of roses and strange symbols that looked black against the light color of the silver. Four heads touched as they all leaned forward to get a better look at this precious object.

They watched in amazement as the dark symbols began to shift, making their exact shapes unclear. Five indistinct configurations of circles and lines with swirls and strange twisty things running through each showed starkly against the shiny sheen of the box but didn't stay formed long enough for the Keepers to properly identify them. Sharing one thought, the group almost laughed aloud together. Even if they had been able to see the symbols, it was doubtful that anyone other than Braccus would know what they really meant. They had some of what they had come to find, what they had given their lives to discover in this place and still, had no idea how to use this object to destroy their enemy. Both James and Thomas glanced at Sara, feeling her frustration at not having all the answers. Why would she be here if she didn't have the ability to use this thing? When she willingly went to her death, it was with the understanding that she could make a difference, but now that she had achieved her goal, she had no insight as to its purpose. Feeling a strong need to touch the box, make contact with this all-important, world changing object, she reached out, lifted the heavy lid and looked eagerly inside. Staring in fascination, they were anxious to see if there was something inside that made the box weightier than expected, but there was nothing.

It was empty, lined only with a dark smooth material that might by velvet, the texture slightly furry and so soft. She continued to explore the lining with her fingers, running the tips across the material in case there was something hidden beneath it. She was surprised to find the sides dry, but the center wet and sticky. The thick cloth was soaked all the way through and when she pressed it, it felt soggy and unclean.

It reminded her of the last time she had seen the box, the memory came to her sharp and clear as if it had occurred just minutes before. She had been lost in a dreamland for four years, and one day had discovered the box in the house that Olie and Thomas had made for her. While wandering through several different rooms trying to find her way out, she found items made both by her mentor and her boyfriend as well as a few that Braccus threw in as he tried to make his way to her. She had found the box during her travels through those rooms. It was sitting on a table, in a creepy room furnished with rickety furniture; she could still remember how "not right" it felt for her to be in that room. The small, elegant container had looked out of place in its gloomy surroundings, drawing her to it immediately. She had picked it up to examine it more closely, having just enough time to notice the musty smell coming from inside it. That was all she had time to notice before it melted away and disappeared, as if a vivid part of someone else's dream; a dream she wasn't a welcome part of. She had a vague memory that it was wet inside at that time too and had been convinced that there was a strong smell of blood but didn't understand the significance of it then, and she still didn't now. All that she did know was that the damp box lining made her fingers burn when she touched it, as if she had briefly brushed against a hot stove. Thomas pulled her fingertips to his lips and soothed away the stinging sensation, earning himself a small smile from her. The gesture was more sweet than logical, dead flesh could not be harmed. If indeed she even had flesh; she was pretty sure she hadn't taken her body with her when she left the living dimension. She didn't really want to know what had happened to their corpses after their spirits had vacated them. As much as Braccus hated them, her especially; they were bound to have been destroyed in the cruelest way.

Sara's hand rested on top of Thomas's, channeling his energy with hers as she tried to reach out for the power that had used her earlier to find this box. Nothing happened. No convenient mini-movie running through her head telling her everything she needed to know about Braccus and his connection to this thing. It seemed for the moment that Shalsar had abandoned her.

Choking back her disappointment at this development, she tried to force her way past the emptiness, reaching for the other part of her that lay stubbornly dormant, giving her absolutely nothing. What she did feel was a slight hesitation on the part left of her guardian spirit; the part that was so closely entwined with her. It was the hesitation that both frightened and angered her. While at first, there was nothing but eagerness to get her to the container, there was now an almost regretful vibration inside her. As if maybe in this time, this place, there was hope that this situation could be different. Maybe he, meaning Braccus, could be brought back here to this environment by what she had almost seen in him. Her dead heart fluttered in her chest even though it wasn't supposed to. Sara was waging a war with herself and the irrational feelings put out by a powerful soul long gone from the worlds.

Thoughts of what a wonderful being he could have been if all the temptation of lording over people, places, the very fabric of the universe hadn't been a factor in his existence, entered her head. Maybe if he were away from it all, in this place he had made for himself and not in competition for everything with an entity he could not hope to better, he would be content and would be as she wished him to be. So angry that she had to take a deep breath to fight back a scream, Sara pushed away at the foolish, childish thoughts invading her head. All the memories of witnessing his cruelty, selfish pride, deceit, and destruction of all that the creator had made and loved, returned with a vengeance; aimed specifically at the section of her brain housing what was left of Shalsar's being. She made a point to recall the miserable wasted image of her guardian when they had found each other in the dreaming place. Forcing the recollection of when Braccus had managed to capture Shalsar and treat her cruelly, torturing her soul for years before she had gotten away from him. It had been during that brief meeting that Shalsar had told her she was going to give everything up, her powers and what was left of her connection with Sara and return to Iam. In that place where reality and wishful thinking were firmly merged together, Sara and her guardian had actually touched. One dead woman and a girl in a coma had made contact in a place where both were solid and real.

Even though Shalsar had been dead for hundreds of years, she had dwelled inside the young Keeper for most of her young life, giving her power, wisdom, and inner strength to get through some really tough times. When she first became aware of her inner spirit's presence it hadn't felt like an intrusion, it had felt like having met a long-lost friend. Now she was more than a little bit afraid of the way Shalsar had hung on to a big part of her even after she was supposed to have left her completely. It felt like all she had known about her was a big lie. It hurt that she didn't know Shalsar as well as she thought she had.

When the other original Keepers departed, leaving their powers to the new generation of protectors, they did so with the understanding that it was a final goodbye. The ancient souls of their mentors severed all ties and would never again be sharing the bodies of their students. Sara thought Shalsar had done the same, but she never got the chance to become accustomed to her absence; it became obvious as time passed that Shalsar was still in her head. She seemed more present every day and her thoughts were not rational for someone who had died to make sure that Braccus did not win. She had seen her guardian soul's intentions toward Braccus from the beginning and it had been one of cautious mistrust. How was it then that she suddenly felt all this resistance to ending his existence? Nothing about this situation made any sense.

Sara gripped the box so tightly that she dented the thick silver, leaving the impression of deep fingerprints there. She was determined to force answers from it. It would tell her what she wanted to know. There was another part of this thing, something that went with the box. Obviously, it wasn't this container that she'd been sent her to obtain; it was whatever had been inside. Having had enough teasing tidbits of information passed on without any real help, she pushed past the blocks that Shalsar had put up, dropping her own protective wall at the same time.

It took a minute or two, but her aggressive action worked. Fizzling grey stuff exploded before her eyes as she saw flashes of the past. A figure moved rapidly across hills and valleys, barren fields and stormy seas, its footprints leaving burnt impressions in scarred ground. The surface protested mightily by shaking and cracking when the land itself became aware of what was truly crossing it. A bluish black trail led to misty mountaintops and beyond to even taller peaks from which smoke billowed freely, belching out red trails of lava. It didn't end there, going still further to a place she could not quite make out, but the direction itself was clear.

Studying the course she was reluctantly shown, Sara smiled with satisfaction. They knew at least where they should begin to look, even if they still did not know what they were looking for.

The group had to go back, even further into the evil places, passing once again into the smaller and smaller protected area of the deceased Keepers and then back up into the worst section taken by Braccus's demented, demonic thoughts. All that lay before them was ugly and warped and they would have to pass further into it to gain what they wanted so desperately to find. This was where it hid. It, being the other part of his secret, which she felt would not give in to her easily or suffer to be found without a tremendous struggle.

Turning toward the wavering doorway Braccus had escaped through, Sara thought of all that lay so teasingly close. The living world was just on the other side of the glowing opening. Maybe they didn't have to stay here, after all. Maybe Iam would help them now that they found part of what she was supposed to find. But even as she told herself this, she knew she was being foolish. Sara reached out her hand in the hope that she was wrong, that maybe there was another way to do what needed to be done. They were so close to the entrance back into the real and solid world of the living. A place that she longed for so strongly she wanted to cry and throw herself back there. The liquid warmth flowed from the portal, teasing her with the promise of escape from this nightmare. She just had to know if what her father had been trying to tell her was true.

His last message to her before she left her parents behind in the protected Afterworld was that it might be possible for her and her companions to return to life somehow, if she just did the right thing. Maybe taking a chance this way was the right thing. Sara turned toward the exit, the lure of escape calling to her so strongly that she thrust her hand into the opening. Her hand shriveled as soon as it hit the light. With a startled cry, she pulled it back quickly. The message she had just received was clear, there was no going back, at least not at this time. There was only one direction they were allowed to take, and it would lead them into places she did not wish to go. Allowing Thomas to take her suddenly restored hand in his, she reached for James and he, in turn, took Diandra's hand. They turned as a unit in the direction of the ugliness that they must go back through, all aware of what they would have to face as they went toward the prize they sought.

Chapter Eight

Eric faced the prettiest woman he had ever seen. He smiled as his eyes focused on all the familiar features that time had advanced at a rapid rate. He could see that she was looking at him with the same amazed admiration and love he was showing her and he was overwhelmed. Hands shaking as they held each other's arms, the couple stood face to face, seeing each other in the darkness through Eric's remarkable night vision. A yellow glowing light bathed everything he saw and of course, Finola saw it all through his eyes.

"We did it," they both said in hushed tones as if afraid that their voices would be overheard, making everything unreal. The will that had allowed them to bend the very fabric of time and remake themselves as they wanted to be had been incredibly powerful. Where before there had been two young people feeling very vulnerable and alone with no support system, there now stood two people in their twenties. They had chosen the ages they felt would give them more respect and confidence. If they were going to go out there and face these people head-on, they were going out as impressive grown-ups, people to be reckoned with, not as children to be intimidated and forced into hiding.

Finola's long dark curly hair fell gracefully around a heart-shaped face that had become a little leaner with age. Dark cocoa-colored eyes with heavy lids stared at him with triumph as she saw what they had become together. Full lips smiled at him and his heart pounded with joy; he was so much in love that he couldn't stop smiling in spite of the fact that things had not exactly gone in their favor lately. Finola was doing the same; he saw himself through her eyes as a full two feet taller with wider shoulders, a muscular solid frame, and a strong chiseled jaw that made him quite fierce-looking. He liked the way she saw him because her eyes saw him at his best.

Shaggy red hair fell to his shoulders and he actually had a little stubble on his face. He would have to learn to shave soon since this was a one-way transformation; they wouldn't be able to go back to what they were. It didn't matter to him anyway; as long as they could stay the same age together he was happy. He caught the words *Wow, you're handsome,* from Finola's mind, which, of course made him smile even wider. They were both very impressive, stronger-looking, and every bit what they would have expected two powerful beings should look like to ordinary mortal people. Mission accomplished!

It had been a long-shot. They weren't sure if it would work or not - but it had. The idea for this had started because of Finola's fear and frustration at being trapped here. Enough was enough! She wanted to be taken seriously, not like the little girl who the group had felt perfectly comfortable with chasing into this dark place and screaming threats at. They called on every memory they shared from a time long ago when trying to learn how to adapt their current physical forms to something more intimidating and awe-inspiring. Eric would do anything to help Finola feel more secure and confident, make the hurt and anger she was feeling about all that happened just go away. If she had asked him to morph into some kind of purple dinosaur that could sing and dance, he would have gladly have done so. He had given her everything, pushing his power to the limit as he pulled an image from Finola's head of what they wanted to be and let their combined energy take over. It was ambitious but had definitely paid off.

Power had ebbed and flowed from their pores, tingling through them until the hair on their arms stood up. Bones popped and creaked beneath skin that was being pulled tighter and tighter against muscles, joints, and tissue shifting rapidly upon command. Finola made a point to hold onto all the feelings that Eric was having, this little escapade was causing him pain and she hated that. He was doing this all for her; it wasn't his first choice of activities for the day and she owed it to him to share this, to know what he was going through just for her. She loved him all the more for it.

His actions humbled her, and she held on to him tightly, taking in some of his discomfort. It reminded her that this was happening because she had gotten them into this situation in the first place. Eric tried to protest and make her stop buffering his pain, but he was so uncomfortable he could only concentrate on their metamorphosis. He'd let her know how he felt about this later.

Eric's skin felt stretched, his head ached, and he felt a little woozy. Finola took what she could of this feeling from him until nausea threatened to overwhelm her. The room spun around them sickeningly until they became used to the changes they had made in themselves. Aging several years in a matter of minutes was bound to take a toll and they both consciously slowed their hearts a bit until they became used to the larger frames they now occupied; refitting their souls to these grown-up bodies until they felt more at home. Breathing deeply, they sat on the ground trying to get used to their new twenty-year old forms.

They were overjoyed, yet for all they had accomplished, they were still unable to contact their fellow Keepers. Without any backup to speak of, they had to make a move to get this situation under control. Problem was that Iam would still frown on harming or killing those he sent them to rescue. They had to find a way to make the refugees listen, but it would be really hard to do so when all they seemed to want to do was hurt them.

Rising to stand on the thick grassy surface that Finola had created to keep busy, she breathed in the fresh scent of growing things, trying to get comfort from the feel of the life within them. She felt the plant's love, their gratitude for having been saved and given another chance to survive, produce and continue to grow down here, and it calmed her. Focusing on them and not the remarkable thing she and Eric had managed to make happen, she took a deep breath and hugged Eric tightly. All that mattered was what they were going to have to do now. Stopping to consider what they had just managed to accomplish was not going to help them get anything else done. As cool as it was, it was still merely a shape changing trick; it didn't make them any more powerful. There was no strong inner knowledge that this transformation would affect any other part of their mission.

Looking intimidating might not be enough to get them through this situation; it had to be resolved with a little bit more tact than what they currently felt like using. The now older versions of Finola and Eric stood uncertainly at the exit, all ready to go forth and fix the mess somehow. Even though they could not currently make contact with their fellow Keepers, there was a rising sense of urgency coming from deep inside that told them haste was called for. Eric knew part of it was coming from another source, the others were waiting to break through.

The connection was blocked, not broken; they felt a strong steady rhythm as if many hearts were beating at once, but it was distant and not accompanied by the shared thoughts and visions. It was both frustrating and lonely to not be able to get past the separation of their mind connection. But there was that other thing they sensed, the underlying shift that indicated the bad stuff was about to get worse. Changes were taking place in the universe around them, a pressure was rising, and it made their teeth ache. Hate, fear, intense anger radiated through the air, generated by some event they had not witnessed but felt like a building storm. It was as if the very air was being squeezed in a giant fist until the pressure built to a level of extreme discomfort. It took the pleasure away from their recently accomplished aging trick, so they didn't have time to enjoy it. What to do, what to do...? The combination of all they had gone through and all that was going on around and inside of them was suddenly making them quite shaky and doubtful of their next move.

Eric and Finola were about to wildly throw caution to the wind and walk out into a crowd of very unfriendly, scared individuals, looking very different from when they had left them. Hoping that just maybe they could think of something wise and useful to do by the time they reached the end of the tunnel. It was apparent, to their insides at least, that trouble was building to a critical level and drastic action had to be taken soon.

While the couple stood together, contemplating things, a sudden quiet descended over the area. Eric had only been half listening to the other section of the caves but he hadn't heard much lately. It was almost like their pursuers were deliberately being quiet so as to not be heard by him. The silence was eerie, leaving a sizzling, staticky sound in place of the noise. He was not used to this at all, having been able to control sound in all its forms at his will. Fine tuning his hearing, Eric tried to get anything at all from his surroundings that he could use, the drip of water on the cave walls, the chirp of the crickets that had taken refuge among Finola's growing things. He had to fight to get even these small sounds to come through; maybe it was exhaustion from all that extra effort they had put out to make their change happen. Having always been in touch with his powers, he had never experienced this weakness before and it scared him. Sweat was pouring down Eric's face as he strained his ears to hear all the things he normally would have been able to hear. He felt like he had cotton stuffed in his ears; it was all so muted, and he could not seem to adjust the volume. He wanted to hear what was going on beyond the rows of bushes Finola had put up between them and the refugees in the central cavern. He needed to know what they were doing so he concentrated harder on pushing past his weakness. Eric tried to force his powers to kick into full strength, aided by Finola who was giving him everything she wasn't giving to the plants to make it all work right again.

The extra help paid off. He started to hear a few things more clearly. The crackle of a distant fire a few hundred feet beyond their sight, a few bugs scurrying across the surface of some leaves. But it was the simple soft voice of a young woman that sounded loudly above the faint scratching of mouse feet that caught his attention because she was calling him by name.

Chapter Nine

Charlie watched as his friend Franklin spoke to Vincent. Troubled expressions broke out across their faces. They all now realized what disturbing things were going on right under their noses. At this point, it was pretty obvious that they were sharing this space with about twenty-five dead people. These dead people were roaming around the room mingling convincingly with the living refugees. It had taken the Keepers a few days to notice the differences that separated them from their companions. It was the slow but noticeable decay of the bodies that was beginning to give them away. The changes were showing in the small way the arms and legs were losing their basic functions. The skin on the bodies was slowly rotting as evidenced by the way it was peeling in spots while other areas were discolored and soft-looking. They did not smell yet, but he was sure that it was only a matter of time before that too began to occur.

What were they doing here? The Keepers had been certain that the doorways were protected, the bad things were not allowed to move through, but all three men were very aware that whatever was housed in the bodies of these Marrikans was not good. It was disturbing to note that all this was happening right in front of them. Something evil had slipped in where it should not be; slyly hiding amongst the others, as if waiting, learning all they could about those they moved among before making a move to destroy them.

Charlie was ashamed that he had not noticed the dead ones earlier; he thought he had gotten to know all the Marrikans very well and was embarrassed that any of them could have changed so much without his detecting it. He used to know all kinds of things before they happened; there was no evil that walked the worlds he couldn't identify. Until now. All those years he had been part of the protection forces in Sherrin, controlling what was allowed through the different dimensions, and now he couldn't stop a force he should have been able to recognize immediately. He sighed heavily as he realized that this was yet another sign that his time, like that of all his peers, was coming to an end. Charlie was terrified at this turn of events, not exactly for himself, he would have gladly fought the enemy until his death just like his people had. But these good souls didn't deserve to die out; the enemy could not be allowed to destroy the last of this truly remarkable civilization. The Surren had watched all the worlds from a distance. He had interacted with them. They had given him trust and respect, and he would miss this feeling of belonging when he was gone; it would only be a matter of time before he left the worlds and he knew it. He had spoken with the five dead ones from time to time and failed to detect anything different about them. It was almost as if they were not even aware that there was something different about them themselves.

He had sensed real living souls in those bodies and they were good ones, not evil, but it had been like a switch had been flipped and that the good things were suddenly gone. All goodness had left them, and it wasn't until then that he sensed their absence. The pure and certain living souls had been replaced with something that was not familiar with the equipment it now occupied and was having a difficult time operating the bodies. Charlie knew now that they had been able to avoid detection because the original owners of the bodies had hung around for a while. For some reason the good souls were oblivious to their own non-living status. Hanging around out of sheer habit, because they didn't have the slightest idea how to let go of their fleshy homes, they had given the dead things enough clues as to how to blend in for a time. When they were forced to face their own extinction, they left a huge void their deceased hitchhikers could not fill.

Something had to be done soon. Charlie noticed that all twenty-five of the living dead had moved into separate areas, each standing close to a small group of people. And it seemed to both Vincent and Franklin that they were making efforts to connect with each other but in a bumbling sort of way, shuffling and grunting a little without making much headway. It seemed their efforts were hampered by the fact that they were not able to focus their drying eyeballs on any one object, making them look wild and stiff, turning their heads instead of moving their eyes. They couldn't make eye contact and they weren't speaking aloud. Gradually, it appeared that they were adapting, getting through to each other somehow because they were all moving to isolate the small pockets of survivors into even smaller groups, like they were rounding up stray cattle. Without intending to, the normal people were helping these zombie-like creatures in their efforts to control them, because as time progressed, they were getting more and more anxious to stay away from those that were showing more noticeably unpleasant differences. The Marrikans moved away from their strange acting companions in a clumsy kind of choreographed dance planned by the dead things. The anxiety of those few people's increasingly odd behavior made them move where they were intended to be, corralled in corners, sitting ducks for a sudden direct move by the enemy.

Charlie wondered if maybe there was some other kind of communication going on, something they had failed to notice because the five things had all cocked their heads to the side as if listening, and small crooked smiles broke out across their saggy faces. Charlie joined with the two Keepers. Together they tried to catch any signals that might be traveling from one pasty body to another. Still listening intently, the three of them separated and moved into the crowd to counteract whatever was about to happen. They were able to make out some sounds after a minute or two of concentrated effort. Strange mumblings filled the air but neither he, Franklin or Vincent was able to make out exactly what was being said.

As for Vincent, Charlie was receiving very clear messages from him, messages of true panic. Panic at the sudden realization that he could not kill what was already dead and how he would now have to revise the way he approached this enemy. For the first time in a long while, he was dealing with beings he could not hurt but could hurt him very much. It wasn't that he was afraid of them, it was just that he didn't know how to function in this situation. Charlie looked on with pity as he listened to Vincent's puzzled plea to his close friend Franklin.

Franklin, what am I supposed to do? Vincent's voice popped into Franklin's head. *The only people I can possibly kill are the ones I'm trying to protect. I can't touch the living, and if I touch the other things, I'm sure it won't do any good.*

This battle they were about to engage in would be more challenging than any he had ever fought in before because he and his rivals were on an equal playing field. This would call for care and skillful defensive tactics on his part, two things he had never had to use. At this moment, he wished he had been bestowed with such gifts. It was all very good and well to advise the Marrikans on what they should do to defend themselves, but he had never had to do that for himself.

Franklin looked over at Vincent and tried to appear confident for his friend's sake, while inside his own head he was trying to come up with a calm and logical approach to isolating the dead ones from the crowd they had so skillfully infiltrated. He even tried not to show how upset he was when three of the dead things managed to get quite close to a few small children. With a quick message to Vincent to calm down, Franklin moved forward slightly. He felt nauseous watching the ghastly grins that suddenly lit up their faces, and he knew that the creatures were thinking the same thing Vincent was; the only threats in this room right now were Charlie and Franklin and they were going to use the people around them to create confusion and interference to get to them specifically.

The more Marrikans that died, the more hosts they would make available to the spirits seeking a way down here. Franklin received this message as clearly as if he were Alice herself. She didn't like to share this kind of thing, even though he knew she could do it. Somehow her knowledge of things as they stood with the dead things was in his head. It wasn't exactly the type of communication they were used to sharing and he had only been able to see her past experiences when they met, but she was sharing a new thing with him somehow. Distant and fuzzy as it was, he had a feeling this was her desperate attempt to relay this important fact with her Circle members, relying on the unique bond they shared to get through when the other way was blocked.

The time had come to stop trying to be subtle about this. They had spent all lot of time preparing the refugees. Things had now come to a head. It was time to act. Raising his hands above his head with a warning cry to all the Marrikans in front of him, Franklin unleashed a fiery rain that fell into the crowd. With the powers of the Keeper giving them courage, the refugees fought back. Grabbing whatever was closest to protect themselves against these ugly version of themselves, they struck at the mushy bodies closest to them. At the command of the adults, the children around the dead ones took advantage of the distraction to fall to the ground and crawl away. Using the flexibility and fleet-footed skills available to only the very young, they hid in the narrow corridors. The only one not fortunate enough to make it away from the interlopers was a four-year-old girl pulled violently aside by a shorter pasty man whose hand moved faster than Franklin thought possible. The moving corpse dug his crumbling fingers into the poor girl's neck, holding her fast as she screamed in terror.

Franklin ran at the creature, each second dragging out as he watched the thing begin to choke the girl. It cannot be happening this way, he could not witness this! Desperately aiming a stream of flame at the thing's head, Franklin continued to run, believing it would break contact to save its shell. He was distressed to see that his action had no effect whatsoever, that the creature was still choking the child. A figure moved in from his left and he was surprised to see the flaming villain fall to the ground, his grip on the girl loosening as he shifted his now fully engulfed arms onto Vincent's body. Franklin and Charlie rushed forward, trying to find a way to help the man they couldn't touch because of his deadly gift. Helplessly they watched, distraught, as he screamed in pain.

Chapter Ten

At first, the call Eric heard was low and hard to make out, part of the interference he had been experiencing lately, but due to the persistence of the person calling, it eventually made itself heard. The person spoke unceasingly, repeating over and over again her wish that he return to the cave to help the people there. Each attempt to reach him became louder and more urgent until the voice began to yell his name loudly. The woman who called out was saying that things were getting very bad in the caves. She was telling him that their pursuer's focus had shifted from coming in to get him and Finola to the disturbing behavior of some of the people that stood right next to them. The voice was begging him in tones full of fear. After a minute or two, the screams of those surrounding her burst through at full strength. Alarmed, he and Finola quickly moved their new grown-up bodies into the tunnel. Fear for the people that had caused so much distress earlier had made them respond without hesitation after it was clear their help was needed.

Finola pushed the thorny bushes aside as they ran through to help the very people that had driven them into hiding, neither of them thinking about the consequences of going back to a hostile group. A few more rows of super-reinforced vegetation slid quickly out of the way, making an opening for the Keepers as the plants whispered words of caution to the woman who had made them. Though her outer appearance had been altered, they knew her well and stayed as closely connected as ever. What the plants conveyed to her was a growing sense of the danger waiting at the end of the tunnel. The words they spoke to her were not of any language to be understood by humans but rather an internal knowledge of every fiber and cell they were composed of, as it was related to her soul. She was part of them as they were part of her. As a result, every root, leaf, stem, and flower that sprouted out of the ground shared its experience with her.

She felt what they felt, saw what they saw, if you could call it actual sight, it was more a collection of things drawn from the atmosphere around them. In an intimate connection between parent and child, they shared everything. They were telling her of the wrongness happening just beyond the barrier, that there were many things unnatural moving amongst them. They were also telling her that the sickness that killed many of them on the surface was now down here, and they were scared for her as well as hopeful of her ability to rid the place of these things so they could not kill again.

The doorways were supposed to be blocked. What could possibly have gotten past the fortifications that Alice had been maintaining? Finola wondered as she ran headlong toward danger, toward the somewhat familiar portals. In the past, she had made them appear without being quite sure how she had managed to do it. There had just been this strange warm tingling feeling that came upon her and a glow that led to many strange and unpredictable places that had just opened up out of thin air, giving her and her companions a way out of their current nightmare.

84

She hadn't been able to recreate this little parlor trick after the first few times it happened and eventually Alice had taken over the task of defending them as they were, but even she couldn't make them appear. Her Circle mate hadn't let go yet, she felt her power even if she couldn't currently talk to her. The barriers were still very much in place at the portals. The power at the doorways was designed to keep bad things out, only good things could still gain entry if they needed to reach the safety of the underground places. So how had anything bad managed to get down here?

The last of the barbed defenses curled back and reluctantly let the Keepers pass into the main cavern, currently in a state of chaos. Stopping suddenly in mid-flight, Finola and Eric froze and stared in confusion at the struggle going on around them. The refugees that had aggressively chased them into hiding now seemed to be at war with themselves. Using both stones and branches broken from her beloved trees, they were beating at each other with terrified looks on their faces. Well, some of them, anyway. The others, the ones they were hitting, seemed to have a strange yellowish glaze in eyes that held no expression.

Three men with unusually pale skin were pursuing a young woman across the rocky floor, their hands covered in blood that must have come from the bodies lying on the ground behind them. Some of the injured were moving, while others were still and lifeless. The pools of blood surrounding the bodies showed Eric that those still moving would not last much longer and would soon join their companions in death.

It was much the same in several areas, with some very lively and normal-looking but horrified people aggressively defending themselves against creatures that kind of resembled them, except for the extraordinary ability to keep moving while sporting wounds which should have proved disabling. Crushed skulls and broken arms and legs were present in one form or another, but while those that were normal suffered from their wounds, the other half of the room seemed unaffected by them.

The pasty men, fresh from the fierce struggle with the dead and dying piled on the floor moved stealthily toward a slender female with black hair. The fierce snarls pasted on faces promised no mercy on their part when they caught up with her. The creepy men continued to advance as she backed close to a wall. Shuffling at a surprisingly fast pace on legs torn and bloody with pieces of bone sticking out here and there, the men seemed fixated on reaching her in particular. The young woman raised her head as Finola and Eric burst into the area. With a mixture of relief and fear, she called out to them. "Eric, do something!" As the words came out of the woman's mouth, one of the men with the impossibly painful injuries lunged at her, fingers slapping stone when she dodged aside at the last second. Hugging the wall behind her, she screamed again. "Finola, stop them before they kill any more of us!"

The message was loud and clear, the enemy was cleverly hidden within the ranks of the refugees.

While they had managed to make it this far undetected, the differences between the two sides were painfully clear now. The bodies of the attackers were beginning to rot, making them far uglier and smellier than the other inhabitants of the cave.

With a definite objective now identified, Finola let loose on the rapidly decaying body of the man who had just days earlier been the one to encourage the destruction of her plants. Roy, or whatever he truly was called; was her first target. She had a score to settle. It helped tremendously that she was pretty mad at this guy and he wasn't really alive, so she no longer felt bad about smashing his face to the ground.

With a small smile, that expressed more determination to complete this vengeful act than joy at having to perform it, Finola called on the feelings that had caused so much self-recrimination earlier, unleashing them all. Dead things were fair game, and she didn't hold back. Snaking, slimy vines curled around decaying ankles, cutting into them in two. Strips of skin sloughed off and fell to the ground with a small plopping sound before jerking the bodies back and downward into the hard surface. The sound of bones breaking echoed in the already noisy atmosphere. Eric, seeing his lovely companion wince at this sound, even as she continued to pound away at the dead things with her viciously effective growing gifts, dimmed the sound so she wouldn't have that to suffer it.

Standing her ground, even as she began to attract the attention of the zombies, Finola unleashed the full extent of her talent on the killers. The plants grew twice as fast as they ever had, the need for revenge being fed both by Finola and themselves as the connection between them became blurred and she let her anger guide them as a unit. Rough green tentacles snaked across the stone beneath her feet, branching out to reach for the evil beings, making violent and effective contact with almost all the invaders, effectively pushing and pulling them away from the living refugees before rendering them unable to attack. The wounded and traumatized quickly ran to Finola, hiding behind her as she attacked the enemy on their behalf.

Eric watched her; she felt his immense pride for her actions. He was unable to use his gifts against beings that didn't need to hear and didn't care that the eardrums of their hosts were burst but she was making significant progress in ridding this place of them. Despite the temporary handicap of being unable to use his gift, he did his best to help the people around him. Grabbing a thick stick from the ground, he went on the attack. Swinging the wooden club like a bat, Eric struck a large specimen that had two children cowering against a boulder. The blow had its intended effect, breaking several ribs, and piercing a lung that was no longer able to provide air to the body anyway. This action got the things attention away from the children and onto Eric, making the chunky dead man turn and lash out at him with swift and violent force.

One massive arm reached up, hand closing around the red-headed man's throat, cutting off his air supply. Eric struck out at the beefy arm intent on

88

making him as lifeless as it was. Chunks of puffy skin and tissue flew up in the air as his blows landed, but still the hand squeezed tighter and tighter, unaffected by his defenses. Throwing a punch that tore out the side of his attacker's face had absolutely no effect either; he struggled to break the steely grip without success. Whatever damage he inflicted upon the dead thing was useless because it didn't have any interest in maintaining the body that was decaying so fast now. It would be just as easy to find a new shell, maybe even his. In dismay, Eric looked at the ugly creature sporting a wide repulsive grin with teeth showing through his skinless cheek, exposed jaw moving in a soundless laugh, seeing his doom in that evil thing's soulless eyes, seeing Finola's future without him, growing older, maybe finding someone else to love. This was not what was supposed to happen! He was a powerful man, strong enough to make himself as she wanted them to be. He wanted to be that man that she saw, wanted to live with her for as long as he could before he was called back to be with his maker. That time could not have come so quickly. After all they had been through before they had stepped on the surface of this world, it could not be so easy to end his existence. Pushing and lashing out, until his body was no longer able to fight, Eric felt his airway close off until he was gasping like a fish out of water.

The world became black. Eric lost all control of his power and the room became very noisy once again. His soul spent a brief moment above the struggle, watching as the large man threw his limp body

89

aside and turned toward the children once again,
Finola's anguished cries sounding below him.

Chapter Eleven

Alice knelt on the floor, watching the doorway as the visitors she had been expecting shuffled in. It seemed like an eternity before they crossed the threshold but when they did, she almost did not recognize the figures as those of Isobel and her three cronies. At this point, the rate of decay in these borrowed vessels was so advanced they bore little resemblance to the people she had first seen when they arrived in the caves. Bones peeked through skin flaps that were peeling off like pieces of old plastic on a broken toy. There was no blood, because that particular fluid had long ceased to flow through their veins, and the repulsive odor that wafted from them was enough to cause a weaker person to gag and retch.

Alice was sure that the smaller figure, still acting as the leader in death as she had in life, was Isobel. The graying hair that hung to the scalp in clumps was one of the few clues left as to her identity, that, and the half section of face that still stuck to the skull. Looking at it was a reminder of the woman who had stared so hatefully at Randall before she used her influence to take him away. The men who were with her were completely unrecognizable. Alice couldn't really tell them apart, their size the only indicator that they were once large and strong. What was left was not so much impressive as disturbing. Muscular masses once covered with skin showed a grayish-purple color as they went about the act of moving what was left of the bodies in a slow jerking gait.

The stumbling quartet stopped suddenly as dead Isobel pointed at the pale, exhausted Keeper standing before them. Alice was now officially stretched further than she had ever been, appearing transparent without even trying to hide herself, while the world around her wavered in and out of focus. One minute she was seeing the true and solid world that housed the living and the next, the shadowy section that played host to what had never been but wished to be.

Grey became black as each world struggled to dominate. She was a Keeper, destined to be in control in both, but right now she was too weak to do this properly. She wasn't in just one place or another, she was flitting between them and couldn't seem to anchor herself in either. In one world she saw the corpses staring at her with interest, and in the other, she saw the hideous shifting forms of unformed evil with yellow eyes. Whatever their appearance, both forms were mocking her, laughter echoed first solid and stable as it came from the figures in the cave, then echoing and distant when they came through from the dead places.

Struggling to stand up straight, she reached out with her mind to check the shields around the two men she was trying to protect. The thin barrier held but she was surprised to find that the men behind it looked a bit stretched and thin behind the wavering wall of protection. Confused, Alice shook her head in an attempt to make everything look much clearer, only to find her vision becoming more and more distorted with each passing second. She felt the two innocent souls so close to her that she couldn't possibly have been mistaken about their presence and it reminded her of what she was and why she was here. There should be no doubt about her next action, she was determined to protect them with all the strength she had left.

Turning with a slight stumble to address the threat on her other side, she found the corpses had almost reached her. laughing and mumbling through ruined vocal chords. She couldn't understand a word they said but their intent was clear, they wanted to kill both her and the two men with her. Standing her ground, Alice used her hands to create hundreds of thin white strings which she threw out in front of her like a fisherman casting out a net. The thread-like projectiles flew through the air and settled just above the four images in front of her. Hovering, they were ready to be used against the ever-changing enemy. It was all so confusing, she had to force herself to concentrate really hard to keep centered and on task, it was becoming more and more difficult dealing with each universal shift. She was barely able to maintain everything for now and a movement to her right almost made her drop the net in shock. For a split-second, she was sure a familiar form had passed very close to her and she had to fight hard to regain what little control she had left. Shaking her head from side to side, Alice squinted and tried to look further into the darkness, stopping stopped just short of going fully back into the dead lands to see if the figure had gone there. She could have sworn she saw Eric move through the room, cross to a stone wall, and disappear. This could not be true! It had to be another cruel trick on the part of the enemy. And it had worked, providing enough of a distraction for them to spread out in a wider line in front of her to evade her trap. One of the figures had made it close enough to reach out a ruined hand to grab her arm. She felt air move as the hand descended on her own and attempted to grip it with fat, flaky fingers. Scaly pieces of skin stuck to hers when the fingers moved across her arm, trying to clamp down without success.

The proximity of the enemy made her jump back. Her reaction made the small form that had once been Isobel smile with eyes so wide an eyeball popped out and lay on a sunken cheek to stare at her from its odd position. This action both grossed Alice out and made her more determined to spare the two young men behind the fate these poor people had suffered. They were not going to die and have their bodies used to harm others. Without glancing back, she reached out with her mind and felt the men standing strong and bright behind her. In order to keep the enemy back, she needed more strength and drew on all of her resources to accomplish this. The time had come to ease the burden of overextending herself, so she began to drop some of her other shields; the ones covering the doors had to go. With the shields down to ensure the safety of all the places, she had to close each one. All over the worlds, the magical portals began to disappear, much to the amazement of those around them. The openings snapped shut with a final sound that was both depressing and scary, but it was the only way she could think of to keep the others safe while she wasted away. At this point,

Alice didn't know how long she would last, what with the lack of sleep and this hopeless feeling she had without the support of Randall and her Circle members. She was so alone.

Alice didn't feel *real* anymore. She missed Randall so much it hurt, she couldn't feel him, couldn't talk to him anymore; maybe he really was dead. She didn't want to believe it but maybe it was time she did. If he was gone then she really didn't want to be in this world anyway. Resignation began to set in. Maybe this was her fate, after all, to disappear into nothingness and deal with the things that dwelled there. If this was how it was supposed to be, then fine, but it was still important to keep the refugees safe. With the added boost of not having to maintain the doors, Alice gathered the strings closer together and began to move her fingers in a circular motion. Knitting the net together, the beautiful Keeper strengthened her trap. Fine threads infused with the strength of steel closed and pulled tight, each splitting off to form four tentacles that reached for the dead things and drew them in to the center of the web.

Four very angry masses were jerked roughly from their sheltering solid forms and pulled backwards into the shadows. The nothingness was forced to give up claim on their borrowed vessels and though they fought to regain control, Alice's power was still too much for them. Dark clouds of ugliness were sucked back into the nothing they had come from. As their cursing screams died down, she sank to the damp, cold floor once again, a place she was becoming far too familiar with. This time she couldn't work up enough strength to raise her head to check on her two companions, but she still felt them with her and wasn't surprised when, once again a hand gently touched her arm. She was surprised, however, to feel a slow steady warmth spread through her body, giving her the ability to raise her head just enough to see the last person she would have expected to see in front of her.

Chapter Twelve

A foul-smelling wind blew across a dark landscape. The only light in the area came from the four clean things moving through it. At the moment, the sole thing that kept the filthy ugly things around them from approaching was their shining goodness. A brilliant glow clung to the Keepers' forms and lit up ground that had never had to tolerate the intrusion of anything like them before. Everything was distasteful and out of place here, even the surface beneath them seemed to try to shrink away, loathing to connect with the substance they were composed of. The four travelers were walking above the ground. A welcome phenomenon, because they did not like this place any more than it liked them. Like the pleasant section of the Afterworld, every second they spent here seemed to drag on for an eternity, an eternity they did not want to endure.

They wandered around in this land of permanent midnight in search of something that could end the affliction that was Braccus. Whatever it was, it didn't want to be found and was now being helped by an unlikely ally. Someone who had fought so strongly against everything Braccus stood for was suddenly having second thoughts about completely ending his existence, causing Sara a lot of internal distress.

Perhaps this made her see something that threw her confusing world into further chaos. She was almost certain that when she turned toward one of the last existing untarnished places in this section of the Afterworld she saw someone that she had known from time to time through Iam. This person had knowledge of her through visions that she and Iam had exchanged through the years. Their distant connection was needed to keep him and his other Circle members going during tough times. He was a little bit older than when she had last seen him, brief as their encounter had been, but she was sure it was the Keeper called Eric who turned to look at her briefly before moving through a portal, appearing suddenly as the orange burst of color behind him. The vision smiled and nodded his head before passing through the opening again in a manner that left her puzzled. She didn't feel his loss like she had her two Circle members. Dead or not, a connection still existed between the Keepers, but she didn't sense his wonderful essence, diminished as it might be here. No, he was not part of this place, so she put the whole experience down to another trick of the enemy.

He could not possibly be dead because she would have known that, even as separated as she was from the living worlds, she would have known if he was like she and her companions. It couldn't be real. Not wanting to disturb her fellow dead people with this sight apparently only she had seen, Sara put it behind her and forced herself to move on.

Their destination, a line of broken black mountains, kept getting closer and closer. Traveling there had been a certainty not too long ago but now, with Shalsar remaining steadily silent, it seemed questionable. It was all up to Sara to draw what she could from the few memories she had been given at the beginning of this journey to find her way.

It was terrible to be at war with herself again, especially when the part of her she was fighting had been her constant companion and strongest supporter for most of her life. It was as if everything she thought she had known about her guiding light, the woman she had inherited her powers from was a lie and she didn't know what to do about it. Shalsar may have lapsed into silence but she wasn't resisting at this moment, she just wasn't helping. To Sara this was just as disturbing because she just felt the wrongness of the situation. It had not been too long ago that Shalsar was fighting Braccus just as strongly as she was. What had caused this sudden change? How had it been possible for Shalsar to be so secretive about her true intentions?

What was it about this 'thing' they were seeking that had made everything so different? Pushing on while all was relatively quiet in her head and she wasn't fighting the remains of powerful beings that seemed to want to hitchhike and run her brain, Sara was determined to end all of this as soon as possible. Trusting in what she felt certain was her last reliable recollection, Sara held fast to her connection to James and Thomas and moved straight ahead, all the while quietly listening, keeping her senses open for any sign of the enemy. Instinct had her continuing despite all the doubts at the back of her mind.

They had left the gruesome town where dead bodies roamed freely awhile back and walked into a desert-like setting that was the opposite of any they had ever seen. As usual, everything here was far uglier than anything Iam created. This darkened version of

Iam's arid sunbaked atmosphere was teaming with odd things; ratty creatures the size of large cats skirted around their light, casting ominous shadows on the sandy ground. Scorpions, equal in size to rodents, with stingers that extended out from the body like a long knitting needle, ran around stopping occasionally to jab at other creatures before moving into the darkness beyond. All around them, black sand moved in a hot, foul-smelling wind that whipped and swirled and broke off to form several mini-tornados. The small conical-shaped formations shifted constantly, looking for one second like human forms, and the next like mythical monsters with many arms and distorted features. These useless intimidation techniques did not impress the Keepers but were working quite well on Diandra.

The young woman held James's arm so tightly that he was sure her fingerprints were now permanently embedded in his skin. She regretted that, he could tell, but James didn't mind. He remembered what her internal warning system had done for him not so long ago. Diandra had saved him from the greatest mental torment and kept him together so he could battle the enemy. The result was that he and his fellow Keepers survived to fight another day; and so he endured the minor discomfort and kept her close to his side. It would have been far more painful to be without her.

Shaking with fear, Diandra avoided looking from side to side, preferring to look straight ahead; her primary focus on the back of Sara's head. The distraction was enough to still the shaking and loosen her grip on her boyfriend's non-real flesh. James didn't complain, even though he felt the pain just as keenly as if he were alive. He understood that, as much as she had been through, she had been a gifted human and not a Keeper and had not seen everything they had. But she had one thing most people dead or alive didn't have, she had him and he tried to pass that knowledge to her. He was hers to draw from and he wanted her to know that, no matter what, their connection was her safety, and her safety was his salvation.

A small smile curled up the corner of her mouth as she caught that thought. It was so nice to have this time with him… Diandra stopped herself from going any further, quietly censoring the thought before James could pick it up. Puzzled, he smiled at her brief, totally odd thought, considering where they were, this could hardly be seen as a nice time. He patted her arm comfortingly and prepared to move ahead with her, but they didn't get far.

Sara's feet stopped moving and she turned to look at the red-haired girl who saw things others of her kind could not. Blue eyes gazed into purple searchingly as each and every thought in her head was looked at carefully. Diandra stared back in fascination, caught up in the magic of all she saw swirling around in those two orbs. Water, she saw water, lots of it, and she felt herself slipping under the cool wet surface to view the many wonders underneath. The truth was swimming there, many versions of it, some of which she wished were true and some she was sure were not. The special young dead girl felt Sara gazing into her soul, knowing she was fully aware of all that went on inside her head. *Do you want him to know?* Sara's voice sounded softly in her inner ear.

This particular conversation was private, intentionally hidden from the man they were discussing. But to her surprise, Sara felt Thomas in her head even stronger than before. He was becoming better at getting past the barrier she had put up against the others. It was another sign that their bond was growing. Being persistent was paying off for Thomas, he was learning things from hanging out in her head constantly. She could feel his disapproval of the way this conversation was going; he didn't want to keep anything secret from their Circle member. He didn't speak, continuing to listen silently, even though, at this point, she knew what he was thinking anyway. That this kind of secret could be devastating to them all, but he didn't have a good answer for it because telling it would be almost as bad.

No. If he knew what has already happened, he wouldn't do what he needs to do, go where he needs to go, Diandra whispered back sadly.

Then he won't know, but I don't think even you realize what it all means. It will be as it's meant to be, and nothing can change that. Diandra was listening but wasn't sure if she heard exactly what she was being told. The feeling she got from this conversation was neither hope nor despair, it just left her numb. The dead girl who traveled among the Keepers forced herself to walk forward with a neutral expression to avoid giving away her feelings to James, but there was so much more beneath the surface.

The whole encounter lasted less than a second, but the conversation held so many meanings for Diandra, none of which she particularly cared for, because they showed a future that she didn't want to know about. She may not be a Keeper, but she was going to do what she could, go as far as she could to make sure this had a successful ending. A slight tug on her arm had Diandra looking into James's eyes as he urged her to move forward to catch up with his two Circle members, who were so far ahead they had could barely be seen. Dark puffs of smoke began to swirl around Sara and Thomas's forms, threatening to engulf them and hide them from view. The glowing light surrounding their bodies prevented this from happening entirely, cutting through the dusky cover enough to keep them in sight. It also showed the shadowy forms hovering above the light waiting to swoop in and make their move on the vile intruders should an opportunity ever arise.

Spurred on by an inner sense of urgency, Diandra moved forward quickly, practically dragging James along behind her. The ground they weren't even making contact with began to throb underneath them. The sound and feel of it promised that once again, things were about to change. It must mean they were getting near the source of all the problems of the worlds, and she wanted to be close to her friends when she disappeared forever more.

Chapter Thirteen

Bodies fell quickly, both dead and living, in all the separate underground areas. The refugees that had the assistance of the Keepers were lucky and had a higher survival rate than those that did not. The others saw lots of good souls leaving their poor defenseless bodies at the mercy of the dead things that had slipped into their midst. The few normal living souls left alive ran and hid in the deepest part of the caves, shaken but determined to live until the special and powerful ones they'd heard about arrived to help them.

It was during a few horrible surprise attacks when they were beaten, and some killed by those they thought were friends and family that the refugees discovered the truth about those were sharing space with. When all pretense at life had been abandoned by the interlopers and savagery had taken over, the living learned quickly that it was possible to defeat the corrupted bodies if they waited until the rotting had started. These lessons were learned the hard way, in the middle of pain and loss, out of a need to survive.

The corpses were only effective when they were fresh because they were hard to detect, when they looked just like everyone else. So the living had to be careful to avoid becoming victims. They took their chances only when it became apparent the enemy was at its weakest. When the decay started, they could attack and remove all parts of them that could do harm. If it meant ripping off arms, legs, and poking out the occasional eyeball to disable the invaders then that's what they were going to do. Thankfully, it took only a few violent encounters before they learned the minor differences that made these things not one of them anymore. There was a change in the way the living saw things, as if invisible fingers were pointing accusingly at the imposters, giving away secrets, exposing them for what they really were. The refugees couldn't have known that the spirits of the Keepers were doing what they could to protect them by revealing the minor flaws of the departed in ways that drew attention to their deadly nature. Flies appeared in mid-air and began to land on the spots that had subtly became soft from decay. Mysterious sparks of light drew the eye to the shuffling gaits and arms that were becoming stiff and harder to bend.

The helpful warnings had the desired effect. Those that had not been attacked in the initial ambush, had begun to look around them suspiciously at their companions. The enemy had used their initial panic and mistrust to drive them further and further apart, but after the differences were made clear, the last of the living normal ones were able to join forces and fight back. Successfully breaking away, the small groups waited terrified, angry, and hopeful for their promised saviors to arrive before they became like those poor possessed shells they had been forced to kill for a second time. The gifted ones kept them as calm as possible with stories of their visions about the Keepers and what they could do for them.

In the other underground places, it was equally nightmarish, even in places with the good fortune to have the Keepers. The group with the highest survival rate was, of course, those that were with Robert and Maryann; he was at this point the oldest of the Keepers left in the world of the living and his powers were just as potent as they had ever been. When the evil thoughts had invaded the bodies of the dead and dying, he had been quick to detect them and had therefore managed to isolate them from the rest of his saved people. His was the one area where only five deaths occurred; the first a man who would not listen when told to move away from a woman he had known as his wife for fifteen years.

The man in question had not known she had been killed just before they arrived in the underground place. The couple had been separated for a mere twenty minutes when she had fallen and broken her neck. Her husband had seen her fall but when he reached her, she had seemed alright, and he assumed it was not as bad as he feared. Relieved at their good fortune, he helped her up and they had run to safety with the others. Robert had spotted her, noticed the difference in her, and tried to separate them, but the man grabbed the woman's hand and pulled her closer to him. Robert watched in horror, as the possessed female's hands reached up as if to cling to her husband, then deliberate twist and break the male's neck. As she committed this horrible deed, she was staring straight at the Keeper, smiling, apparently enjoying the effect her act had upon him.

He also managed to trap four other decaying people in a corner far from the living refugees. He stopped their advance rather quickly, using his powers to prevent them from taking even one step toward his people.

With an anguished cry, Robert raised his hands, becoming a dragon-like creature, letting loose a stream of fiery hail upon the bodies of all the possessed ones. The fight was over here before it had started, and the shocked villagers huddled together near their powerful savior, watching the ashes of the evil things float around the cavern. Grief-stricken at the loss of his people, Robert changed back to his original form, struggling to show a calm front for those around him. Stress had him reaching out for a familiar, comforting bond that had carried him through battles for centuries. Low and distant, it vibrated in the air just enough to be felt; bringing an inner peace he missed so much. He felt his brother's presence move in the air around him, encouraging him to remember what they had accomplished in the last great struggle. Reviewing all the horrors he had survived to this point gave Robert strength. He was still alive to fight evil and that, in itself, was a victory and something to build on. Robert gathered his people closer and they sat in stunned silence as he and Maryann exchanged worried looks. They were the only two here seeing quite clearly what was going on in the other worlds, the struggles the young Keepers, who were like children they never had. In particular, Maryann had seen an unmoving Eric lying on the ground. Together they watched another

108

place, where two other Keepers faced another crisis, their thoughts and actions playing out like a bizarre movie before their distressed eyes.

In the less fortunate areas of the worlds, Vincent was facing a terrible crisis as he fended off bodies that were not afraid to touch him because he could no longer harm them. For a man that had longed for human contact for most of his life, this type of touch was not exactly what he wanted. His instinct for survival kicked in as the blows landed on his body. He hadn't had to deal with this before and received several painful punches and a deep cut to his right arm before he managed to strike back at the three zombie-like things that had ganged up on him. Ripping off the arm of one of them, Vincent used it to beat back the hideous trio. With a great deal of effort, he managed to get far enough from the shuffling things that scratched, bit, and tore at his body to allow Franklin to set fire to them. Vincent stumbled backward to watch the bodies flail around as walking fireballs, shocked at how helpless he had now become. He hurt all over and blood seeped from the many wounds inflicted upon him before he remembered how to fight back. Wiping away a stream of red that dripped into his eyes; he watched his good friend burn all those monstrosities while also directing the groups of good people around them to use improvised weapons to defend themselves. It was the first time since they had known each other that the tables were turned, and he was the weaker one.

He was glad to see that most of the enemy had been herded into the center of the room by armed refugees who were now doing a very good job at destroying their uninvited guests. Franklin had no problem reducing the rest of the walking remains to a pile of ashes as the empowered villagers watched with the satisfaction of those who had fought hard to survive another impossible situation - and succeeded.

There was no sound for quite some time except the crackling flames and protesting screeches from the lifeless evil thoughts forced from the bodies. They had no place to go except back out into the in between areas to watch the forms they could not enter now. There were no longer any candidates here for occupation and the doorways were all closed to any type of travel.

Standing and watching the ashes of the bodies float upwards, Franklin walked over to Vincent to check on him. He looked pretty banged up, with several cuts and bruises but he didn't sense anything serious. He regretted that alone he wasn't able to fix the damage, but his friend would live, for now he would have to heal slowly, like a regular person.

"Can you stand?" he asked as he looked around for Charlie, who he hadn't seen in awhile.

"Yes," Vincent said, rising. He too was thinking about the little man who he had come to like a lot. A short search of the area revealed no sign of him dead or alive. Where had he gone? They had little time to worry about this new predicament, for they were soon besieged with a flood of information from everywhere. It was as if the dam had burst and all that had been kept from them was suddenly flowing into their heads. It was a wonderful distraction to find they were connected once again and could now hear what was happening with their groups. Vincent and Franklin exchanged horrified looks as both stood sharing a vision they did not want to see.

Chapter Fourteen

Finola was crying out Eric's name over and over as she directed her plants to pin the dead things to the ground. In a desperate shrill voice, she urged him to get up and come to her, knowing full well that he could not. She couldn't see his chest rise and fall, didn't feel his oh so wonderful presence in her head as she continued to use her plants to their deadliest effect. Row upon row of spiky plants tangled around wasted ankles, anchoring them down, wrenching feet off completely. It seemed the corpses were now falling apart at a much faster rate; aided by some unseen force which was working on their side for a change. Flesh seemed to melt away from bone while figures were held tightly to the stone floor, flopping around until all that could be heard were Finola's anguished cries and the clanking of bones against the solid surface. A strong authoritative voice inside her told her to hold the trap until there was nothing left for the ill thoughts to use as vehicles for their deeds. The force behind the command was strong and she couldn't disobey it.

With the knowledge that she could not break free until it was safe to do so, Finola used all her inner strength to keep back from Eric. It was not what she wanted to do; it was what the voice in her head commanded. This act of obedience was killing her; a tearing pain in the vicinity of her heart was almost more than she could stand. She couldn't look at him and not go to him, so she had to look away. With tears in her eyes, the young Keeper focused only on destroying the abominations in front of her until she felt the voice free her from its command.

When it had faded away, she surveyed the scene before her. The last of the possessed things lay unmoving on the ground. A gentle internal nudge by the same force that had held her in place made her aware that she was finally free to run to Eric now. She wanted to scream and cry at the heartless way she had been kept from him. How she could be serving an entity that would deny her going to help the man she loved when she knew he was no longer breathing. Finola experienced a moment of pure rage that nearly saw her turn her back on all she had ever known.

How could she have been denied the right to save him! He had been just a few feet away and she could have gotten to him so quickly! The voice in her head spoke loudly, breaking into her thoughts at the moment she would have thrown everything away for the loss of her soul mate. She didn't want to be here anymore if he was gone. Stern yet filled with compassion, Iam talked to her.

You couldn't have saved him; you were meant to save the others. Saving Eric was her job. The sentence ended very softly, as if her creator were speaking to a small child who'd just thrown a tantrum. He was letting her know that he understood her distress but would not tolerate disobedience from her before he freed her to go to Eric. The whole message of reprimand and hope happened in less time than it took for her to turn away from the tangle of bones and overgrowth to the place Eric had fallen. The sight that greeted her was both puzzling and alarming.

Eric was still lying flat on the ground but kneeling next to him was a darkly beautiful young woman with jet-black hair, smooth ivory skin and eyes the color of coal. She was stunning but scary. Her skin was so pale it shined like moonlight in the dim cave; a nightlight among the neutral almost invisible living things around her. Her whole appearance screamed walking dead, like anything she touched would become as cold and lifeless as she was. If she hadn't been moving and looking around, Finola would have assumed she had been killed by the enemy days ago. Dressed all in black, she reminded her of one of those goth-girls she had seen during her time at school. Looking like a horror movie extra, this stranger was hovering over her boyfriend and Finola had to do something to save him.

The urge to run forward and push the girl away from Eric was strong but she was held back once again as the voice told her to wait and watch. This stranger took hold of Eric's hand and his chest began to move, rising and falling with each restored breath. Then he opened his eyes. The first thing the resurrected young man did was to look straight at Finola. Now free to move, she ran straight into his arms. Breathing in his familiar scent, she buried her nose in the soft material of his shirt which quickly became wet with her tears. Instinctively, she used their familiar connection to make sure that this was indeed still Eric and not one of the uninvited things they had just gotten rid of.

His soul was clean and still very much intact, but with one slight change: he felt whole; the empty area she had felt in him before was smaller, having shifted to include a part that had been previously vacant. A sudden breakthrough had been made. This change had something to do with this one incident, and it wasn't just the fact that he had been dead and now suddenly wasn't. This girl had just brought him back to life, which meant she was not just an ordinary human being. It had to be that she was the last Keeper, the one that made Eric's Circle complete. She had to be Vincent's other half. It made perfect sense. He could bring death and she could bring life.

Reluctantly letting go of Eric's hand, Finola moved back slightly to study the girl that sat next to them a little more closely. She was a bit frightening with all the darkness about her, but she didn't feel bad to Finola now that she was near her. Over the years, Finola had developed an internal warning system that made her study everyone very carefully before letting them close to her. It was a shame that they had spent so much time separated from the refugees because she could have sensed the dead ones before they had a chance to infiltrate like they had. She was thinking this very thought as she looked the girl over carefully, guilt for her earlier actions and relief for herself and Eric hanging in the air around her. The feelings must have been stronger than she thought because it seemed to trigger a response in the woman, who reached out and touched her arm. Upon contact, she immediately felt better than she ever had in her life. She felt hope, love, and an awakening in her heart for all good things possible in these horrible times.

"Her name is Marlaina," Eric said with a smile, as he confirmed what she had just figured out. He had already connected with the woman without ever having spoken a word to her. She had reached out for him with her soul and called him back from the great beyond. Unfortunately for him, that was the closest they got to what they should be, the connection was already fading as he fully returned to his body.

Finola shared his thoughts as he showed her that for a minute or two he had actually been dead, walking in the shadows and watching all the madness in the cave that now went on without him. He had moved through a glowing doorway totally unlike the other portals that seemed to have been closed off entirely. Eric had seen many strange sights as he moved through the opening, it was like looking at many different scenes at once, seeing the lovely living things and the ugly dead things as each side went about the acts of surviving in the worlds any way they could. He could also see the things that moved in the gathering darkness, things that seemed to be growing more dominant even in the Afterworld where he was. The creepy areas he saw here were disturbing because they seemed to extend throughout most of this place, with small pockets of light fighting to keep back the darkness.

This was not how he had always heard death was supposed to be. It didn't seem peaceful and he saw no sign of Iam or the wonders he had made for his faithful souls. He was so scared to see this turn of events. Did this mean that it was hopeless, that Braccus's powers extended even into the restful places that were promised for those that passed into death? He didn't have long to dwell in the unpleasant place his thoughts were taking him to, because even as he wandered into the deteriorating Afterworld, he saw in the distance a sight that changed his outlook on the whole situation. Shining in the middle of the darkness were three of the brightest and most special souls he had ever encountered. Eric had been told that there was a reason for their deaths, so what they sought must be here somewhere, which was very good news.

He watched as they moved above all the ugliness around them, the woman walking tall and proud, golden hair showing up like moonlight against the darkness and the men with her both carrying different shades of darkness about them. The darkness they carried was bold and pure, glowing like a dark pearl that cut a clean hole in the murky blackness that was around them. Sara, James, and Thomas, the worlds' hope, passed within his view. Eric stood still and observed the progress of the small group which included a female soul he did not know. They all moved toward a craggy mountain range in the distance.

He smiled, and Sara's attention was drawn to him at the very moment he heard Marlaina calling him back. Turning to answer the commanding female voice he could not ignore, Eric moved back towards the living world. The whole episode had taken less than a second in time in this place. Eric felt that Sara had made more of an impression upon him

118

than he had on her, but at least he had encouraging news to pass on to his fellow Keepers.
Eric's thoughts of the Keepers seemed to break through the barrier that had existed between them. Just a few minutes after his arrival back in his body, the floodgates opened and they all started talking at once.

Chapter Fifteen

Alice looked into Randall's eyes while touching his face with trembling fingers. She wasn't quite sure what she was seeing was real. Maybe she was dead, and she was seeing him in the in-between place. If they could be together there she wouldn't have minded the dying part. She wished with all her heart it were not so for his sake, but oh his beautiful face was so good to see.

She had to get herself together and focus; everything was so confusing. It helped that the doorways had been closed. With that burden removed, she had enough strength to partially sit up but that was about all. Alice was no longer able to maintain security for all the areas and at this moment she wasn't sure she could even keep herself safe.

If this wasn't really Randall then she was going to either have to make an effort to kill this thing that was looking at her with such loving eyes, or it was going to kill her. Either way it was a bad situation with no hope of a good ending. It bothered her that they were usually so closely connected but she couldn't tell the difference in her current state.

The voice that spoke to her as if from a great distance sounded like Randall's, it even made her heart thump with joy at the memory of her love for him. Echoing dully in her head, the sound was calling her back to him. "Alice," he said softly in her ear at the same time as other loud gravely voices shouted at her in the background. Vile voices were cursing her for removing them from their borrowed means of transportation and were doing their best to keep her trapped in uncertainty. She didn't know what to do. Was she even awake? Had she given in to exhaustion and was merely having a bad dream? It was hard to tell because lately both reality and nightmares had a lot in common.

Digging her fingernails deeply into her own arm to test this theory, Alice gave herself a savage pinch, drawing blood, proving that she must be conscious because it hurt so much. The Randall figure was kissing her cheek and calling even more insistently, trying to break through the misty veil that separated her from the solid plain of existence that should be grounding her. She didn't know if she could, or should, listen.

A hand touched her shoulder and she turned to face yet another thing that was trying to capture her attention. Steven and Ray were standing behind her, looking on with concern, small smiles turning up the corner of their lips when they realized that she saw them too. She had not responded earlier when they spoke to her, simply stared into empty space like she was seeing something they could not. It was hazy all around this place. Whatever she had done to those evil dead things that had been after them had changed the atmosphere here, and now it was hard to see anything but her. The rocks were hidden by mist and they couldn't feel the ground underneath them, but she was as bright as a full moon on a really dark night. All they could see of the area around them was the light that she put out. She saw them now and was listening to every word they were thinking.

The two men were understandably drawn to her as she was the center of everything here, their rock; grounding them in a very scary world. After fighting so long and hard just to make it to this refuge, they felt far from safe. The young men had always watched out for others; keeping them protected both above and below ground. It was getting so hard to continue battling in situations that were more and more outrageous, with creatures that were constantly changing, becoming increasingly difficult to overcome. They had always been big strong men and used to boldly going into danger for their people, but this young woman, smaller and more delicate than they, had stepped willingly into danger for them. Thoughts and feelings passed between her and them without words.

The warriors knew how tired and worn out she was, had seen the way she staggered beneath the enormous weight of all she was responsible for, yet she still managed to put herself in harm's way for them. This courageous act had humbled them and had earned their respect and loyalty. If only they could get her to Jacob, it would be the start of something positive for their people. It would be a win-win situation. With her and Randall together, they would have an edge over the evil ones and she would be looked after while she got some much-needed rest. Maybe they could help each other out. They gazed at her adoringly before she just disappeared and heard so many people talking at once.

Blinking rapidly as she lost the two men for a second, Alice felt solid and focused as each of her fellow Keepers broke through, all talking excitedly as they felt their connection restored. Randall was holding her face in his hands. When their eyes met, and he knew she was totally with him again, he gave her a warm enthusiastic kiss. On returning his kiss with as much strength as she could muster, she heard a shuffling of feet followed by a low cough and a few male voices chuckling in the background. Looking behind a very relieved Randall, she saw three men watching their exchange with amused embarrassment.

While all handsome and rugged men, with an air of goodness hanging around them that was easy for her to make out, it was the man in the center that caught her attention. The glowing green aura that she had become accustomed to seeing around good souls was enhanced by a golden tint that marked him as special. That small clue combined with the fact that this man looked so much like Steven, told her right away who he was.

This must be the Jacob she had heard so much about, and he had found Randall! This was so wonderful! Steven would be so happy, he was just thinking about taking her to find his brother. She never thought she was able to read the living like she just had, but both he and Ray were coming through to her so strongly, maybe this was a new feature of her continually changing gift. Delighted at this sudden turn of events, she stared straight at the seer and addressed him by name. "Hello, Jacob,"

Her voice got stronger and louder as she drew strength from her Circle mates. "I'm so glad to meet you. Look, Steven, we didn't have to go far to find him. He came to us." She turned back to the two young men standing in the shadows that were becoming a little bit fuzzy and out of focus for her. "Steven, Ray!" she called out, straining to hear them as she saw their forms moving as close as they could. Something seemed to be holding them back from her. Alice felt her two Circle mates slowly coming back into her head, but she wasn't yet able to pull out everything they said. She continued to swim through the muck that was her surroundings in the hope that things would continue to get clearer. Why could she only see part of this world? Surely, she should be able to see all her companions.

Randall was alive and very real; she could feel his touch and his presence in her mind again. There was no doubt that he was with her as she touched his face. Maybe the weakness was still getting the better of her; she had been through a lot with the dead things and she just needed some rest.

Randall held his girlfriend, thanking Iam over and over again in his head, knowing full well that it was his help that had gotten him free from Isobel and her group and led him to the one person who could help get through to the traumatized people here. It was just too perfect. They had wandered into this dark place and found Alice when there were so many possible places for her to be. He was relieved and grateful to find that they were not as alone as he had first thought.

Kneeling and hugging her slender body close to his, he tried to give her everything he had left of his own strength to give. She was in his arms, but she was still so far away from him somehow. She was still seeing things he could not, and he knew it was because she was partially dwelling in between the living and dead places. He wished he had the power to bring her back. Calling her name over and over until he was sure she heard him, he reached out with his spirit for the connection that had always brought them together. It seemed like forever before he got any kind of response from her. She kept looking behind him and smiling at something. When the other Keepers managed to break through and make their presence known again, he knew she had finally seen him and was in the same place mentally. His heart swelled in his chest until it fairly burst with joy. Then he was kissing her and never wanted to stop.

The noise that broke them apart brought his other companions to her attention and she addressed their leader by name. Randall watched the same man react to her greeting with a small nod, as if he was not surprised that she knew who he was. What happened next was a surprise, however. The minute Alice began to talk to someone named Steven about Ray, the Seer turned pale, looking like she had just punched him in the stomach.

"How do you know Steven?" the strong warrior choked out through tightly clenched lips. This exchange really disturbed him, and Randall couldn't figure out why. Randall had been with Steven and Ray for a short time before Isobel and her men had taken him but had not seen them since. They were brave young men who seemed capable of taking care of themselves and as far as Randall could tell, no one seemed to dislike them. What did Jacob know about these two men that caused him to be so upset by the mention of their names?

The man approached the Keepers, eyes wide as he dropped to his knees next to Alice and reached for her hand. Alarmed by his look, Randall's fingertips crackled with building power as he prepared to defend Alice against this man who he thought was on their side. "Can you see Steven?" Jacob asked again, this time softer and with less urgency. Alice looked at the large muscular man with the red hair, noting the scar that ran down the side of his face, proof of a life spent fighting a brutal enemy. She saw determination in his eyes and another stronger emotion that she wouldn't have expected: sorrow. Placing her hand on Randall's to still the energy that flowed there, Alice spoke to Jacob.

"Yes, I can," she said softly and turned back toward the darkness to see the two young men staring at her with hopeful eyes. "Can't you?" The two men had moved forward until they were standing right in front of Jacob, reaching toward him with both hands, but Jacob didn't react to their presence at all. "He's here?" Jacob asked in a hushed voice, barely containing his emotions, but she saw the sadness in his red eyes, the eagerness to hear something specific in the flush of his cheeks and the way he held his breath in anticipation of some profound statement on her part. She must have taken just a bit too long to answer because when he spoke again she could hear the tense note in his voice, indicating impatience and a little desperation. He moved closer to Alice; close enough to make Randall zap the floor at his feet to warn him away. Sparks flew from the stone, but it barely kept him back. It was as if he couldn't help himself, he wanted an answer from her and he was going to have it.

"Right in front of you," Alice answered, afraid of the reason he couldn't see the men standing in plain sight, looking at him with sad smiles on their faces. "In front of me," the husky warrior fought back tears as he spoke the words that Alice was dreading, "How is it that you can see my dead brother?"

Chapter Sixteen

The skies got darker as a strange black mist rolled in to cover all the landscape of this area of the Afterworld. It was getting hotter and hotter as the seconds ticked by. The appearance of the dead place changed from that of a desert to a volcanic sea as if a television channel had been flipped. Red lava bubbled up from an unseen source, sloshing freely around on the surface, swirling and dipping on its way to no particular place. The steaming liquid was moving constantly, following the four bright entities that floated above it, watching for any opportunity to get past the brightness that surrounded their repulsive goodness. Crackling sounds filled the air, a sign of the growing tension in the atmosphere as the dead things reacted to the presence of something it hated and feared: the Keepers. Even though dead, they were just as threatening to what occupied this place because they had invaded "His" space and were looking for" His" secret.

Still eager to please their source, the evil thoughts here wanted to make their move on the Keepers, waiting for Braccus to give them just one chance to get close. If they accomplished their goal of killing the one that could get to the thing they had been ordered to protect, then maybe he would honor them with a newly dead body.

The things that never really had life had seen many bodies piling up in the living worlds below, and were anxious to get a chance to feel what it was like to have something solid to occupy. The few entities that had made it back here from down there had told them that their experience inside the shells had been exhilarating. The fight was on to get back inside a body while the envious crowd around them waited like panting dogs to bolt toward a source. It would be harder to get into a body now that the underground was sealed, but maybe, if they pleased Braccus with a truly gruesome sacrifice, they would be able to get through somehow. With this goal in mind, they continued to try and find a way to get at the Keepers walking through their territory.

Gnarly stumps popped up from the red soup that bubbled over from some unclean place. Another surge of energy helped to form fingers on the doughy, slop-filled stumps. Long skinny digits reached toward the light, groping ineffectively at the glow that invaded their space. Screams erupted from the half-formed blobs as contact with the Keepers caused them to break apart into a finer mist before reforming in another spot to try again. Reading their intent easily, Sara watched all this as she moved. She had been thinking more often about what she was almost sure she had seen not too long ago. What she had originally considered merely a trick of the enemy was suddenly a disturbing possible reality, and it scared her far more than the grotesque display she was walking through. Uncertainty had her taking just a moment to pause and reach out for the one soul she thought she had seen pass through here briefly. As time passed, she found herself reviewing that encounter in her head more often and was becoming less sure of what it meant than she had before. Nagging doubts were tugging at her; she was blind to the worlds' perils. It was so unlike the time when she could have easily moved anywhere and helped out; now she was handicapped by death. She just had to know what was going on below. It was still hard to accept the limitations that had been placed on her when it came to helping her friends.

Working on the theory that he might have actually died, she sought the trail Eric would have left as he went toward the light. Iam's light should have guided him towards safety in death. He would have either gone to Iam as was instinctively programmed into his soul, or he would have been drawn toward his fellow deceased Keepers. She didn't feel him anywhere and felt so relieved by this, it meant only good things to her. She had detected him for less than a minute, so for whatever reason he was here, he had not been required to stay. Had Iam wanted her to realize that something significant had happened below? Was her creator trying to remind her why she had to finish the job she started? All these questions floated about in her head without receiving an answer. Without any decent theory formed on her part, Sara continued to seek an answer from within; her mind endlessly cycling through the possibilities of what she had seen. So Eric was dead and then not dead. What was that supposed to mean?

Sara looked at her companions; the three shining beautiful souls that floated above it all with her. She knew for a fact they were dead just like she was, and, despite what her father had said about the possibility of living again, she still had no idea how that could be achieved. So how could one of the other Keepers have done it? She wanted to know what was going on down there so badly. The view of the living world as it rolled along below them earlier was no longer visible and that made it harder than ever to stay here. The unknown was eating at her with its finality.

Are you okay? Thomas's voice sounded softly in her head, like a whispering in her ear. When she didn't answer, he said something else that couldn't have surprised her more. *I saw him too, you know? and I really do believe he went back.* She hadn't exactly gotten used to him knowing exactly what she knew, when it had been so easy to hide things from him in the past. James remained silent in her head, but she didn't feel him quietly listening. He had chosen to keep his distance lately because of her and Thomas's new relationship.

James was looking at Diandra with adoring concern, so she was sure he had no clue yet about her earlier conversation with the girl, but she still had to be careful because he was stronger too. Lately he had been able to do things she hadn't realized he was capable of doing. And she had a feeling there was a lot more he could do but hadn't shared, either. She had a lot to think about as they got closer to Braccus's secret. Things were changing and there was so much she needed to consider but had no time to do it.

The ugliness around her just seemed to become uglier by the second as she guided her companions toward a mountain range that popped out of the ground with such force that the air vibrated. The troupe stopped suddenly, staring at this new barrier between them and what they sought. Shadows shifted in front of her and it became harder and harder to see, making her fear that the things she and Diandra had witnessed were about to begin far sooner than she hoped. Resigned to face the inevitable, Sara moved into position to begin the fight she knew was coming.

Chapter Seventeen

As Jacob reached out, Alice closed her gaping mouth. Randall moved in once again to prevent this, but she gently pushed him back. She knew he was afraid for her, but she got the feeling that Jacob was more sad than scary. It all began to make sense now, the strange half here, half there feeling she'd been having for quite some time; she had been trying to protect two dead men from several other dead people. A deep sadness filled her, and she wished she could offer more support to this noble man.

"Steven is here with Ray," she told him quietly, trying to give comfort along with honesty. "They have been here with me for quite some time. Your brother and his friend watched over me when I was not able to watch out for myself. Steven was anxious to bring me to you; he wanted to help his people." While she spoke to Jacob she watched Steven staring at his brother with an anguished look. She felt his strong need to contact his brother. Her heart went out to him and she was anxious to help.

"When did you die?" Alice asked the young blond man hovering close to the man in front of her.

"I'm not sure," Steven said. "I think it was shortly after Jacob and the others made it down here. We were outside the entrance, trying to cover their rear flank when we were attacked by these big gray monsters. Ray and I were gravely injured but managed to stumble through the doorway where those things could not follow. Jacob came back and found us. I think we died shortly after that. We didn't want to go. We never wanted to leave them to face what was going on here." As Steven spoke his hand hovered over his brother's head; but death prevented him from making contact. "Ever since the madness started in the worlds and the monsters appeared I, we, have been at his side." Steven's companion Ray nodded his head sadly but said nothing. Watching his friend, Steven asked, "How is he going to get through this without me?" Alice's heart ached for the man as he looked at his brother, wanting so badly to continue to help him. But she could tell that he already knew the answer to his own question. There was a brief pause as their eyes locked and he began to speak again; this time to answer questions that had not been asked but needed explanation.

"Randall saw us because you saw us. You were so tired that you passed on visions of us as living souls to him. It was all so real to him and the fact that Isobel and her followers saw us too almost made us believe that we really were still alive. But then we started to remember when Jacob buried us in the caves. We saw him dig those shallow graves he placed us in and all those rocks he put above us, but for some reason, once we left our resting place, we couldn't seem to find our way back to it. It was good for us that we could not."

Steve sighed deeply before going on. "Those things you stopped from approaching us, the dark things like those inside Isobel and her followers have been searching for our bodies. We heard them saying that they wanted to use us to walk around in. I think

136

Jacob knew somehow and made it impossible for them to get to us." Steven finished speaking and all was silent for a minute as his stunned brother Jacob watched the young woman in front of him intently listening to something he could not hear.

"Are you talking to Steven now?" Jacob asked with a pained expression, trying to look behind him to see what she was looking at, hoping to get a glimpse of his brother, wanting desperately to see what she saw.

"Yes," Alice answered, reaching out to hold his hand, to offer him comfort. "He wishes he never had to leave you." As their hands touched, Alice felt a comforting flow of energy that was slightly different than what she felt with the other Keepers. It was also different than regular people and she knew that it was because Jacob was one of the special people that would help things progress as they should. Maybe it was because he was different, and his will was strong, but this time she was able to share, just for a second, what she was seeing. Jacob was treated to a brief but very clear vision of his brother and Ray. With a bright smile, he reached out to try and touch his brother's hand. It was not to be however, the man shimmered out of sight and the vision was broken as Alice removed her hand from his.

When Jacob grabbed her hand again, she pulled back and stood on shaky feet, leaning on Randall as she tried to explain. "I'm sorry, Jacob, I wish I could show him to you again, but I can't."

"They look so alive," Jacob said, backing away, barely controlling the urge to pull her roughly toward him and force her to help him see Steven again. Her gift had to be practiced with caution, the dead were still dangerous to the living. It was more common for the ugly soulless entities to creep into the afterworld areas, watching the living with jealous eyes while waiting for an opening into the bodies they wanted so badly. She didn't want to risk giving them a way in.

"You saved him and Ray from the dead things. You covered them so their bodies couldn't be used." Alice saw the truth in his eyes, the sorrow at having to scratch out enough dirt from the solidly packed cave floor to house Steven and Ray's bodies.

Jacob spoke again, and his voice was tight with restrained emotion, "Steven was the only family I had left, and Ray was just as close as family. My brother and I have been friends with Ray since we were very young. I lost two brothers at the same time. It happened so fast and, for all the things I know, all the things I have been able to do to help my people, I still couldn't save the two that meant the most to me."

"Tell him we will always be close by," Ray spoke up for the first time, standing very close to Steven who appeared to be too consumed with emotion to speak. "We died defending our people, it was the only thing we could have done. Jacob did the right thing; he protected us. Do you know how horrible it would have been to share our bodies with those things? You know what happens at first, our souls would have hung around, not being aware at first that we were no longer in control, but then we would find that "they" were in there with us. We would have spent a few terrible weeks watching our flesh rot as we did things we would never have done in life. The cruel things we would be made to do as our horrified friends and the others that had grown to trust us watched. He did so much to help us, and we will stay by his side in death as in life to do what we can for him."

Alice slowly stood up and spoke as her fascinated audience of Randall, Jacob, and two of his faithful warriors watched. "Why can't you move on? There is a greater power waiting to give you comfort and help you on the other side of this world. Surely you have felt Iam by this time?" Her heart grew icy as she heard the answer.

"We can't talk to him now; the other side is also in chaos. The souls of the dead are lost, unable to move on because the battle is occurring there too. It is becoming harder and harder to get through to Iam, he is pulling his trusted guardians the Artregeans close to him while the darkness moves closer to his protected area. He would have given us safe passage, we could feel that, but we also knew that it was more important for us to stay here and fight. It isn't only the living in danger, the dead are too. There will be no rest, no happily ever after for any of us until this is all settled. We intend to help change all this. It is important that we stay close to you; you are our connection to both worlds. We can help each other." As the men said this they quietly faded away, but she knew they were there, would always be there.

Not wanting to alarm Jacob, Alice merely told him the two men were going to stay close to him for a while.

"They are not ready to move on yet," she said. The tall man looked down, holding her gaze, a million unasked questions hovering on his lips. The thoughtful look on his face told her that he suspected she was holding back a bit, but he wisely avoided asking what he knew she would not answer.

"Your brother will not leave you," Alice said softly, trying to convey her regret to the man. "I will protect him from now on. He and Ray will not have to deal with the ugliness in there, I promise you. They will be safe until they choose to move on. Please know that every step you take, Steven and Ray will be taking with you. I apologize for rushing you through this, it's the best I can do in this situation. It's very important that we make it back to the central cavern, the people need us."

The tall warrior nodded his head slowly and turned to lead the way back toward the people he had sworn to protect.

Chapter Eighteen

Eric looked at his Circle member in fascination. He had seen her from far above when he was dead, in that strange kind of half-dreaming state he'd been in. He saw how she had remained out of sight among these people, waiting patiently in the shadows, keeping herself isolated. Not fully connected with the girl, he watched passively from beyond life itself, surprised by the fact they had not known she was even in the caves. He felt as if he should know her better, but something was keeping that complete connection from being made. Despite the fact that he didn't know her as he should, Eric still felt some of what she felt, and what she felt was fear. She was terrified of the refugees that she watched from the darkness.

Her fear of the people here was well-founded. Those in the cave were afraid of anything different in a way that made them dangerous to even her gentle soul. Eric had to admit that this line of thinking made sense. She certainly didn't look like any of the people around her. Marlaina's pale skin and black eyes stood out starkly against those she now moved amongst. She didn't know how to deal with the negative energy caused by the villagers' fear. From what she had told him of her past, Eric learned she was used to being adored and appreciated by everyone she was around, despite the way she looked. Her aura projected love but instinct made her avoid contact with most people, keeping close to just the small group she lived among.

The difference between what he knew about his other Circle members and what she was sharing with him was, that it was necessary for her to tell him about herself. He was only able to catch a few fleeting images of her life because she'd let him see them in her head. It was not easy, and she wasn't so great at it, having no real experience at sharing with others this way. He was impressed with her effort though, as she had imitated the vibrations passing between him and the other Keepers to do it. The connection between them was not natural and not immediate like the one he shared with Randall, but it was there nonetheless.

"For most of my life, I haven't felt whole, something important was missing," Marlaina said softly, trying to pass on what she had been through up to this point in time. It was what was missing that made her very vulnerable to the harmful forces in the world because she was not capable of hurting others. Bringing people back to life didn't leave her with much skill to protect herself. Staying away from people for the most part had been her way to deal with her shortcomings. She had lived in a small secluded community where her safety was ensured by being familiar and well-liked by those around her.

Never having known her parents, she grew up in an orphanage, surrounded by other parentless children who needed the comfort she was able to give them. She was loved at that place and felt so safe that she had stayed even after she was old enough to leave; she had no other place to go anyway. Now in her early twenties, she used the education they provided her to become a teacher at the orphanage. She had been happy with the work she was doing but felt lonely even when surrounded by adoring students. She stayed in Eric's head, sharing his isolated early life with an understanding that only someone who had that kind of life themselves would know. It was a strangely personal interaction with a slight amount of detachment; he wished there was more.

Eric showed her his connection with Randall but sensed something strange when he included Vincent in their circle. She went a little bit paler, if that were possible. The internal visions ceased, and she began to speak, withdrawing a bit, as if the distraction were better than discussing the very person he was sure was an important part of her.

He let her speak, watching her face as she tried to mask her confusion, a small frown creased her forehead before freezing in a neutral mask for him to look upon. He tried to read her thoughts on the subject, but got nothing, just static in her head as the sound of her voice came to his ears. The switch in form of communication was a sign that she wanted to focus on what was going on now and not something she wasn't too certain about.

"When the monsters came, I saw a glowing light outside the orphanage. I was drawn to the light; I wanted to leave but I couldn't resist. I went toward it because I felt I was supposed to. I wanted to tell the others to follow me through to escape this nightmare but before I could, I was sucked inside. It happened so fast. It was like moving from one room to another, only this room was crazier than the one I left." Her voice rose and fell while telling her story, echoing softly in the cave around her.

"I wound up in a place with more monsters chasing a different group of people," she said sadly. "I didn't know what else to do so I ran underground behind them; it was either that or stay up there with those things. Here seemed better."

Dark eyes blinking, Marlaina nodded toward her curious audience. "I couldn't let them see me, so I hid, and I waited." Standing in the corner far away, she eyed the cautiously people she had just brought back to life. All the formerly lifeless bodies were staring at her with admiration, and while Eric sensed she was comforted by their gratitude, she was still scared stiff by what she had seen them do to Eric and Finola just days ago.

Marlaina continued, confirming what he was thinking, "I don't know exactly what you two did before I got here, but these people were screaming and yelling for your heads on a platter. I wasn't about to let them know I was here too. Fortunately, there was one girl who was able to make them listen to reason. She told them all about the Keepers, the things they could do, and that's when I realized what I was." The new Keeper held her hand up to show him the red star on her hand; his own mark tingled and glowed brightly also in response.

"I have known for quite some time what I'm able to do, but I really didn't have any idea that I wasn't alone until I saw you. It's wonderful to have someone on my side." A small smile curved up the corner of Marlaina's lips as she spoke to her new companions. It was nice to feel like she almost belonged. She was so anxious to continue sharing with them that she kept talking to Eric as if he would disappear as soon as she stopped.

"As a small child I created an imaginary friend, someone I saw in my head and carried with me for the longest time. I was so convinced that this friend was actually real, that we were two parts of the same person, but sadly, one day, this figment of my imagination vanished completely." She sighed and quickly changed the subject, unwilling to pursue it further; it was painful, and she had no idea where to take the conversation from that point. Changing the subject, she spoke about the seer she had shared the cave with for a short time. It was this girl who had called out to Eric and Finola when they were still hiding out.

"That girl didn't seem to be shocked in the least bit by what you could do." She nodded toward the corner where the girl she mentioned earlier seemed to be waiting to speak to them. "It's a shame she couldn't have arrived before all the trouble started." Moving forward, the young woman in question addressed the three Keepers.

"My name is Ariel," the seer said, as she stood among the people she had been expecting to come and save her fellow refugees. "I'm sorry I was delayed in arriving before it got crazy here. My party and I were in the tunnels and got lost. I used my connection to you and Finola to make my way here. I'm sorry I wasn't able to stop what happened." Her voice sounded regretful as she explained her late arrival. Eric listened to her thoughts, picking up the knowledge that she had not expected all of them. He was puzzled to note that she had envisioned two of them only. The third person who had stepped out of the shadows had been a total surprise to her.

She is not complete. Eric read the thought easily from Ariel as she tried to explain why she missed the third, very effective member of the group she just officially met. The Seer gazed adoringly at Marlaina, whose gift brought so many formerly dead people back to life. She was sad to say something so cruel about this miraculous person. Ariel avoided looking at the crushed and mangled bodies of the truly dead things that could not be brought back to life. The poor unfortunate souls of those bodies were too far gone to be brought back; too much had been done to them. The only good thing about it was that the evil things had nothing to return to either. This girl had brought the miracle of life back to her friends and she was quite troubled to have to report that she did not feel much from her besides her recent contributions.

Marlaina looked at the bodies with the same thought in mind. Eric caught the regret in her mind and felt her wince as she plucked the thought about her from Ariel. Eric looked at his teammate and the beautiful woman he loved so much at his side. Finola smiled when he put that thought out there. They took Marlaina's hands in their own and moved among the people she had saved. The two seasoned Keepers wanted her to enjoy the gratitude she had earned and show her their support. They also had to find a place to talk about their next move. It was time to come up with a plan to reunite with the others whose voices were sounding distantly in their heads.

Chapter Nineteen

Charlie was nowhere to be found. Vincent and Franklin were now among the villagers with no special person back-up. They had already been given the necessary introductions and where no longer in danger of being killed by those they were here to help so his presence was no longer really needed, but very much wanted. He had not just been a means to an end; he had become a very good friend and it made no sense that he was suddenly gone.

With the villagers they had just saved helping them, they moved around the caves doing two things at once, frantically looking for Charlie and hastily, but very thoroughly, burying the bodies of the possessed refugees. It had been necessary to bury the remaining dead because the corpses had decomposed so quickly that the stench was overwhelming.

During their search, they found seven bodies of innocent souls recently killed in the battle. What with all the shock and confusion, the deaths hadn't been noticed and they were horrified by the losses. Vincent and Franklin had thought themselves prepared enough to avoid this altogether. It hurt to realize they were wrong. These good people were freshly deceased and needed to be honorably buried, but there was no time. In the rush to find Charlie, this important task had to be delayed halfway through.

The pale bodies of the slain lay on the ground. He couldn't feel anything bad from them. In fact, he couldn't feel anything at all. That was good because that meant they were just bodies, evil was not present in any of them. Franklin was sure that Alice must have something do to with keeping the entities from coming back to claim these new shells and he sent her his thanks.

Soaked with sweat from helping to dig so many graves, the two young men listened to their friends quietly say hello. There was much whispering back and forth. Their inner voices were trying to wake themselves up and were not yet strong enough to be louder. The distance seemed to be affecting their connection a bit; they were, after all, worlds apart. *We can't find Charlie,* Franklin passed this information on to Alice as he explained who his unique companion was. He tried to not let the worry he was feeling be passed to his fellow Keepers. A being as strong as Charlie could survive anything, that's what he would believe.

Images from all the individual groups were flying back and forth. Those same images were a bit distorted but the messages, though wavering and sometimes a little puzzling, were reaching their intended receiver. Each group had found the special ones, but all were stranded in their respective areas. Franklin was extremely happy to hear Alice's tinny voice answer. *You lost a small pink man with purple hair?* There was no hint of amusement in her reedy voice. He got the impression that she was a bit puzzled as if she didn't quite understand what he was saying to her, like maybe she got this bit of information wrong. Her head felt heavy and unfocused when he spoke to her.

Are you alright? Franklin asked as he walked along the now brightly lit caverns looking for Charlie. It was hard to tell, with the faint connection, but she seemed more than a little bit woozy. He knew that Randall was with her and he felt good about that as they spoke about what needed to be done to get back together. Randall would do all he could to keep her safe.

The doorways have been closed, Alice's voice sounded in Franklin's head again and he couldn't be sure, without seeing her in front of his face, but he thought he heard her yawn.

As he listened, Finola popped up in his head with as a soft voice that, though far removed from him, came through with authority. *She's tired. Keeping the doors safe took a lot out of her and she won't be able to open them again any time soon. They were closed for the people's protection, to keep those things out, but it also means that we cannot get through to where you are at present.* There was a brief pause during which Franklin was pretty sure that Finola was checking on Alice for herself.

But you can open the doors. You've done it before. Franklin passed on memories of their time on that little island in the middle of the ocean when they had desperately needed a way out. The island had been blown away by a storm, leaving five young people stranded in the water in danger of being drowned. Franklin had been one of the people saved because Finola had been able to open a doorway in the middle of the water. That glowing magical portal had led to safety for the whole group.

Franklin could feel Finola's dread at being asked to do this particular task. *I don't know how I made the doorway open,* she said to him in a voice he recognized as hers, only a little bit deeper than he remembered from the last time he saw her. He sensed a slight hesitation in her as he listened; she was trying to hide her moment of slight panic. *But you can do it, whether or not you know how,* Vincent piped in, looking around at all the bodies of people he had helped train. *You have to try,* he added, with a note of frustration.

Franklin could sense his sorrow at being unable to help these people and was worried about Charlie too. Their growing connection was so strong that Franklin was pretty sure he was closer to this young man than his Circle mates. Vincent was taking this hard and trying not to let his outsider status bother him too much. He was still struggling to be something other than the extra guy who just happened to be part of their Circle. Vincent could hear his fellow Keepers but there was no real bond there. They understood him a little bit, but Franklin could sense that it was nothing like their good old fashioned, formed in person friendship.

He felt very bad for his friend until he noticed a sudden change in Vincent's demeanor. Sometime during the passing of information, a different voice had joined in, a voice he didn't recognize. Soft and definitely female, the voice had a strange echoing quality to it, that had the most interesting effect on his friend. Franklin watched Vincent's eyes well up, as it triggered a vague memory which flashed through his mind into Franklin's. Visions of laughter and the joy of conversations that didn't need to be had because all that could have been said was already known, came into his head. He turned and gave Franklin the strangest look; like he wanted to ask a million questions but didn't know where to start.

Franklin wanted to talk to Vincent, but the death toll of the innocents was high, and this new voice was saying something amazing. *If you get me through, I can help them.*

What do you mean you can help them? Franklin asked, puzzled by the feeling of certainty he got from this new voice in his head. *They're all dead, how can you help dead people?* Even as these words slipped into his head, he knew she was telling the absolute truth and he began to understand why. He knew what Finola knew as she stood in the middle of a group of people who had once been deceased but were now breathing again. He felt Eric's surprise at being so close to something he had waited so long to find but not quite feeling all that he expected to. His Circle member was determined to help Finola find a way to get this person to the other worlds as soon as possible.

Vincent's other half? he asked excitedly. He was rewarded with a faint *Yes,* and his heart filled with joy at this turn of events.

Chapter Twenty

The four worlds lucky enough to have Keepers suffered the least deaths, but there were three other worlds that existed. The worlds of Relgar, Farlan, and Earth as it was seen on the ordinary level, were left without the benefit of the protection they so desperately needed. It was to these worlds that the souls of the original Keepers went. Being currently vaporous and unable to affect anything directly, they rushed into the unprotected worlds through portals that remembered their clean souls, having welcomed them in so many times in the past. The ancient dead beings tried to help the frightened refugees in any way they could.

These long-departed souls sent messages to the Seers in each area, making sure they got their fellow cave dwellers to safety. Unfortunately, they still weren't able to save everyone; there were many innocent souls killed. It was confusing and upsetting to both the Keepers and the Seers that what they were able to do hadn't been enough to prevent the loss of precious lives.

Scattered groups of survivors hid out in dark places shivering and shaking as they tried to come to terms with what had happened to them. The Seers in these worlds sat back, just as stunned, listening quietly to disembodied voices that told them exactly what to do. They had been expecting actual living people to contact them. What they got instead was this strange humming noise followed by a couple hollow-sounding voices whispering urgently for them to take action.

The four Seers, two men and two women, latched on to the voices in their heads, eager to get through the madness all around them. Following on without speaking, they guided their charges through the danger. Where were the Keepers they had been led to believe would be walking among them, making everything so much easier?

Silvery shadows, visible only to the gifted ones in each area, hovered around the cave, watching the struggles. The deceased Keepers encouraged the Seers to show the refugees how to kill the possessed bodies that were killing them. Invisible guardians cheered each victory and cried with every loss of an innocent person.

Damage their heads and remove their hearts, they instructed the Seers. *These are the only two things that will have any effect on them. These are body parts the dead things can enter and use for their own purposes. You cannot leave them anything useful to return to.*

If we get rid of them, will they stay away? the Seer in the land of Relgar asked quietly, his back turned to the people who were looking at him with such hope, such total confidence. It was pretty obvious after a few days underground that he and the others were trapped with something totally not like them, at least not on the inside. His senses had kicked into high gear, as the dark empty shells of people they thought they knew had begun to kill.

The Seer's name was Frill and he had seriously hoped that the Keeper named Eric would help him with his wonderful gift. He had often seen this man in his head, and it would have really come in handy

156

to have him here. At the very least he could have used the sound to bring sections of the cave down on the dead things. Frill had seen all these wonderful images in his head but now all he was getting were distant instructions on how to split an already mushy scalp to destroy a decaying brain. He was also shown how to dig his fingertips into the softest part of the chest and rip out the blackened heart resting there.

Frill shared his knowledge with his people, as did the Seers in the other three areas. What followed the whispered advice was a fierce struggle on the part of the living to stay that way. The dead, for their part, were trying to find suitable replacements for their decomposing shells. Both sides were equally determined to have this situation turn out in their favor and were putting all their effort into making sure they won.

It all ended with the small bands of traumatized survivors hiding in cramped areas watching the dead bodies of their comrades lying next to the shattered and squashed bodies of the things they had killed. But even as the dust of battle settled, and the only sounds vibrating through the air were the sobs of the victors reliving what they had been forced to do once again to survive, more situations were arising that needed to be addressed.

The Seers wanted to tell their people that it was alright, that it was safe to go back into the central areas, bury their dead, and enjoy the fact that they were still alive. But they couldn't. It was the same gift that gave them the ability to help their people see something they would rather not.

The voices that had been so helpful in battle were now once again speaking to them, but rather than whispering, they were now screaming warnings to stay back. They were being shown a horrid sight. Just above the bodies of the formerly possessed people, small black clouds had begun to form. These same black clouds were floating toward the newly murdered refugees, intent on finding a new home for themselves.

The Seers heard alarm in the voices in their heads, followed by a flash of light so bright it hurt their eyes. Screeches and loud grunts sounded in the air around them, noises so loud that the Seers were surprised to see that their followers hadn't reacted at all. The common person could not see what they could, it was apparent by the way their fellow survivors looked at them with tired but hopeful eyes. They soon realized that they were being allowed to see what the Keepers were seeing as they attacked the darkness with all the light they had left.

Chapter Twenty-One

Abruptly, Thomas halted their progress. He stared at the craggy, chipped surface in front of him. It had appeared suddenly but was hardly a surprise to the three Circle members who had been anticipating resistance to their presence here. He had to raise his eyes to look up at the whole thing and still could not see anything beyond the solid stone barrier in their way. It was the last great attempt to stop them from getting through to the one thing that would begin to make a difference in this struggle between the Keepers and Braccus. Whatever came next was sure to be very unpleasant and he opened his mouth to say the words he knew were on his group's minds anyway.

"What's coming next?" The words were unnecessary but seemed to fill the stuffy silence in an oddly comforting manner. The question went unanswered for several minutes, each member going through a shopping list of possible ways for them to die all over again. Only this time it would be the death of their souls; a death that would be permanent. With this depressing possibility hanging in the air, they carefully considered their next move. When a reply finally came from Sara's lips it was surprisingly aggressive.

"We pass through this and find it." Her voice echoed throughout the large rocky terrain, issuing a direct challenge to the things she knew were watching them and waiting to attack. "And we make those who would stop us pay dearly for their efforts." As if to reinforce her conviction, they all felt a sharp snap of electricity pass through their combined forms, an awakening of something dangerous and very determined to overcome the odds despite their current disadvantage.

James nodded in agreement and glanced nervously around him; ready to attack anything that moved in their direction.

Thomas felt his friend's resolve as he asked what they were all thinking, "How do we get through that?" The stone structure in front of them, though it had appeared out of nowhere, seemed solid and indestructible. Since they were not the dominant force in here yet, it would not be easy to get past the enemy's fortification.

It had been hot in this place earlier, but it was even hotter now, so hot, in fact, that dead as they were, they were sweating profusely. If their skin were alive then surely it would have bubbled up and melted away by now but that wasn't really an issue. It was the things Thomas was seeing that were. The climate and intense anger and hatred that radiated through the air was changing, reaching a critical level. Though dead, they were still awfully real and fleshy and not capable of getting past the barrier in front of them. Levitating above the mushy, contaminated ground was one thing, but the oppressive dark powers that occupied this portion of the Afterworld were weighing them down and preventing full use of their power. It wasn't as if they had the ability to walk through the barrier or fly above it, but they had to find a way to pass it. Thomas tried to use his powers to move the stone but, other than a faint jiggling motion in a few of rocks in front of them, his efforts didn't yield any significant results. It could never be that easy, anyway. Not in his wildest dreams could he imagine Braccus just rolling over and letting them gain control of the thing he did not want them to have. At this moment, being dead would be the least of their worries because he had a feeling that there was more than enough hate and desperation in Braccus to make this place much worse than any nightmare he ever had. While his last encounter with Braccus was pretty horrible, Thomas was certain that things would get much uglier in their present location.

His thoughts went back to a time when he had been trapped with Braccus in a place he had created just to keep Thomas with him. They fought for a long time, each inflicting deadly wounds on the other. He remembered the pain he had suffered during that seemingly endless time trapped with that rotten soul. The injuries inflicted upon him were bad but the fact that his body had been repeatedly healed so that he could go another round with Braccus was almost more than he could bear. Braccus had become solid so Thomas was able to fight back, causing a lot of damage to his opponent. But it didn't matter how badly he hurt Braccus; the evil guy had enjoyed the pain, thrived on it. It had all been a game to that evil being, a game he never wanted to play again. Only he had the sick feeling that the new experiences planned for them were going to be just as bad.

Thin lines of smoke began to snake through cracks in the stone, curling along the red-hot ground until they formed a perfect circle around four people that were an abomination to the evil that dwelled here. The puffy black material floated in a slow, lazy motion that belied its malevolent intent. It was studying the beings of light and looking for a sign of weakness it could use to its advantage.

Time had no meaning here, so it didn't matter how long it took to get rid of these invaders, Braccus's evil thoughts were determined to be the victors. Thomas felt this with all his being and it didn't help that Shalsar seemed to still be resisting Sara's efforts to get to this thing they were seeking. Negative, desperate thoughts began to drift into her head and they weren't hers. He knew this because he was also deeply imbedded in Sara's mind and was quickly becoming used to the small dark areas where her guardian soul dwelled. He felt Shalsar struggling to find a way to make her wishes known, trying to make Sara see things from her point of view. The strongest person in their group could now be the weakness, the one the enemy could use if they could attack her from inside her own mind. It wasn't just the silence inside her that bothered him, it was the fact that even though Sara had overcome so much to gain control, Shalsar and Braccus were still buried deep in her head. Death had not expelled them. The struggle went on and he was sure that they were going to start using this connection to their advantage. There was a faint stirring, as if their presence were awaking from a long nap, eager to get her to do what they wanted her to do once again. He couldn't let them use her. Alarm bells were going off in Thomas's head as he waited for something to happen. He was ready to fight them with all he had left to make sure Sara was safe.

He still felt the heat of this scary ugly place, yet his bones were chilled. While the smoke curled around and around the group, Thomas felt the strong need to reach out for his Circle members and hold on tight. Mental fingers entwined as he turned to James and Sara for support. He needed them, and at this very moment they needed him. The strings that bound them together braided themselves tighter and tighter until there was only one single thick cord that acted as an unbreakable chain. He was about to say something to them but the whole place changed once again, and so quickly that the spoken word didn't have time to escape. He was on high alert watching everything with a wary eye when he saw them.

Black bubbles formed in the air to float lazily high above like little planets orbiting in their heads. There were little dark things wiggling around inside the bubbles. These things were hard to see but appeared to be growing larger and heavier by the second. The heavier the bubbles became, the lower they dipped toward the ground. The weighted orbs made their way toward the surface, their eerie, quickly growing contents scrambled around as they struggled to get closer to the four souls moving below them.

Sara's soul was humming loudly in his head like an overloaded power plant ready to explode. Her will was strong as she pushed back at the parasites, but they screamed in protest at her attempts to banish them. Fear for her prompted Thomas's next action.

He called out for James, urging him to forget all that was going on around them and join his Circle mates. The three formerly independent body forms seemed to blend into one as they tried to reinforce Sara's power. Thomas felt this was how it was supposed to be: three as one against their greatest enemy. It was the only way they were going to get out of here.

He and James were merged with Sara. They appeared to the startled girl as a wavering brightly lit figure that looked like Sara one minute, and Thomas and James the next. Thomas could read Diandra's thoughts quite well; her special bond with Sara was now his too. She was scared, the only non-powerful dead being here, watching her companions with terrified awe as they became very separate from her.

The landscape was different to their combined eyes; the darkness seemed to melt away and the sky was a dim blue color. They were now in a place where people were running around with smiles on their faces and looking up toward a figure standing on a hill. This figure was tall and imposing and hard to make out at first, but gradually, through his own eyes he was able to see a shining form that looked very little like what it had eventually become. Thomas was puzzled at first by the admiration they all felt when they gazed upon the imposing beauty of this form since there had been doubt about its truth from the beginning.

They picked up the feeling of complete faith in his goodness and the hope that the brief stain of darkness that had been visible had to have been a

164

mistake, a trick of the light. After all, here he was looking so wonderfully powerful, and the people seemed to adore him. As this male entity stood with complete confidence, absorbing all the worship being directed at him, there was one being that watched from above with mixed feelings. The watcher was also caught up in the magnetic personality and physical perfection of the being it observed that it felt small and weak in comparison. In addition to fear and puzzlement, the intense longing he picked up from the interested observer was another emotion he recognized all too well: love. The viewer was warring with an inborn caution, remembering all that it had been taught since creation: that evil was hiding in plain sight. Evil was charming and loveable and the last thing it would ever show those around it was its true shape. But the love Iam had shown this one from the start couldn't have been a mistake; she didn't want to believe it was. At this point, Thomas felt they were dealing with Shalsar's memories, because he got the very female vibe she was putting out.

While the three companions watched the scene in front of them, hoping for some kind of clue as to why Shalsar was showing this to them, the bubbles dropped lower and closer to the intruders. They stood, a trapped and fascinated audience, while Shalsar's idyllic little episode played out before their eyes.

The Keepers were captivated by what she was showing them and couldn't look away; waiting to find out what happened next. They were hoping they could use something they saw against Braccus.

The cries of adoration from the crowd grew louder and louder until they almost covered up the sounds around them in this hollow place. The furtive scratching noises of the beings scrambling around in the circular air globs grew in volume but was going unheard by those who needed to hear it the most. Thomas only became aware of the situation after Diandra began screaming their names over and over again.

The desperate cries brought the trio out of their temporary standstill. The Keepers blinked, breaking contact just as Braccus's figure turned to them with a triumphant smile on his face. The scene he was portraying for them slowly faded away and they finally saw what he had been trying to distract them from. Thomas saw Diandra standing behind twelve dark glassy objects that had finally landed on the mushy ground around their combined bodies. The bubbles settled nearby in a way that was hardly random. They were in danger. And in response to this new threat he felt a jolt inside their bodies as something in Sara woke up. This something was very alert, very angry, and not willing to let either James or Thomas move away from her. Thomas knew that they were the only thing anchoring her to some sort of reality. The power made the ground beneath their feet spark as each of their forms flashed in and out of view. While Thomas knew Diandra was seeing all three of them from time to time, he was seeing the world around them from his own eyes.

Thomas found himself looking out at the gloomy mountainous area littered with the black balls now stretched outward in spots as whatever was inside them struggled to break free. A faint screeching noise, like fingernails down a chalkboard, sounded loudly in the air just before the bubbles burst. The creatures that crawled out of the slimy orbs were wormlike with thick bumpy skin. Large knobby heads sat awkwardly on top of skinny bodies as if glued there by a child. The difference in the size of the head and body created a bobble head effect, wobbling unsteadily on the skinny body that slid awkwardly along the slop beneath it.

Black eyes the size of coat buttons were stuck in the fat heads; Thomas didn't know if they could see very far, but judging by the way they were moving in an organized pattern around them, he guessed they could see enough to do what they intended. The greenish black skin covering the ugly things had small red pustules that popped and oozed a black liquid as the monstrous beings slid into place. Two lines of the wormy things stood between the three Keepers and the mountain they needed to scale. It was clear that this was a line of defense they weren't meant to pass.

Thomas winced when Sara's voice broke into the stillness to mock the things they faced. "Worms! This is what's going to stop us, Braccus?" she shouted unnecessarily this part of him that refused to give up on his little section of her mind would surely have heard her without the noise. He was mumbling incoherently in his own little space. Still connected like a short in an electric fuse, sometimes he flickered in and out of her mind weakly, not enough to gain control yet.

He also felt James protest the way she was challenging the evil things in this place. *Stop it, Sara,* His voice was tense in their combined space. He was not concerned about their group, they could hold their own; it was the girl with them who was at risk. Braccus may be far enough away from this place to not be a direct threat, but he certainly had many representatives here that would gladly carry out his wishes. He was worried about Diandra who was now separate from him, standing totally alone and vulnerable. James was struggling with his need to be near her, to protect her from whatever was about to happen here and his duty to stay connected to his Circle members.

"Diandra!" James called out, his figure briefly appearing to the terrified girl in an attempt to show her he was still with her. Thomas felt James's desperation while he tried to persuade the creatures swaying in front of them to move out of their current positions and far away from the helpless girl standing just a few feet away from them. The worms swayed from side to side as they tried to fight the compulsion he was giving them. After a brief struggle, the thick fat forms flattened and parted as James commanded.

Inside the group, he and Sara noticed James's confidence grow as his powers began to have their intended effect. James then urged his companions to move toward Diandra, trying to get closer so they could protect her. Hoping to quickly close this distance, James managed to be the only thing she saw, his body flickering constantly into view, effectively shadowing his companions so she would walk straight to him. Thomas and Sara gladly stayed in the background so that Diandra would be comforted and approach the wavering, glowing form they had become.

"Diandra, please come here. Don't pay any attention to the things around us. Just walk to me," James called out softly to her.

Thomas felt the panic in James's voice even though he was trying not to let his girlfriend hear it. Thomas knew she felt it anyway, due to the connection they had already established, but she was worried too, and it required little effort to propel her feet forward. James's main focus was getting her as far away from those wormy creatures as quickly as possible. Caught up in the emotion he was sending to her, Diandra stared at him with loving eyes as she hastened toward James's image, wanting only to be near him again.

Then, as things often did in this place, the situation changed once more. The worms began to sway back and forth, and shadowy shapes began to drift upward from the ground all around them. James was speaking to Diandra softly, trying not to change his tone as he encouraged her to move faster. Thomas and Sara waited, hoping they were wrong about this temporary reprieve from whatever the enemy was brewing up. As powerful as James was, Thomas didn't think this holding pattern would continue. They were in territory where evil didn't play by good's rules and there would definitely be a way for it to work around the limbo James had placed them in.

Step by careful step, Diandra moved closer to James. She had a hopeful smile on her face when she made it to within a few feet of her handsome true love. James was fixated on her beautiful face while Thomas stayed in his mind and rooted for his partner. Diandra was just about there, fingertips inches away from theirs; almost touching. This was as close as she got before what was sure to happen finally did.

The worms continued to sway back and forth, held under the influence of James's power but another force was at play, determined to break his hold on them. A fine dark mist was forming in an area above the worms, hanging over them, dipping lower and lower until it settled on to the backs of the hulking tubular beasts. Mist became solid matter, trickling downward until hands formed in mid-air, gripping the thick skin beneath them. Control needed to be regained and these things, this place was going to take it back. The thoughts and feelings created from anger and hate were struggling to gain form.

Thomas was ready for something to happen, and when it did, both he and Sara had to use all their strength to hold James back. Scrawny limbs wound upward from the hands until they joined a boney torso, followed by a misshapen glob that must have been a head. Clothed in black, these entities remained faceless, but Thomas could feel them staring nonetheless. It felt like icy cold fingers poking at their skin where the unseen eyes gazed at them.

As James watched Diandra, Sara and Thomas watched the headless figures as they raised their hands and pulled tightly on the spongy worms. Sharp pointy fingers dug into the slimy skin beneath them, leaving a thin line of black goo where they tore into it. This action seemed to get the attention of the worms which were forced to obey, breaking loose from the control James had over them. The worms moved slowly along the ground, not approaching the shiny forms that were such an insult to their comforting darkness, but toward the one soul in here they could attack. With a speed they had not exhibited before, the tubular monsters rushed toward Diandra who stood just beyond James's reach. They advanced on the girl with a vengeance, pushed on by their headless drivers who had gained control. Though James's tried to fight back, he wasn't able to get through to them. Diandra's body was whisked out of James's reach in a split-second. Bony fingers dug into Diandra's skin as she was dragged away. Her body dissolved into a fine mist a few hundred yards from where she was abducted; James's frantic shrieks followed her. Without their bargaining chip, the worms moved back into position to block the Keepers' passage. What happened next was a product of sheer rage, there was no force that could have stood against the combined efforts of the righteous trio. The worlds shifted as each side struck.

Chapter Twenty-Two

Marlaina sat next to her new companions, happy that she had actually been able to find part of what she had been looking for all her life. It should have been a really great moment but there was still something important missing. She had waited in the darkness to find something she could connect with, but Eric was just a small part of what she had been waiting for. Marlaina had hoped for so much more from this whole encounter; it wasn't exactly the major breakthrough she had thought it would be. She sensed that Eric knew more about her role in all this, and he wasn't alone, there were other persons involved besides Finola and herself. Though not present physically, she sensed them listening from a distance. One minute it was just her, Eric, and Finola, and the next it was like they had several invisible companions, none of whom seemed to recognize her as part of them.

They were talking to each other, but she could tell she was only hearing what she was allowed to hear. Shutting her out was really easy at this point as she was presently un-present, so to speak. She knew it and they knew it. While she felt a faint tingling of a connection, she knew it was not quite what she should feel, but even then, it was more than she had ever felt around another person, even those she had liked so much.

"How do we get to the dead ones?" Marlaina asked as she looked at her companions. She had begun to hear the voices and was sharing in the conversation as much as she could. If they could move between the worlds like Finola said, then it was obvious what she should do. She might not be able to fight the evil things that had done the killing, but she could undo a good deal of the damage they had done by bringing back many of those they had killed.

As she looked at Finola, Marlaina saw a flicker of uncertainty on her companion's face before whatever drove this strong young woman kicked in. With set lips and a furrowed brow, Finola started to do something that made the earth rumble and the far wall look like soup; all liquid and bubbly. There was a tight, expectant feeling around them that a momentous event was about to occur. Marlaina waited, holding her breath in anticipation of a wondrous sight. Looking at the wall shimmer in and out of focus was beyond interesting, and she was surprised to see the light fizzle out and the wall become just a wall again.

The disappointed look on Finola's face, the shock at having gotten that far only to have it not work, made her want to go and give her a hug. The determination she saw in her fellow Keeper's face, made her stop and wait for the next effort she knew was coming. The little she had learned about this woman during their short acquaintance was that, in addition to being deeply in love with Eric, she was brave and persistent. Marlaina was soon proved right when her graceful mahogany skinned companion raised her arms above her head and doubled her efforts. Powerful, invisible threads moved through the air, each seeking the other by instinct and all moving toward Finola. It was tough

174

being the new girl; she wished she was a bigger part of this but was willing to follow through with whatever her companions started, if it got her where she was supposed to be.

Marlaina's black hair began to tingle, rising from her scalp to wave about in the air. She watched solid stone became flimsy and pliable as plastic. A glowing doorway formed in front of the startled crowd who huddled behind her for safety. Her belief in this reasoning was confirmed when she overheard three young women a few feet away speaking about her.

"We'll be okay," she told her shaken companions. "They can protect us now. You saw what they can do." The blonde one in the group was speaking to her close companions, two brown-haired twins. She paused to point out that Marlaina had brought one of them back to life. "You were dead not too long ago, but you're talking to me now."

The girl in question slowly nodded her head; a slightly dazed look on her face as she continued to recover from her traumatic experience. She didn't respond to the blonde girl but moved even closer to Marlaina, who had looked back to find the crowd behind her had grown considerably. Apparently, a few people had also overheard what was said and the logic of it made them chose to stay close to the girl who could reach out and touch them back to life. Whatever happened, it would be really nice to have her close at hand.

Looking at the rough, rocky ground, Marlaina was unsure of how she felt about the confidence they were showing in her but was glad she wasn't alone.

She didn't want to let on that she couldn't do a thing to keep them from being killed, hoping that her powerful new connections would see to it that they at least stood a chance at not being picked off one by one, only to be revived and find themselves facing yet another death.

With slightly confused smiles, Finola and Eric watched her and the small parade that was quickly growing into a much larger group before addressing the people themselves. "You cannot go with us,." said, Finola, her words, meeting with distressed moans and oh no's from their disappointed audience.

Eric spoke next. "You don't need to worry about the enemy entering here. As long as you stay here, you will be safe and protected. The dark things can't get to you now." Cautious silence followed as the frightened group listened hopefully to him. "You will be better off in these caves until we can arrange for others like us to come and provide more for you. It will happen soon, but Finola has to open a few doors into the places that separate us. There are people in other areas that have been killed and this girl has to help them like she helped you."

The momentary quiet was broken by the sounds of sobbing and frantic whispers from the refugees. After all that had happened they had hoped to hold on to the new-found security of having these powerful beings staying with them. The Seer Ariel began to speak to the anxious group, offering comfort and complete confidence in the Keepers and all they could offer them. The people here had no idea there were other worlds beside their own and, being good, loving citizens of their world, couldn't allow others to go without the assistance they had received.

Conversations started again, this time more calmly, as they dealt with the facts. Finally, a chorus of voices agreed in unison that the Keepers should do as much as they could for the other worlds, then stepped back to wait for the arrival of the others that would make their lives in this uneasy refuge much better. Driven by compassion at the people's change in behavior, Finola urged the roots of her plants to grow again. Marlaina was impressed with her new friend's abilities; after all she had been through with these people she didn't hesitate to provide them with vegetables and fruit as they prepared to leave them.

Finola and Eric joined hands and walked toward her with smiles on their faces. Eric held out his hand to Marlaina, who stepped up to join them and reached out a shaking hand to grasp his. "You can do this," he told her, giving her fingers an encouraging squeeze. She wished with all her heart that she could share all her fears and hopes with him. She couldn't put into words what she wanted to tell him and passing them on to him any other way just wasn't quite enough. Raising her chin to look directly at the swimming doorway, she put aside her own need for comfort and tugged at Eric's hand as she moved toward it.

"Let's go, I'm needed in there," she said as she crossed the threshold, pulling Finola and Eric along behind her. She suddenly felt strongly that there was a reason she needed to be on the other side of

that opening and she couldn't get in there fast
enough.

Chapter Twenty-Three

Robert sat up suddenly, his attention drawn to a flickering light coming from a tunnel to his left. It was the middle of the night, a fact he knew to be true, even though it was basically always dark here. Old habits die hard. The body's instinct for the sun was still there, so when, invisible as it had become, it was formerly sundown, the refugees always called it nighttime and they slept.

In the quiet of the night, the people under his care were all asleep; the only casualty of the minor battle of the dead things was lying in a hollow area far away from the others. Robert didn't feel anything evil currently lurking in the area and his senses were wide open; nothing was going to get past him again. He regretted the fact that this one death had occurred at all. If only he hadn't let his guard down, assuming they were safe because he was here.

It hadn't occurred to him that the shadows still existed. He had heard rumors, of course, but it had been long after the secret of Braccus's true nature had been revealed; a few hundred years after, in fact. There had never been any proof of their actual presence to be found save the vague unease the clean souls had detected hanging in the air from time to time. The origin of the rumors had been unclear, just faint whisperings of alarm, but in their role as protectors of the people, the Keepers had constantly expected danger and waited for the next strike from whatever source it came.

Robert had been foolish enough to assume that, if they had truly ever existed, the shadows were not of any danger to the people. If they had been, he would have encountered them at some point. He had been around for thousands of years and never even seen one. Obviously, he had been wrong; wherever they had been, they must have been shaken loose when the shift in power happened and part of Braccus had been set free. It hadn't happened during the first revolt, but this time was different, he was stronger, more aggressive. Braccus had openly defied Iam once again and had greater success in his efforts. He was reminded of the shadows by Olie; his brother whispered a few important facts about the myths he heard. His brother had said that these extensions of all that Braccus hid from the world were lurking beyond the reach of man and so were no initial threat to the world. But the tide had turned, and they had broken free to wreak havoc on the living and just because they had left the area, it didn't mean they were gone for good. The dead man was to be kept far away from the rest of them, just in case any of the shadows made it through again. Robert felt awful about treating the man this way; he had been a good man, but a body without life and a soul firmly present was too much of a temptation to these things desperately looking for a way to become alive. He had to keep the others safe from this very thing. He didn't want to disrespect the body, choosing to keep it covered and protected, but separate.

Sleep had been a hard thing to come by after all he and his people had been through. He hadn't rested more than a few hours at a time before rising in a panic to check and recheck his safety measures. He was expecting the Keepers to arrive soon. After he heard that Finola was able to reopen at least one door between the worlds, he knew it would only be a matter of time before they managed to move into this world. It couldn't be soon enough as far as he was concerned.

When he had finally given in to his body's demand for rest in the arms of his beloved wife, Robert had slept so soundly that he almost hadn't felt the shift in the air and the soft voices calling him to consciousness. As soon as his eyes opened, the voices stopped, and he saw a light swimming in the distance. Carefully sliding away from Maryann, Robert kept his thoughts isolated in a bubble so as not to awaken her. With slow, soft footsteps, the Keeper walked toward the light, anxious to see what it was doing there.

The short walk down through the darkened hall toward the beckoning brightness brought a peace he hadn't known for quite some time. With all that had gone on in the past few months, the loss of his fellow Keepers, especially his brother, had drained him. It had taken all his strength and determination to put on a strong front for his people and carry on as the last of Iam's original Keepers. The last of the good ones, anyway; there was still Braccus. He had also been around at the beginning of time but could hardly be called good.

Despite all he had felt and seen during the many decades of his existence, before and after his arrival on the solid plain, Robert had never once doubted why he was here or what he was meant to do. Just before he had slipped into a fitful sleep, he had, for the first time ever, begun questioning what he had been created for. The thought had popped into his head like an unpleasant surprise and he was ashamed of it. Shaking it off with horror, he kept his feelings hidden from Maryann, as she looked at him with worried eyes. Giving her a small smile, he simply kissed her and held her close until sleep came.

Now that he was awake and slowly approaching the glowing light in front of him, Robert felt the faint spark of something hopeful and familiar returning. The soft glow was shimmering in front of him, making him feel safe and loved. The light formed itself into two hazy figures that he recognized immediately, and his heart leaped with joy.

"Hello, Robert," Olie spoke to him with a voice that echoed in his head like it was coming from the end of a tunnel.

"Olie!" He was smiling and feeling better than he had in quite some time, especially when he saw who was standing next to him. "Ferd." He shouldn't have been surprised that both men were here together. After all, they fought together and died together, it made complete sense that they would continue on after death as they had in life. He was so glad to know his brother was in such good company.

A shorter form appeared behind them that did take him aback for a second. "Maggie?" He had been under the impression that she had gone on to the safety of resting with Iam in paradise. Knowing what he knew about Ferd and Maggie, it was something else that shouldn't have really surprised him. Despite the fact that she had intended to stay in the hereafter, he should have expected her to find her way back to Ferd eventually. Her desire to help the worlds had been as strong as the love she had shared with Ferd. Iam knew this about his children and Robert knew he was counting on their stubborn loyalty to all they held dear to wake up the sleeping power that was needed in this time of crisis.

"What are you doing here now?" Robert asked, whispering to avoid waking the sleeping people behind him. As glad as he was to see them, he was aware they hadn't come to visit just because they missed him.

"Doing what we can to help," Olie answered, "The people down here are lucky to have you on their side. I am so proud of you. You did well against the shadows." Robert listened with a longing to have his actual live brother standing next to him and not this whitish-gray form that flickered in and out of view. This was all he had left of him and it had to be good enough.

"Sara, Thomas and James are closing in on their goal, but something happened that may cause a problem for them. We intend to solve this problem. An important element from their group has been removed but we managed to get it back," Maggie said as she moved in closer. She was so short he had to look down to see her beautiful face smiling fondly at him.

"We brought you something for safekeeping," Ferd said, and the three figures in front of him parted to reveal a small figure curled up on the ground in a fetal position. The figure in question was a young girl with red hair and very pale skin. Robert leaned over to look at the girl and the reason for the pale skin was suddenly very obvious: she was dead, a couple of days dead at least.

Robert continued to stare at the girl, hoping to find a reason for her importance to the Moon Circle. Looking all of about seventeen or eighteen, she didn't have any obvious injuries on her body to indicate a cause of death. Even if he didn't know what killed her, she was dead nonetheless. What did they think he could possibly do for this girl? He assumed they had a plan for her, but he didn't have the power to bring her back from where she was now.

Olie spoke to him, answering the unspoken question as easily as he had when he was alive; their bond had not been broken by death. "She will come back soon but needs to be protected until she does. You are being trusted with a Seer, and not just any Seer; she has a special connection with James. This connection is strong and necessary for things to work as they will."

"The last Keeper has been found," Robert said with a smile. He knew that Vincent's gift had another half/ life and death were natural companions and Iam always had a plan. It was a mutually beneficial pairing, two halves of a greater whole. He remembered the first pair with love and sadness. There had been two Keepers, Iona and Larkin, now deceased, who had originally been the owners of said powers. They had been the first to go in Braccus's earlier revolt, his skill at manipulating situations to his benefit was well known and he had made both sides of this terrific pair turn on each other. It hadn't seemed possible for it to happen that way; but it had without much effort on his part. All the right elements had come together to create an opening for Braccus and he used it to his advantage. He reached out into the universe with every dirty twisted thread he could throw out and forced things to change in his favor. The darkest of the darkness had been used to make a loved one turn on another. It had been the first of one of his most awful deeds and one he had made sure the other Keepers felt every second of.

The gifts had been pulled away from Iona and Larkin just after they moved on to join Iam and quickly given to two of the neediest souls there were. Beautiful as they had been, these two souls were on the outskirts of the group, despite all the love given by Iam, he always felt their separateness. Iam knew this, had created them with it in mind, to make them complete. Iam had a way of placing the gifts with the people that needed them. Pairing some souls with other souls that would support and encourage them throughout the relatively short period of time they would be sharing the same solid form, one dominant, the other there for back-up, so to speak. Old souls helped by even older souls. The one difference between Vincent and...searching his mind for a name to give the other half of this dynamic duo, Robert was suddenly aware that he had none. The main difference between Vincent, his other half, and the other Keepers, was this pair had never really carried their guardian souls with them. These two had never had any support or guidance from anyone other than each other and that brief connection had been broken far too soon. Now that the giver of life was back, things were moving right along, and he was happy for these two Keepers and for what they would become.

"We managed to get this one away from her world before the evil things got hold of her. It wasn't easy but necessary, all about timing really." Ferd was speaking now. "What they had planned for her was very ugly. They were going to mess up her body pretty badly. She was taken to the Afterworld where she met James and even though her soul had been saved, she was still at risk. The dead things wanted her because she was not as powerful as a Keeper but was loved by one.

"They would have taken her soul and used her form to mess with James in ways that would have hurt him very deeply. He would not be able to fight against this creature they created because he would only see the person he loves so much. So, we stepped in and saved her body. After that, we went to the Afterworld and retrieved her soul. We brought her to you for safekeeping until she can be brought back by our newest Keeper. As long as she has a pure shell, untainted by occupation of anything evil, her soul will be able to find its way back."

Maggie looked at Ferd with a wide adoring smile before she finished speaking for her companion. "Finola is finding a way to reopen the doorways. A gift she had used before, but had never perfected, so it may take her a little bit longer to get them to you.

186

When Alice regains her strength, the Keepers will be moving much more quickly but for now, they are doing what they can, as fast as possible. There are many places they need to be and, once they get through to them, the people will begin to receive the help they need to survive for as long as it takes to turn the tides of fate in our favor once again. Be expecting them soon. We are going to direct them to you first."

"Thank you for that," said Robert said. "I will make sure I go with them to the other places when we are finished here. They will need me,"

"No, you can't go," Olie told his brother, "Your wife and child need you here."

"My child?" Robert's voice choked as he registered this statement. He didn't see how it was possible at his age. He had always understood that the only reason the younger Keepers had come to be was due to the will and power of the originals long before they had any bodies at all. He didn't think it was possible for him or the other body-bound original Keepers to create life. It had not happened in the hundreds of years they walked the planet among the people of the worlds. He had never dreamed that despite all the wonders he had performed that this would be his greatest miracle.

"Yes, your child," Olie said, smiling at his brother. "I am going to be an uncle." He could tell Olie was both happy for him and sad that the closest he would ever be to a parent himself would be through Robert's experiences with this new life.

"This child will be a symbol of hope for the Keepers," Olie continued. "A stronger tie to the people we have always looked out for. It is now more important than ever for you to stay in the Land of the Keepers and look out for the people here. You will be the center of support for the Circles as they move through the worlds. You are their guardian now. We will always be watching but we can no longer do for them what you can. You have so much responsibility now. Can you handle it?" Robert listened to his brother, understanding the meaning behind the question. He had disappeared once before. It was necessary for a time as he had been roaming the worlds watching evil's slow spread throughout. With the loss of the original watchers, the Surren, he was doing what they had previously done, identifying the unclean things that slithered quietly in amongst the innocents of the worlds. Those same nasty things that most people identified as "boogeymen", unpleasant figments of their imagination that seemed to be felt now and then, usually just before bad things happened. Stories of accidents, injuries, deaths, unspeakable acts of cruelty by one person towards another because of ideas given them by strange whispering voices in their heads, he had pursued them all for a while. Driving them away when he could, destroying the more aggressive ones when he couldn't. When he reached the earthly plain, everything changed. One fateful meeting had him doing what no other Keeper had previously done: falling in love with one of Iam's human creations. One look at Maryann's beautiful face and he stayed where she was, losing all interest in completing the tasks he had been given. Finding a job, a home, and simply not using his powers almost had him convinced that he was like the people he was hiding amongst. It was the closest he had ever come to understanding the creations he had watched over for hundreds of years. Like the other Keepers, he had watched over the worlds with a certain detached interest; they loved all what Iam had made but it wasn't as if they had ever felt like much more than concerned observers. But he was an imposter, pretending to be something he could never be. Dropping all effort to please Iam, he turned his back on all he had been asked to do. He had not located one of the hidden Keepers, even though he knew there were some to be found in the world he chose to live in. He had lived this alternate life for so long he was almost able to convince himself that it was going to last. Reality was sharply brought back to him when he had been transported back to the Land of the Keepers, but whereas the young ones had been transported by the Garren, it was actually Iam who pulled Robert back into his world. He knew it as soon as he "magically" disappeared from the street and found himself standing back on the softly humming soil of his maker's first world.

Though he hadn't been told this directly, Robert knew he was the luckiest Keeper in the worlds. He had been given a second chance, a chance to prove himself to Iam by doing what he had been chosen to do all along, be the guiding force to the young Keepers. Iam had been so generous with him, without even knowing it he had married his own Seer. His meeting with Franklin had been intended all along, his chance to rescue the young Keeper from the Garren and get him acquainted with his true friends. Looking back at it all, he realized that he had wound up exactly where Iam had wanted him to be, and when he wanted him there.

Ferd spoke to him next, "Make sure she is brought back, and you will help James immeasurably. The Keepers are counting on you to be their guiding force. The living are safe from the forces above ground for now, but the dead are restless and it is the duty of the first Circle to establish control in the Afterworld. You already know the shadows are seeking a way back in and unless Sara, James, and Thomas intervene, they may do so. Make sure Diandra's body stays safe so that James will have the strength to continue his mission and we will find a way to let him know she is alright."

"Take care, brother. Be on your guard. The shadows are always there on the outskirts of things waiting to find a way back in. This current calm is deceiving, and I wish I could help more on this level, but you know I can't. But there is good news coming, not only are the new Keepers coming together soon but our brothers and sisters have woken up, their spirits are moving through the worlds, doing what they can to help." Olie spoke to him again, his steady calm voice rose slightly as he spoke of his fellow originals. So many memories drifted from Olie's head to his; it had been so long since either of them had been in contact with these clean spirits and they had sorely been missed.

"I feel them moving just beyond my reach," Robert said sadly as his three filmy companions flickered in and out of view. He hated knowing all those wonderful ancient beings he had been created with were in places he could not follow. A dull ache filled his body as the joy of their unexpected news could only be shared from a distance. The connection was fading even as he faced them. The family he had known was changing and he was now acting as parent to all the new Keepers. He was also in the position of being the first Keeper to become a father on the earthly plain. What should have been a wonderful moment was clouded by sad thoughts.

"I never thought it would come to this. That I should be the only one of us left to guide the young ones. I could never be to them what you were," Robert addressed Olie's rapidly disappearing form. "You should be here leading them not me,"

"No, Robert, you are exactly what they need." Olie's last words echoed in his head as he bent over his new non-living companion, gently moving her further into the shadows. He had to find a way to explain her to Maryann and the others in the cave behind him. They would have visitors soon and he would have more than enough to explain without this. With a heavy sigh, he turned and sat facing the central cavern. He would not find sleep anymore tonight, plans for all that lay ahead kept his mind occupied while he waited for his people to awaken.

Chapter Twenty-Four

Fingers dug into thick rubbery skin, ripping and tearing with a vengeance that failed to give any satisfaction to the person doing the damage. The violent outburst happened so suddenly; like a light switch had been flipped, all set in motion after a heartbreaking loss. Grief and rage sounded loudly in the heads of the three combined souls, echoing loudly as they heard what James was feeling. His moment of weakness after Diandra had been whisked away had given the bad guys just the opening they had been waiting for. His concentration broken, the young Keeper had closed the distance between his group and the enemy riders. Without thought of the consequences, James had attacked. His mind was so caught up with Diandra's disappearance that all reason left him. He gave up on controlling the worms and succumbed to his need to hurt them, which, of course, gave the faceless riders even more control over the creatures that had attacked his girlfriend.

Though still afraid of the shiny forms they faced in the otherwise perfect darkness, the large fat worms had been urged further forward by their bony, faceless riders. It seemed the worms were vulnerable to brute force. Pain was a great motivator, and the things on their backs were determined to gain control by any means possible. Hands buried deep inside the gummy flesh, the dead enemy pushed and pulled until they got their lumpy steeds as close as they dared be to the forces of light. Now, with James's compulsion to stay back gone, it was easier for the riders to force the worms to their will. Unable to resist, they moved sluggishly toward the thing they feared the most. The light was like acid to them, but they did as commanded. Determined to block the way until reinforcements took over, they formed a line between the Keepers and the path beyond.

In addition to this growing threat, there were other things appearing from the soupy mess beneath the forms of the good guys. At first, it was just bony hands grasping ineffectually at the Keepers' feet, still hovering above the ground, out of reach. After a few minutes of swatting at the air, the hands extended upwards red, clay-covered arms moved closer to the Keepers. As James continued to lash out at the worms, flinging chunks of the slick worm meat into the sludge below, the figures around his group continued to become taller until there were hundreds of bony-bodied, faceless things between them and the direction they needed to travel.

James, his name was shouted from inside the wavering collected entity the three of them had become. His form was the dominant one, showing clearly while Sara and Thomas stayed hidden within him, captive as he ran amok like a wild man. When his Circle mates hesitated, unsure on how to handle his rage, James was able to break free from the bonds joining them together. Sara and Thomas hadn't held on tight enough, and soon his body had separated completely from theirs. Silently cursing her carelessness, Sara tried to reach out to James, but he wasn't listening anymore.

She had known something like this was going to happen, Dinadra had shown her, but things did not always end up exactly as predicted, and she was hoping desperately that it would be true in this situation. They had stuck so closely together, and James had been so careful with his girlfriend. Somehow, she had managed to foolishly convince herself that she would be able to prevent Diandra's second death. It had happened anyway, but why had she lost control when she did? James wasn't listening to her; he was moving away from his friends. No longer caring about the unity of the group, he gave all his attention to inflicting as much harm as possible on those responsible for his loss. The single flickering form they had been split into three once again and they found themselves standing in their own separate spots, facing an ugliness that was determined to keep them from going any further. Sara watched from behind as Thomas and James moved toward the blockade, trying to make an opening in the line that stood against them.

Sensing the need for unity, Sara struggled to bring them all back together, to glue them into a central unit to face the growing threat around them. She should have been able to do this easily. This was, after all, what she had been prepped for. The building power was like an acid in her gut. Watching her friend suffer wasn't making her feel better about what she needed to do. James's violent outburst had to be quickly reigned in for all their sakes. Gooey worm material fell to the ground with a splash as it hit the liquid surface. Screams and moans, and wild laughter from the faceless things filled the air with a piercing hollow sound. Though intended to intimidate, the noise was the least of her worries. Control needed to be restored, at least among the three of them.

Closing her eyes, Sara reached inside, pulling at her two companions who were very preoccupied with working their way through the enemy forces surrounding them. Thomas was all for backing up James. Without considering the consequences, he too begun to rip and tear at worms, temporarily losing sight of his vulnerable girlfriend. A few of the creatures collapsed, toppling their eerie riders into the slop below. But there were still so many waiting to take their place. This was all going wrong, and the pain and loss Sara was experiencing at their momentary desertion was crippling her. She had lost their attention long enough to have given her internal enemies an opening. The small presences in her mind that she had kept at bay for the longest time were showing her what fate awaited her when they won this battle.

James, Thomas!! Flames erupted inside her head, making her scream as she saw the death beyond death. She was being dragged down into the muck by a hazy figure with a familiar feel to it. It was a soul she had carried with her for the longest time. It was heartbreaking to know that this same remnant of a soul that had been so clean and honorable was dragging her toward her ruin. Worst still, she knew that her companions would be there with her before too long.

196

Sara had not only condemned them to this place when they foolishly followed in death, but now they were doomed to go someplace even worse, courtesy of Sara's guardian soul Shalsar. This was too horrible to believe, especially since she knew how hard Shalsar had fought everything Braccus was for a longer period of time than most people could even imagine. How could this be possible? She would have felt it long ago if there was anything unclean about her guardian soul. This woman had seen her through the most horrible times of her life. and to just turn like this was beyond her comprehension. But there was worse to come. In the blink of an eye, for just a moment, she was in a place so terrible she couldn't have imagined it in her worst nightmares, and she was there alone.

The smell around her was even fouler than the decay and sulfur of her previous surroundings. Fetid beyond imagining, this place stank of total despair. If eternity spent with a lack of hope had an odor, this would surely be it. It was also very hot here; much hotter than the spot she had occupied just a second before. The feeling around her was pure, never ending misery. She could hear high-pitched screams coming from everywhere, even inside herself. She was drowning in the ugliness she had been dragged into.

He can make this better, Shalsar's voice sounded softly in her head; echoing with a tinny sound as it strove to make itself heard, even as Sara forced her back into the smallest corner of her mind she could. Not even wanting to hear what she had to say because it hurt to know what her internal companion had begun to do. She was obviously talking about Braccus, who, for his part, was a mere echo from far away. She could feel an angry buzzing from somewhere in the worlds, just out of reach, and knew it was him. The implication was that if she just gave up and no longer went looking for Braccus's precious object, things would suddenly be alright again. He was distant but still trying to give the impression that he was the immediate threat.

His weakness hadn't made him give up, it just meant that he would use whatever influence he had to make sure she was trapped in this stinking pit forever more. And he would use it with a vengeance. It was so unfair that he was able to manipulate Shalsar in a way that hurt like she had been stabbed in the stomach. For just an instant, she felt like a small child back in the Finklestein household, totally at the mercy of forces she could not hope to overcome.

All that garbage she had been told about what she could do was simply that: garbage. She would never be able to make a difference in the worlds. Braccus would win. He always won eventually. She should just accept that and stop fighting. The voice that had gotten her through the worst moments of her childhood was urging her to give up. It was breaking her heart and sapping her energy in a way that no actual physical threat ever could. Her blue eyes dimmed and the solid form she had occupied in the Afterworld suddenly began to flicker in and out of view as she began to accept her inevitable second, and final death.

Then, a sharp voice, like a slap to the side of the head, caught her attention. *Don't you dare forget what you are!* The strong male voice was filled with outrage as each word snapped into her inner ear. The command was accompanied by a sudden gust of air so cold that it turned the ground to ice beneath her very feet. This, of course, was some accomplishment, because it was unbelievably hot here.

I did not make you to be afraid! You survived for years with less knowledge of what you could do, and she was a big part of that. The male voice continued speaking, anger making each word sharp and distinct as it addressed not only her, but the lingering influences in her mind.

Now when you are where you are needed the most, you will not shrink from things that are less powerful than you. It was this statement that made Shalsar slink even further into the recesses of her mind, no longer trying to make her presence known. Long after it stopped, the voice continued to fill every single fiber of her body with its stern tone. Its intended effect had been well and truly made.

It was a shaming wake-up call, a reminder that she had been created for greater things. She couldn't have ignored the message if she tried; it commanded attention, overpowering the agonized screams of things she could not see. What had before been unbearably loud was merely annoying background noise. The small voice inside her head shrank from this voice of authority, respectful fear keeping it silent; she could still feel it trembling like the aftershocks of a terrible earthquake.

It was her second contact with Iam. The first encounter had been far subtler. He had appeared in the shape of a person who, to this day, she couldn't exactly identify to anyone. The only thing she could tell for certain was that he was male. His shape had changed when she tried to focus on his features, but this disembodied voice made even more of an impact on her. It was a scary but welcome reminder that he really was out there and terribly interested in her success. She was grateful but still stuck in the ugliness all alone. As if in response to her thoughts, Thomas's hand suddenly appeared in hers, gripping so tightly, she couldn't quite tell where hers left off and his began.

She could still sense that part of him was with James, but he couldn't make himself stay away from her. It took less than a minute to follow once he felt her slip away, but it had been a very long agonizing minute. For his part, James was too distracted to join them, his grief overwhelming him to the point that he wasn't thinking of the group, only of his own loss. It was important that she bring him back to his senses, back to them.

Whatever she was destined to be at the end of this, it would be nothing without her Circle members. They had walked into death with her and she was going to get them back to the real, solid world any way she could. With Iam having reached out to her, and Thomas's appearance in this miserable place, she felt better. Not quite so hopeless.

She listened to Thomas as he spoke to her, filling the sudden silence with his love and concern. She drank in his voice, letting it soothe her, "I'm so sorry you were pulled down here alone. I wanted to be with both of you, but I waited just a second too long." He was trying to remain calm by keeping his voice low and smooth, but she could tell he was panicking both about what had happened to her and what was going on above them.

James should have followed the thread that joined them, but he hadn't. He didn't even seem to care that he was being flanked by the creatures all around him. Thomas's essence was with him, but very little of Sara, who had given in to self-pity and fear for a moment too long. Her image was standing above, but there really wasn't anything that went with it besides a few moves that amounted basically to a sharp slap on the wrist to the enemy forces, barely keeping them back. Everything was out of control and it needed to stop.

"We must go and get him back. We will not abandon him to his anger. We will not let him leave us that way," he said, referring to James and the distance he had placed between them. Sara nodded. Renewed in spirit, she began to use her gift again with great results. The ground began to ice over, creaking and cracking as their feet moved over it. Protesting howls erupted from unseen places in this ghoulish inferno, this unwelcome change in the temperature. The panic she had felt a moment before was gone, replaced by a sudden knowledge that she could get back where she needed to be. Concentrating on her boyfriend's solid hand grasped in her own, and with the sound of Iam's voice still ringing in her head, Sara let her gift take over. Thunder rumbled, lightning flashed. Their source being not from nature but from Sara and her connection with Thomas. In the middle of this impossible chaos, a fierce rain began to fall. Fiery spots crackled and sizzled upon contact with this foreign substance. The unholy stench became worse. Two figures flush with power and light rose upward, struggling through the slime and ugliness to get back on the field of battle.

Chapter Twenty-Five

With a flash of blinding light, Finola, Marlaina, and Eric passed back into the Land of the Keepers. As soon she crossed through the portal, Marlaina felt a difference; this place was so unlike all the others. The air made her skin tingle and her blood bubble slightly, like one of those fizzy drinks she had tried once. The energy here was stronger than Eric and Finola's. It made the air electric and wonderful and she was drawn to it like a cold person toward a heater. This type of connection to other powerful people was taking some getting used to. Her new friends, however, seemed to be quite at ease with the energy. She could see the relief in Finola and Eric's faces when their feet touched the stone floor; they were coming home. The power here seemed to feed their souls; they looked refreshed and happy, their smiles became brighter as they looked around them, expecting something wonderful. They didn't have to wait long. The wonderful came in the form of two figures walking toward them.

A man and a woman greeted her companions with open arms. Her heart ached at the feeling of pure love they brought with them. The woman was beautiful, with long dark hair and very tired green eyes. Marlaina had become used to the power she felt rolling off her companions. It had drawn her to them in the first place, but this woman was a little different in a special way. Marlaina looked into those green eyes and saw a deep understanding of many things that went with abilities she herself did not have, and this insight gave her a different kind of power.

She had a little something extra about her too, the aura that she projected was bluish-red with a stronger feel than those around her. It took the new girl just a second to realize what the difference was: this body carried not just one life but two. As someone who could restore life, she knew what it felt like when it was beginning anew. The knowledge of this made her smile, earning her small smile in return from the woman quietly studying her from over Finola's shoulder.

Marlaina was enjoying the exchange and the hopeful feeling this lady gave her and she didn't want it to end. She tried to hold the connection and never let go, but it was broken as the big man standing behind the woman came forward.

Intimidating to say the least, he had a strange mixture of human and animal hanging over him. It was one of the side-effects of her gift, the ability to see things people hid inside themselves; traits good and bad, not seen by most. Thankfully, he was good; he was letting her see inside him, but she had a feeling he was capable of blocking her out if he chose to.

He let her see what he wanted her to see but he could not lie to her, she would know if he did. A funny thing happened when someone lied to her, the air around them looked all hazy and red. These people didn't project anything like that, but she knew without his saying so that he had something important for her to do. Whatever he was going to ask, she didn't have an option to say no to; this she knew for certain. Whether or not she was fully aware of everything going on with the Keepers, she was one of them and was therefore obligated to help. It wasn't that she didn't want to, it's just that she didn't know exactly how she fit into this whole situation and would go in any direction the Keepers suggested.

Marlaina waited patiently as he spoke, addressing her by name without ever having been introduced. She got the impression that Eric had already passed the information on to him somehow, with all the silent conversations she couldn't quite tune in to yet.

"I am so pleased to meet you Marlaina. My name is Robert. We are grateful that you found your way to us. Your gifts are sorely needed at this time." Marlaina stood staring in fascination as the handsome older man spoke to her in the gentlest voice, eager to do exactly what he needed her to do.

"There are many people in the worlds that lost their lives when the shadows attacked. We need to bring them back as quickly as we can. The shadows are being suppressed for now, but I don't know for how long and I don't want them to have any bodies to take over. As soon as they get an opportunity, they will try to get back in. I need for you to start here and move through to the other places." Robert paused for breath. Marlaina knew that there was something more he needed to say but despite her wide-eyed encouraging look, he didn't continue. Tired of being lonely, even among those who had accepted her, she was eager to learn more about these people; eager to belong. She moved to touch the Robert's hand, carried forward by instinctive trust, allowing herself to be led toward the empty space she recognized as death. The body waiting for her had been laying there for a day or two, the air above it shimmered slightly with a silvery presence only she and the man could see.

This poor man's soul was hanging around his pale lifeless body, looking at it with grief-filled eyes. She knew he couldn't move on because he had been told to stay. A force greater than either of them had commanded his spirit to remain close to a body growing soft and grey with the passage of time. The rate of decay on this shell had been slowed dramatically; days without life appeared only as hours. Regardless, quick action was called for to give this soul a useful body to return to.

Death would not be allowed to permanently claim him, he was loved too much; he and the others waiting for Marlaina to save them. These people were the last of the wonderful life forms Iam had created and he refused to lose any more of them. She was here to preserve as many living creatures as possible, so his legacy continued past this nightmarish time.

"I know what this costs you," said Robert said, gently squeezing her shoulder as they stood together next to the fallen man. "I knew the woman who originally had your powers. It is not as easy as just restoring the life force is it?" It wasn't really a question, just an acknowledgement that he understood what actually happened when she gave life back to an uninhabited corpse.

For just a second, as their eyes locked, she wanted to cry with relief. She'd never been able to talk about her power with anyone before. There had never been another person like her to question.

 "What do you mean, originally had my powers?" she asked, initial relief giving way to cautious fear. It sounded as if this person was no longer around, as in not alive and, if that were true, what had happened to them?

"Your power was handed down from a wonderful spirit who passed on hundreds of years ago. The gift was released into your body after a time spent waiting for the right vessel; it was needed too much to be allowed to vanish from the worlds forever."

An awkward silence followed this bombshell statement. At first, she couldn't think of anything to say to him; the conversation would take far longer than the time currently available. You don't just say something like that to somebody you just met and expect it to be left at that. She wanted to know so much more.

Robert's memories of this other spirit he had mentioned were painful and she could tell, by what he had let slip, that he regretted having brought the subject up at all. "I just wanted you to know that you are not alone. I…*we* will help you. This gift is a blessing to those around you, but more of a challenge than the others know. I understand. You deserve more information, but it is all I can give you. Please accept my sincere apologies for that."

There were tears in Robert's eyes as he told her this before he lapsed into silence once again. This told her that some things could be so bad they had a profound effect on even the most powerful beings. She felt it had cost him a lot emotionally to mention this person, even after hundreds of years had passed, but she was grateful that he had shared it with her.

Marlaina couldn't have explained to anyone else exactly what simply touching a dead body cost her. It was more than just an uncomplicated act without consequences; it could be painful and scary at times. The emptiness called to her, urging her to let it take over and claim what it had been offered. Sometimes she heard voices echoing in the nothing place, the tinny sound of things that had never been real made her skin tingle uncomfortably. Goosebumps raked at her skin when she did what she knew she had to do, despite the distant threats of retaliation.

When the bodies were a few hours old, it wasn't so bad, but when days had passed, as with this man, the dead things were more difficult to call back. She was even more afraid to ask the other place to stop fighting for the bodies they felt were destined to claim. The soul of the good ones often didn't stay around long because Iam had led them onward to a wonderful resting-place, and if she didn't get to them soon enough, there often wasn't any point in bringing them back at all. Iam was the one constant in her life, a legend often spoke of reverently by all those around her.

The stories of him reached epic proportions until they were like wonderful fairy tales. But to Marlaina they were real; she knew this deep inside. Who else would have arranged for her to have these powers? If she were able to call the souls back to their bodies, it was because Iam had a special reason to let them return. Her gift had limits, if Iam did not want her gift to work on a certain someone, it would not.

 For a second, her mind strayed to a time when she had tried to bring a beloved pet cat back to life after it had been attacked by a neighborhood dog. She had a feeling as she reached for the soft fluffy body that she wasn't supposed to ask Muffin to come back, but she had wanted it so badly. When she touched the little broken body, it had responded by jerking violently, as if having a seizure, before rising stiffly to its feet in a grotesque imitation of its former self. She would never forget the look in the cat's eyes, a mixture of agony and hatred that haunted her to this day.

Poor Muffin had limped away to hide in a clump of bushes and she had been too afraid to follow. The next day, he died once again and was buried by a compassionate neighbor, while Marlaina watched from a distance.

"You are a blessing to us," Robert said encouragingly, his voice stronger as she reached for the soft flesh on the dead man's arm. The sickening lurch of her essence stretching itself out made her gag as she began the difficult process of reversing death. Calling insistently to the spirit hanging so close to her, Marlaina saw it waver uncertainly, first looking at the ground below her, then directly at her fingertips touching its arm, it shimmered in and out of sight. The soul in front of her was afraid. He wanted to come back to his body but there were things here that did not want him to go. She strengthened her command, calling the spirit back home. Her call was more urgent than the nothingness around the soul and it enraged her invisible opponent. The thin apparition became clearer by the second, inching closer and closer to its unmoving form below.

Hissing sounds filled her ears. Anger invaded the space like a heavy blanket, covering her and making her gasp for air. She wanted to let go and curl up in a little ball until the ugliness stopped focusing on her and went away. Knowing she couldn't do that, Marlaina held on, waiting for the next punishment in the long and painful fight for this spirit. Lips pursed tightly, she was determined to force death to give up its hold on this man. The inevitable burning pain came as the icy cold grip of death seeped into her skin, sucking all the warmth from her, transferring it to the man lying in front of her. For a second, her fingertips actually turned blue, the sudden demand for a heat source required robbing it from the closest human form.

To those watching the process from afar, she was simply touching a man's arm until his skin turned a warm peach color and his chest rose and fell with breaths that were at first hesitant then confident as the memory of the act returned to its owner. Marlaina's pain and fear never showed; she looked calm and composed as the silvery soul was drawn through her body on its path to its original receptacle.

Black eyes snapped open when spirit and life returned. Sunken cheeks plumped up; formerly soft spots there became solid and firm. The man sat up and looked at Marlaina with shock, eyes gradually returning to their natural brown. All memories from his life came rushing back. She could always tell when everything worked well and the shell in front of her was truly a living person once again. Awareness of his surroundings, of her and who he was came through as he spoke to her in a croaky voice, unused for days. "Thank you,"

Stumbling, the young woman nodded without speaking, allowing Robert to steady her as several of the man's friends rushed in to greet him and marvel at the miracle that was his re-entry into the world of the living. A small sigh escaped her lips when she looked up at the tall man, knowing that he had an even more important task for her to complete here; her work was not done, not by a long-shot. Marlaina and Robert quietly walked away from the small group, including the Keepers and the special woman, all of whom seemed to know better than to follow. Robert led her even deeper into the darkness, to a place where a dim light hung over another body no-one else was aware of.

Chapter Twenty-Six

It was like being reborn into something bright and beautiful, a being of hope and wonder; all things this place hated. The fear and anger around Sara intensified as she erupted from one horrific place into the mess above. She and Thomas appeared as a blinding white light from the depths of the darkness to assault the senses of the evil things. Bright blonde hair floating around her body as it rode on the wave of static electricity that was building up, Sara stood next to Thomas and called out silently to James.

James stop, her voice mingled with Thomas's, carrying a tone that commanded his attention. *Look to us,* they said together *Join with us.* But James didn't respond, his anger had carried him so far away from them, he was hard to reach. Thomas shared a worried glance with Sara before silently agreeing they needed to stop being nice and make the necessary happen. A sharp crack of energy and lightning struck at James's feet, making him stop moving for just an instant, just long enough for his companions to make their move.

Thomas and Sara disappeared in a puff of smoke only to reappear right next to their third member, pulling him into them without waiting for his cooperation. The conjoined form of the three stood amidst the terror and unleashed an assault Iam would have been proud of. Together Sara and Thomas drew on James's rage and used it to keep them in solid form with a crescent moon glowing bright-red against their pale hands.

Sara closed her eyes, and with the power of sheer will, made hers the dominant form; her male companions appeared as filmy cutouts underneath her skin. Her light showed brighter with the rage and determination they all shared. Raising her arms high above her head, she forced the enemy toward her, issuing commands they could not resist. There was a force radiating from her that could not be denied, and it caught the attention of all the creatures here. The worms, being the weakest, were the first to respond, enraging the stronger ones as they struggled to keep them in line.

The large slug-like animals moved forward slightly, while the things on their backs ripped off long strips of flesh to keep them from moving any further away from their current position. A few minutes of intense tug-of-war broke out between Sara and the evil dead things in which she dragged the worms towards, only to have them stripped of several more layers of skin when their foul riders restrained them. Blue eyes glowing with an unearthly light, she increased her demand on the mushy minded beings. She was patient as they moved first closer, then back, then forward again, before ending up exactly where she wanted them to be. Whispered curses and threats filled the air around the trio, but their tone was less than terrifying now. They had never been challenged in their own territory; the authority Sara carried with her had never been felt here before.

The scraping sound of bone meeting bone echoed hollowly in the air, followed by splashing noises as more otherworldly occupants rose to defend their territory. Acting as lookouts for their combined forms, Thomas and James's spirits called out warnings from inside her.

There are more behind us. James's face replaced Sara's for just a second when he regained control of his gift and commanded the enemy to stop moving. The advances ceased but the clattering continued as bony legs moved in place without gaining ground. Hundreds of faceless skeletal beings filled the area, surrounding a single figure that stood out like a nightlight in the almost perfect darkness.

The surface began to slosh underneath the three that were one. Thomas's face replaced James's, and everything that could be torn loose from its foundation, was. Jagged pieces of black rock cracked and flew at the fat wormy bodies and swampy walkers. With newfound strength, Thomas had finally managed to break through the layers of thick material Braccus created for a barrier and was using the stuff to damage his special place. Black ooze flowed freely from the broken areas; it was the closest thing to blood this place was capable of producing, and Thomas smiled at the results of his efforts.

The injuries caused to the formerly impenetrable place were wreaking havoc all over the worlds. The armies shuffling on the surface pounded on the ground savagely, unable to gain access to those underneath or give aid to the dead place that was protesting so loudly, and on a level only they could hear.

The shadows running loose in the living lands were clawing at the closed portals separating them from the bodies they longed to possess. Being unable to

215

enter, they attempted to go back to the dead place they had come from, but this exit was blocked also. Screams of anger and terror erupted into the air from the empty pockets of space they were trapped in. The ruckus they made could be felt even in the Afterworld, causing tremors to shake the surface like mini-earthquakes. The only effect the disturbances had on the dead Keepers was to increase their efforts on their opponents, knowing they were doing exactly the right thing by the reaction they were witnessing.

Rocks sailed through the air with such force that they severed sections of flesh from the worms, sending them flying back into the slushy underground with loud plopping noises. Larger pieces hit the bony riders, driving them back down into the slop they came from, but a few broke free long enough to make a desperate lunge at the offending lights. Crooked fingers turned into sharp razor-like claws as they grasped at flesh that, though painful for them to touch, was still solid enough to cause harm.

One of the hands connected with the figure of light, scratching and pulling its way upward until it stood faceless in front of the form. Sara heard its thoughts as it held on to them, despite the intense burning pain it was feeling. Desperation to please its master drove it to hang on in spite of the fact that sections of it were turning to chalk when it met the heat of righteous anger. The creatures wasted both time and energy, because ripping and tearing at flesh only resulted in the release of more dreaded light causing them to crumble into dust.

216

Sara brushed the crumbling pieces off their solid form, calmly pulling fingernails out of her arm, from fingers that had disintegrated. The tears in her arm did not bleed but remained there for a second, dark and deep before filling with light. More hands tore at her hair as she heard James and Thomas protest loudly at the attack on their combined body. Black projectiles hit the brittle forms, knocking them away from Sara before they split into three separate entities once more. Free to touch her again, Thomas shook the crumbling digits out of her hair. He knew they were beyond true physical harm and that anything they felt now was transitory, but he and James could not stand to see her attacked like this.

Still joined mentally, the friends moved forward, separate but together - what happened to one happened to all. They moved on with one goal in mind, getting through this last barrier between them and the item Braccus held so precious.

Sara looked up at the crumbling wall in front of her, visions of all they had lost up to this point running through her head. As if giving form to her thoughts, flickering rust-colored images appeared in the dimness directly in their path. Pain and regret filled her heart as she recognized people who had sacrificed their lives for this mission to be fulfilled. Bodies passed before her eyes like holograms walking through this unholy land. Her parents, James and Thomas's too. Olie, Ferd and Maggie paraded before her, and lastly, the one person she hoped had survived despite the odds: Rianna. Her beloved guardian smiled sadly and without saying a word, pointed to the center of the blockade in front of her. A single tear slipped down Sara's pale cold cheek, the only indication of how these truly deep losses had cut into her soul. Shaking her head to force herself to focus beyond the sadness, she concentrated on doing what she knew Rianna wanted her to: bring down the mountain.

Rocks cracked and shifted in time with the fluctuations of blue, brown, and green eyes while the power that drove them now gave its full attention to removing the craggy barrier.

They raised their arms and an avalanche of stones came crumbling down in front of them. Displaced slop from below flew around, combining with blackish white dust to create an even bigger mess than before. After a minute or two, the rocks lay crumbled all around them and the way through was clear. With the loss of the mountainous barrier, the heat gave way to bitter cold. There was a sudden whoosh of air followed by total quiet. Silence, like the holding of the collective breathes of millions of faceless beings, sliced the air like a razor, and a brown string appeared wavering above the fetid swamp ten-feet in front of them. Directly underneath the string in the middle of an icy blue fire, Sara recognized that elusive silver box.

Triumph glowed in three sets of eyes as Iam's three representatives in the underworld called the string to them. All it took was a gentle tug and the heavy container landed firmly in Sara's hand.

Chapter Twenty-Seven

Giving the gift of life to this woman was so strange. She felt like this body had been dead for weeks, but it looked like it had been only hours since she passed away. The soul wasn't hard to call back either, it was eagerly awaiting a way back to its body. Marlaina reached down and gently brushed back the soft red hair from the young woman's face and whispered an invitation that she didn't need to make twice.

It was strange that Marlaina didn't feel as drained or fearful about bringing this person back; it seemed Iam was especially eager to see this woman alive again. As if confirming her suspicions, the Afterworld was strangely silent during the rescue of this soul; the unpleasant dead things holding their tongues for the first time ever. No mocking or threatening comments echoed in the air, and she spent an entire minute enjoying this while she guided the spirit back to its proper shell. The feel of this returning person was strong and clean, slipping eagerly back into the pale, still form it remembered so well.

The living, breathing, young woman sat up and looked at Marlaina with the brightest purple eyes she had ever seen. To the life-giving Keeper's surprise, a smile lit up her newly revived companion's face, and she found herself the recipient of an enthusiastic hug. She was even more surprised by what happened next: the woman spoke and addressed her as if she were a long-lost friend.

"Oh, Marlaina, I'm so happy to see you!" Her grateful patient planted a kiss on her cheek. "I'm so glad I got some of my vision completely wrong. I didn't expect that I would be one of those you brought back. When I left them, I thought it was to come back to Glendt and hang around my mutilated remains. I was so sure that those horrible monsters had killed me and torn my body apart. I'm so glad I was wrong, so glad they didn't get to me; that I'm still in one piece."

"Who are you? And how do you know my name?" Marlaina said, finally able to get a word in while the girl drew a breath, looking down at her intact limbs in wonder.

"Oh, I'm sorry," her new companion said, trying to keep a straight face as she stood up and held out her hand in a belated attempt at formality. "My name is Diandra and I'm so very pleased to meet you." They smiled and shook hands.

"I knew your name the minute you called me here. I had seen a few things before I came back but they weren't clear. I thought I had it all figured out, but I guess I didn't..." Diandra stopped speaking for a minute, composing herself when she realized she was talking too fast and not making sense.

"I'm a Seer, like the girl you met when you were in that other place with Finola and Eric." Marlaina's eyes widened. Remembering Ariel from the cave where she first met Eric and Finola, the one who had called the two of them back out of hiding. Ariel had the same shining blue light around her she now saw around Diandra.

220

"Before you called me back, I was in the Afterworld with Sara, James, and Thomas." There was another pause as if she expected Marlaina to know exactly what she was talking about.

Wincing at the disappointed look in Diandra's eyes when she failed to recognize the names, Marlaina looked back at Robert who had moved closer and was listening carefully to every word Diandra said. The look on his face, like he had just won a prize, made her wish she were more of what she was supposed to be.

Marlaina heard snippets of excited remarks in and out of her head from those distant Keepers involved in conversations she didn't quite understand. With raised eyebrows, she turned and urged Diandra to give her a little bit more information.

"You're a Keeper and you don't know them?" Diandra said in a cautious tone, looking to Robert, whose reaction told her he knew what she was talking about.

Robert moved even closer, placing his hand on Marlaina's arm. Through him she saw a young blonde woman, a dark-haired man with olive skin, and a bronze-skinned man all standing side by side with the image of a crescent moon hanging above them. The three people before her were shockingly pale, too pale for any living person to be. She didn't have to be a rocket scientist to know they were dead, but not in the usual sense. They felt and looked like much more than the silvery souls she was used to seeing in the air waiting to be called back. She saw them as she knew they should be, somewhere beyond death, in a place not with Iam, but important to all of this.

If they had been with Iam, their fates would have already been sealed, with no hope of any return but, by what he was sharing with her, Marlaina got the impression that their situation was not permanent. The brightness of these formerly living bodies was intense even for a vision, and it gave her an idea of how important these people were to the Keepers. She was grateful to have been given this introduction into their world, even if the full extent of it was not totally apparent.

"They sacrificed themselves to find something that would save Iam's people." Marlaina shivered as Robert sent her another vision. A man whose aura hung around him as a foul grayish green light, his form alternated between handsome and horrifying. She heard the name Braccus associated with the man. Like Iam, this name was familiar to her but in a much different way. Braccus was spoken of in hushed tones with much looking over the shoulder, as if the subject of conversation might appear out of thin air to teach the speaker a lesson for mentioning him at all. While Iam was all that was wonderful and good associated with creation, Braccus was all that was evil and destructive.

While she didn't have a full grasp of all she was a part of yet, she now knew enough to scare her plenty. Obviously, the gift she had was hard enough to deal with, but the reason she had it was doubly so, especially now the reasons for it were becoming clearer.

Diandra had been watching her closely in the brief moment of silence and growing understanding of what was going on. "You are the one who will bring them back. Because of you, I will get to see James again." Addressing both Marlaina and Robert at the same time, Diandra stood and waited for a definite answer. All three people Marlaina had been shown were important to Diandra but the man James; she was in love with him. It was obvious by the way her face lit up when she said his name.

The hopeful look on Diandra's face crushed Marlaina because she still didn't have enough knowledge to make this whole thing work out the way she seemed to hope it would. Power didn't always immediately come with full knowledge of all things attached to it. While she knew how to draw the soul back to something right in front of her, she was sure she couldn't track down bodies of Keepers she had never met, or reverse a process that had been intended to happen for a reason she was not aware of.

Nodding his head in understanding of things she hadn't said, Robert reached his hand out to both women and drew them to the center of the cave. Introductions were made to the people there before he nodded to Eric and Finola in a silent summons to follow him and Marlaina to an area further away from the crowd. A brief conversation followed in which Finola was encouraged to open yet another door. After several minutes, a glowing exit did indeed appear before them.

Maryann watched from behind, holding lightly onto Diandra's arm to stop her from following the group.

A whispered word or two between the women left
the younger seer watching Marlaina with a sad
expression. She would not be allowed to go with the
others.

Listening to a silent command, Eric and Finola each
took hold of Marlaina's hands. and they walked
through the door. There was a strange kind of
buzzing in Marlaina's head which she didn't have
time to consider before the light hit her, and she was
pulled into the warm doorway once again. Where it
was taking her, she could only guess. The butterflies
swarming around in her stomach told her that
wherever she was going, it would be toward
something that would change her life even more
drastically than it already had been changed, and
she was both scared and excited at the prospect.

Chapter Twenty-Eight

Alice woke up alone. The sound of thumping and screaming from overhead was terrifying. It sounded as if the enemy was trying to break through the ground to get to those they despised or, failing that, shake the earth down on their heads. Something significant must have happened while she slept to have caused all the renewed desperation on their part to destroy the refugees.

Before she had passed out from sheer exhaustion, the refugees had come to understand that, after the attacks, they were safe in this underground place. The survivors had the comfort of knowing that all the Keepers would be able to travel to them and help them thrive, even if they could not go back onto the surface. Alice had stayed awake long enough to check in with her fellow Keepers and assure the now accepting crowd around her that additional support would be arriving here soon.

The situation she had left and the one she came back to were very different. What happened to change things so much? She silently called out to Randall. Their bond was strong enough to assure her that he was alright, but she needed to hear him talk to her.

What's going on? Alice blushed as Randall sent her an image of a soft kiss on her lips before answering. *I'm glad you woke up, sleeping beauty.* An image followed of him standing next to the startled refugees with a puzzled look on his face. *I have spoken with the others and, as far as I can tell, nothing has happened in the underground places.*

All the refugees are safe, and Robert says the other worlds we have not reached yet are safe also. He says they are being looked after by many powerful spirits who say that the changes are not occurring in the living world. The evil army's distress is being caused by something in the Afterworld.

Alice wanted so badly to connect with Sara and find out if it were possible that she had something to do with all the rage pouring out of the enemy. There was a shifting in areas others could not see, and she hoped it meant that wherever the Moon Circle was, they were accomplishing what they set out to do. It was so hard not to be able to confirm this; she simply had to know.

Reaching experimentally for the connection she had once shared with Sara, Thomas and James, Alice heard only annoying static that had kept her from seeing or hearing anything connected to them.

There were other things to hear though, many angry hissing voices protesting changes in one of their most sacred areas. What she couldn't get from her departed friends, she was picking up from the dead things in the in-between spaces. Their anger made her happy.

The disturbance was building. Smiling and standing up, she called out to Randall, who must have been close because he got to her side rather quickly. With strong arms he hugged her and kissed her enthusiastically. "You look so beautiful," he said, as he rested his forehead on hers and they both caught their breath. Dust swirled in the air, shaken loose by the constant assault of the enemy. The earth rumbled but held steady, braced by Iam's strong fortifications.

"Looks like someone's making progress," Randall said, helping Alice to her feet. "It's them, isn't it?" The question didn't require an answer, he could feel her certainty, but she nodded anyway. There was a chorus of pleased voices from a distance, both from the living Keepers and Keepers long since gone. Alice was especially interested in this development. The original Keepers were out of the in-between place and roaming the worlds. This was a major event and a good sign that things were moving in the right direction. Their faint sounds of approval made all the earthshaking fury seem less terrifying and more like the beginning of the enemy's downfall.

All the chuckling and congratulations suddenly faded into the background when a voice Alice didn't recognize broke into their conversation. *They are on their way to making this right, but it is far from over. Braccus will not give in so easily.*

Who are you? Alice whispered, not sure what to make of this uninvited visitor in her head. As if in answer to her questions, a strange vision of a short man with purple hair, pink skin and bright pink eyes appeared to her. She and Randall exchanged startled looks as they remembered a conversation shared with Franklin just before she had fallen asleep. Something about a friendly, but slightly scary small man they had befriended while in Marrik, who had gone missing after the possessed dead attacked them.

227

Charlie? The name came to her before he could answer her question. She was rewarded with a nod from the little man.

Are you dead? She had to ask this question because his appearance was less well defined and a little more wobbly than the otherworldly visions she was used to seeing. He wasn't dark and evil, but he wasn't sharp and clear like the good dead ones either. It was almost as if this man was stuck halfway between death and life, traveling the fine line between reality and final endings.

No, I am doing what my people have always done, passing through the dead lands to fight the threat to the worlds. Tell Vincent and Franklin I didn't mean to leave abruptly. It's just that it occurred to me that things were well in hand after the refugees learned to fight back and I was needed elsewhere. I felt the change in the Afterworld and knew I had to go and help. My people, the Surren have always been able to travel the in-between places and I have faced enough evil to know what and where it hides. She found what she was looking for but doesn't really know what to do with it. She needs me; I have to go help her.

She? Alice said slowly, though understanding was beginning to dawn on her. *Sara?*

Yes, that is what she is called now. The power is what drew my attention; it used to go by another name. Shalsar used to carry it, but I sense a change in her; she is causing Sara some problems. The Circle of the Moon is in need of my assistance and I am bound to give it. A brief pause followed, in which she saw the pink man walking in a mist-covered place. At first, the mist was light and cloudy, but it quickly turned dark and scary. This did not have much of an effect on the little man who showed no fear but just kept walking and sharing his thoughts with Alice alone.

There is someone who needs your guidance, she is coming soon. The giver of life needs to meet with the bringer of death. These two Keepers will be stronger together, but they need to be taught how to deal with the things from the Afterworld. You have a connection with the dead places and the power to make them fear you; they will need these skills to do what is required of them. The Keepers will have to start moving through the worlds soon and you will have to stay with Randall's group for a time to help the last two members of the Sun Circle adjust to their role in all of this.

Alice looked at Randall and smiled. There was nothing she wanted more than to stay by his side. She felt a pull toward her own group but sensed they were alright for now. There would be a time when they needed her more, but not just yet. *What is their role in all of this exactly?* Alice felt compelled to ask because she didn't know much about the other members of Randall's group. It was noticeable to her now that she had no feeling about them at all. Knowledge of them did not freely come to her and this was strange because what Randall knew he shared with her. A shake of his head showed her, as far as he could tell, Eric was his only other true Circle member. Vincent was as much a casual acquaintance as he was when they last saw each other. Occasional visions shared by these two new people did not make them a unit by any means. *The two opposite gifts will equal everything out; what one took away, the other can return. The job that was started in the world of the dead must be finished in the world of the living. The time will come when the Circle of the Moon must come back to complete what they started.*

Is that possible? Alice asked excitedly as the little man continued to walk into the mist. *Can Sara, Thomas, and James come back?*

Anything is possible when the Keepers are called to gather in their Circles. It is not time for that yet; for now, you all need to pull together and unite the worlds. You must provide for the people as the Keepers always have, you are their chance for a new start. Iam will guide your actions, make the caverns a place as productive and hospitable as the surface ever was. Charlie walked on until all that was visible was a patch of purple hair. *There are many wonders underground. I have traveled many different paths there myself. It will be beautiful again when you are through using your gifts. The giver of life will be part of all this, she will come to your group soon and you must travel with her and Randall to the other places to steal the fallen back from death.*

So Randall's new Circle member was a girl. Well, it would be nice to have another girl added to their ranks. Taking Randall's hand, Alice moved down the corridor to a now active portal. A golden glow spilled from the doorway, she felt the gentle waves of heat flowing outward, followed by a flare of light outlining the forms they were about to cross through.

Chapter Twenty-Nine

Sara held the solid silver box in her hand and stared at it in wonder. The last time she held this object she had been in a state of deep sleep. Living only in her mind for four long years, she had wandered around like a lost waif until she found the pagoda Thomas and Olie had made for her. The box had been sitting on a table in a sheltered area created to protect her mind from Braccus. Unfortunately, shortly after she picked it up, it had fallen out of her hands and smashed to pieces. Now here it was once again, teasing her with the promise of solving all their problems. The box's finely engraved surface was rough against her skin, leaving little dents where the designs rubbed against it; she remembered that from last time too.

James and Thomas's hands hovered over hers where it rested on the lid, wavering in and out focus until they appeared to have one hand. That single hand became solid, slowly pulling the lid open to reveal the same velvety lining she had seen before. Only this time it wasn't empty; there was something solid and dark nestled in the center of it. Curiosity moved their hand to pick this all-important item up, to get a closer look at it.

Roughly the size of a peach pit, the object was thick, heavy, and so cold that even their pale dead hands felt the chill. White skin turned first red then a dull purple until fingerbones became visible, causing the surprised Keepers to drop the icy object back into the box. The single hand became three, solid and whole again, before Thomas snapped the lid shut on its mysterious contents.

Though small enough to fit in the palm of Sara's hand, the container was still too large to stuff in a pocket and carry away. There had to be some way to take this thing through an area controlled by an enemy hellbent on taking it back. Sara looked down at James's shirt. It was a blue and white checked flannel number that he seemed to be stuck with for all eternity since he had died in it. With a slight nod of his head and a small smile, he reached up and pulled the entire left sleeve off. Placing the silver container in the center, he tied a tight knot close to the box, leaving two long strips on the end which he threaded through the belt loop of his pants.

Sara balked a little bit as he did this, not because she wanted to hang onto the horrid thing any longer, but because she was responsible for it. This was what she had been charged with finding so long ago and, of course, the enemy wanted this badly enough to go after the one who carried it.

Tight-lipped irritation was the answer to her not very well-concealed thought. *I'm just as responsible for this as you.*

She nodded in response to his thought, the memory of Diandra's loss still hung between them. It wasn't all about her and what she could do or what she wanted to happen. They had sacrificed just as much to be here, and it wasn't over for any of them. They couldn't rest any more than she could; death was just the beginning for them until this mission was completed.

I'm sorry. Once again you have reminded me that I can be so selfish. Let's get out of here and find a use for that thing. A sad smile pressed James's lips upward as he acknowledged her apology. His eyes restlessly scanned the area around them. It was a bit too quiet now for his comfort.

All activity around them became hushed and expectant with the enemy being unsure how to react to their failure in protecting Braccus's sacred secret. If death could fear anything it was certainly Braccus, and the silence was proof of it. It was as if shock had muted their pursuers.

The moment of quiet was broken by the wails of a frustrated enemy. The brightness around the Keepers was blinding and their surroundings became darker in protest to the insult inflicted upon their precious haven.

While the Keepers were safe for now, the atmosphere around them was becoming more oppressive and they needed to find a safe place to consider their next step. The enemy was held back by their light, but it was obvious that they would continue to come at them as long as they stayed in this area; it was a distraction they didn't need right now.

What they did need was time to figure out what they were supposed to do with this much coveted object. They had died to find it, but there were no automatic set of instructions on how to use it against Braccus. Other than the fact that it was painful to touch, they didn't have a clue to its purpose. The light dimmed slightly as the group stayed immobilized by indecision, giving an opening for one determined foe. A moment was all that was needed for one of the stringy skeletal things to lunge at Thomas. Strips of skin were ripped painfully from his arm. It did not bleed but caused enough irritation on his part to crush what was left of the enemy's rapidly burning body to bits with a barrage of coarse stone.

Thomas's pale skin flapped loosely along with the fabric of his shirt, causing Sara and James to look at it with needless concern. The skin reformed slowly in a parody of the healing process they had once enjoyed in life, but it was clear that being here was an unnecessary risk. Sara raised her head, looking out into the darkness for a way out of evil's refuge. In the distance she could see an area that seemed little less dark than their current surroundings. Her interest in that area soon caught the attention of her companions. They all turned and moved toward the dimness, anxious to get back to a cleaner, more tolerable atmosphere, one in which they had more time to decide what to do next.

The trip back through the ugliness was made much easier by Sara's use of her light to shoot rays out into the darkness, effectively frying anything venturing close to them. What few the light didn't hit were knocked down by what was left of the rocky barrier. For his part, James kept busy by turning the wormy beasts against their riders. Forcing them to fight back with gory vengeance. In the center of all the chaos, the well-lit trio moved toward what was left of the goodness that dwelled here.

Dark silver air streams gave way to wispy, ebony fluffs. Still they walked, eyes only on the light gray and white clouds hanging teasingly just ahead of them. The closer they got, the more they began to sense the pure feelings flowing from the air just a few yards ahead. The light was within reach. They felt its pull, thinking of nothing but getting out of this ugliness.

They were so close. The surface beneath them bubbled and hands rose from the mess again, making one last desperate attempt to keep them from leaving their seat of power. Sharp talons ripped at feet just inches above them, almost making contact. The wounds wouldn't have hurt them much, but the hands were more intent on dragging them downward and holding them there until the box could be removed from their much-despised hands.

The level of desperation was so great that the dark entities, in typical self-serving fashion, were more than willing to sacrifice their allies to get the credit for nabbing the Keepers. Rotting meat bodies threw other dead beings at the light-filled souls in the hopes of making enough of a distraction to dim the light once again. Agonized screams erupted as the filthy dark attackers sizzled and burned, leaving a foul stench, worse than the bad smell already hanging in the air.

If the Keepers let their guard down just one more time, it would give them another chance to gain Braccus's favor. They could not let this object leave the sacred place! So each evil thing lost was replaced with yet another, trying to stop the Keepers from making those last few steps toward the clean place. One strong hand broke through the muck, fingers making contact with Sara's leg, hanging on despite its flaming fingers. Thomas jerked at the corpse, ripping savagely at molting skin and shaggy hair, sending clumps falling back into the fluid pit below with a soft plopping sound. Arms erupted into a flame so hot that the bones in them crumbled away. James pulled her back from her attacker whose large body burst upward only to crumble away in a puff of black gritty dust.

Stumbling slightly in the air, the companions were surprised to hear what sounded like breaking glass followed by a golden glow in the air just yards ahead. A stairwell appeared in the lightness above them. On the bottom step stood two figures, one it pained them all to recognize, the other it amazed them to see.

Chapter Thirty

Vincent paced restlessly through the streets of Marrik, trying to keep his mind centered. Franklin had told him there was a lot going on in the other worlds. Some of the Keepers were moving, working miracles for the good citizens hidden below ground. He had also heard something else, a muted excitement in Franklin's voice as he spoke of an addition to the ranks of the Keepers. He stopped short of saying anything else, at least to Vincent, and that bothered him.

He wasn't used to Franklin hiding things from him. The feeling that Franklin, of all people, was concealing something hurt him a lot, and he wanted the feelings of betrayal to go away. He didn't know how to handle this sudden change in their relationship. He didn't want to distrust Franklin; there had to be a good explanation for what was going on here, because if there wasn't, he would be alone again, and he would hate that.

The people of Marrik, though they liked him for all he had done, gave him a wide berth. They were all aware that contact with him would mean instant death, and the closest they could get to him was a cheery greeting from a distance., while waiting anxiously for the help they were told was on its way, real help from Keepers that wouldn't kill them. To top it all off, Charlie was still missing. They had looked everywhere for the little pink man but had no idea where he might have gone. Vincent had so much going on in his mind that he just couldn't stay still, so his back and forth journey continued while his audience watched with concern. "Would you please hold still?" His estranged friend appeared in the center of a flaming mass, both getting his attention and to avoid being bumped into.

"I couldn't find him," Franklin said, after his request was granted and Vincent stood looking at him cautiously.

Knowing he was talking about Charlie, Vincent nodded absently not surprised by the answer. He hadn't expected the results to be any different than the last dozen times they had searched this place. With access to outside doors blocked and only one portal available for the Keepers to pass through, Charlie had nowhere to go, and why would he leave, anyway? He wasn't dead, but he wasn't here; it was a mystery they couldn't solve at this time, and he suddenly felt the strong urge to be somewhere else. He had to know what was happening in the places he couldn't hear or see. There was an all too familiar longing inside him to find what he had lost so long ago.

"Okay, out with it. What's making you so jumpy?" Franklin spoke again, apparently tired of waiting for him to respond. "Are you mad at me?" The look on his face made Vincent feel guilty, maybe he was wrong about what he was thinking. They had become so close and had been through so much to get this far, a twinge in his chest made him have second thoughts. He took a deep breath, let it out, and tried something he was usually bad at: communication.

"Yes," he said, knowing his voice sounded tight and unfriendly. In fact, he was sure his whole body was one big unfriendly message board that practically screamed his anger and disappointment at his close friend. "What are you hiding from me?"

"Hiding from you?" Franklin repeated, but didn't really deny anything, and Vincent got the impression he was avoiding answering the question.

"Yes, hiding from me!" Vincent's voice rose in frustration, hoping to get the conversation to where he needed it to be. "Come on, Franklin, I can tell something different is going on and it's time you told me what it was I'm not hearing." He moved in his friend's direction, stopping just a few feet from him. Franklin refused to move, but it didn't matter anyway, he wasn't really trying to scare or hurt him. He just wanted to get a better look at Franklin's face when he finally got around to answering the question.

Franklin's pupils got bigger as they stared at each other. The staring match ended with Franklin lowering his eyes, the flames in each area of his body dying down slowly. "I didn't know how to do this, because the answer can't come from me. The others are saying that there is something coming for you. What it is can't be told, it has to be shown." His smoldering body flared up again in spots when Vincent shot him a mean look.

"You realize that sounds pretty lame and I'd appreciate something better from you." Vincent was sure his face was red, and he stepped back until he touched the wall. His anger had reached such a level, he was terrified to be close to anyone. The slightest reaction on his part, walking too close to anyone and throwing his arms out in anger would have disastrous results, so he dug his fingers into the rock and stood very still. For the first time in his life, he almost gave in to the urge to move even closer to Franklin, to make him see how angry and hurt he was. He was tempted to use his gift in the most horrible way, as a threat to someone he cared about.

"Vincent, I'm not trying to hurt you! Why are you acting so strangely?" Franklin's puzzled expression made him pause in the middle of his jumbled angry thoughts. Memories of all they had been through together at this time didn't quite match up to the conspiracy theory he had formulated, and he began to feel a little foolish. Especially after what Franklin said next, "I would never let anything bad happen to you and I'm sure they wouldn't either."

There was a lot going on in his head, it was very distracting, and since Franklin was not helping him in the least by clarifying what was happening to cause him all this distress, he just wanted to pound his fist into something. It was like everything was shifting. What did he have to be shown? The other Keepers hated him. What if they were on their way to destroy him? This something that Franklin talked about before, perhaps his payback for killing Sara, James, and Thomas. He didn't feel hate from Franklin, but when it came to the rest of the Keepers, well, they were a different story. He wasn't sure he would want to take them on and he certainly wasn't going to ask Franklin to get in the middle of that.

It's just that… his mind struggled to focus, but there was a great big something that kept getting in the way. Without being aware of exactly when he did it, he found himself turning toward the glowing doorway hovering a few feet away. His neck was becoming strained from turning his head at an odd angle to see the opening that would surely bring his doom. Maybe they were coming for him and that's what he was feeling. The tension in him was building to an uncomfortable level and he felt like crying.

He tried to speak to Franklin; aware that he was watching him with concern, as were the refugees, but all effort to form words was useless. His feet having a mind of their own, turned and guided him toward the portal; drawing him closer to the beckoning light. As Vincent approached, the light inside the entryway got brighter as it always did before someone passed through. Vincent could tell that if he noticed this then so did Franklin. He could hear him shouting a warning in the background, clearly worried that whoever passed through would be literally walking straight into the hands of death.

"Vincent! Get away from the door!"

"I can't," he shouted back, "I don't know why, but I just can't!"

Blurry figures appeared behind the light and he knew that a person was going to walk through any second, but he just couldn't seem to stop moving towards the opening. As he closed in, the doorway flared up, and the outline of a body was clearly visible as a person prepared to step into their cave. Flames shot up in front of him; Franklin using his gift to keep him back, creating just enough space between the portal and the cave for the person to make it through and avoid contact with Vincent. It was an act of compassion, meant to keep the newcomer safe and Vincent from accidently committing murder.

Vincent stepped back, the heat of the barrier warming his face for a second before the flames went out. It was almost as if an unseen hand had reached down and snuffed them out. Startled, he looked back to see the shocked expression on Franklin's face; that he was sure matched the one on his own.

This had never happened before. Was it all part of his punishment? Was Iam in on this too? He couldn't think of anything they had encountered that had been able to shut down the Keeper's powers. Braccus had been a powerful enemy but he had not created a creature that could compete against the Keepers like this. Vincent had never felt as helpless to resist the commands he was receiving to get to that doorway.

The only power he could think of that would be able to make him act like this was Iam, which didn't make sense because, in killing Sara and the others, he had only done what had been asked of him in the first place. A cry of despair broke from his lips as he moved forward, compelled by a force he couldn't resist. A hand appeared through the door followed by a flash of dark hair, a pale face and dark eyes.

"Don't touch him!" Franklin screamed a warning to the young woman then stepping into the cavern, but it did no good. The dark-haired beauty reached out for Vincent and he, without thought of doing anything else, reached out to her.

Chapter Thirty-One

The embrace between the two women was long and fierce; Sara loved Rianna so much and they had been apart for so long. Rianna was here and, even though it was for a bad reason, she felt like this was the second greatest moment of her life, well, death, since meeting her parents, because she had assumed she would never see her guardian again.

Why did it have to be like this? Why couldn't this reunion have happened without the tragedy? Soft crisp material caressed her cheek. She breathed in the all too familiar smell of lemon-scented perfume that she remembered and cried for what seemed like hours, which, in this place, was just a few minutes.

"How?" she asked, pulling back slightly to look at her guardian.

"I never fully recovered from Braccus's possession, my soul was almost lost. In order to salvage what was left, I had to give up the body I was occupying and just let go. I truly believe that Iam showed me mercy when he let me come here. I was finally able to leave Braccus behind. He no longer has control over me." Though her tone was light and happy, it cut through Sara's heart like a knife.

The silence that followed was deep and filled with sorrow as Sara caught the unspoken message that this was Rianna's only place of refuge. The knowledge came to her that she had been declined entrance to Iam's place for her refusal to let Sara go. Rianna had known there were consequences for her actions and chose to pursue her anyway. Their eyes met, Sara's still wet with tears and her guardian's clear, bright, and filled with joy.

"I have no regrets," Rianna told her, "I know I was able to help you and that's the last thing I remember clearly. The rest of my life was a bit of a blur after that. I have a vague recollection of seeing Finola for a time and feel that it was upsetting to her, but it was mercifully ended, and I was able to see that she was okay when I got here. It was the only choice I could make, Sara. I know she doesn't understand why I chose to go after you; but your fate was decided. If I had never followed you, if Braccus had never been distracted by toying with my soul, many people in the living worlds would have died and she would have been one of them. Your situation is reversible, hers would not have been."

There it was again, that comment that this death might not be permanent. Sara was still processing this as Rianna continued on. "I had a vision of what was going to happen before I went searching for you the first time, a vision I didn't share with anyone else. I knew you were destined to die, all the Keepers knew that, but I don't think they knew what would happen if you did not.

"Back then, you weren't ready to face Braccus, he would have won, and it would have been the end for all of us. That is why I left Finola to follow you; Iam knew I would, it was a choice I hated to make because I love you both so much, but it was the only way I could save both of you. I hope she knows how much I love her; I try to send her those feelings every day, but I haven't been able to get through. I don't think she's ready to hear me."

248

A sad smile briefly appeared on her face. "The other original Keepers are moving about in the worlds, but I chose to stay here to wait for you. I knew you'd need me at this time. Shalsar is giving you some trouble; I feel it."

Reluctantly pulling away from Rianna so her guardian could greet James and Thomas, Sara turned to study Rianna's strange companion. She knew what he was, of course, having seen him through Thomas's memories. She had been in Sherin once, but its miraculous occupants, the Surren, had all been gone by then; killed when Braccus's forces crossed through the portals, overpowering them in their home territory. It was another sign of the shifting in power that such greatness could be overthrown. His being here was proof that they really were all dead.

Soft tufts of purple hair graced the pink scalp of the four-feet tall person speaking to her. He looked just like the Surren Thomas had described to her months before. She stood staring at him in amazement as he took her hand in formal greeting; so much strength in such a little body, but there was something else about him that made this situation remarkable.

As soon as their hands touched, Sara noticed something so shocking that she spoke louder than she intended, "He's alive!" Her puzzled excitement was contagious, and her companions reached out to touch the little man's arm to find out why she was so convinced he was not like them. His skin was warm; their super-sensitive fingertips could feel the blood running through his veins. Fine tuning their ears made it possible for them to hear his rapidly beating heart, the sound of it becoming louder since there was nothing else like it in this place. It hurt for a moment to be so close to someone that had what they desired so badly: life.

"How can you be here if you are still alive?" James piped up, his brown eyes growing bigger as the impact of what they were learning hit him. Without waiting for an answer, he asked another question of those around him: "How can he be alive when we had to die to be here?" Though not trying to come across as bitter, that's exactly how he sounded. Sara could hardly blame him; it had been a terrible journey from death to acceptance and the only things good about this place - his parents and Diandra - were taken away again, to be replaced with more fear and misery. She felt his pain and joined with Thomas in offering him comfort, while she considered the possibilities of what she had learned.

The Surren waited for Sara and Thomas to help James deal with his presence here before speaking. "I have been through here many times. In fact, I sent many an evil spirit to the Afterworld. I'm very familiar with the rotten things that die and have to be contained. I have no problem with removing them from the worlds' so they can do no harm. It's a job I was entrusted with for thousands of years. Some evil we let stay but most we disposed of; it's all part of keeping the balance. We always knew there were areas here that, out of necessity, evil had control of because they could not be in the same place as the supremely good souls. Now that I am here again, I feel parts of Braccus running freely through most of this formerly blessed place. There are things here that have not lived in the worlds." For just a second, this very old and wise being paused, a puzzled expression crossing his face as he tried to express the effects the recent changes had had on him.

"He had a lot of time to release that much of himself in this place, must have taken thousands of years at least, and we did not know. I have no doubt that Iam knew something of this and I have accepted that he has his reasons for keeping us in the dark, but we had been given so much power, how could we not have been given the opportunity to stop this before it got that far?"

"You are the last Surren, aren't you?" Thomas's voice filled the silence, earning a sad smile from the ancient being.

"Yes, Thomas, I am. I'm sorry I wasted time sharing my regret." The strong soul steeled himself to continue to what he came here for. "My name is Charlie."

"I am so sorry for your loss. Your people were remarkable and will be sorely missed." Thomas took the man's hand and held it for a minute as they shared memories of Sherin and all that it had meant to the worlds.

"I was forced to leave when it was obvious we were losing the battle. It was decided that I would be of value later since I had visited the Afterworld more than some of the others. Even so, it has been hundreds of years since I last saw the Keepers that dwell here; darkness seems to occupy most of this place now."

As he spoke, a loud scream erupted behind them and yet another bony dead thing shot upward from the soupy surface. Flames rose from the remains of the enemy when it tried to touch them, once again filling the air with the foul stench following its destruction.

"We must move on," Charlie said, gently pulling Sara's arm to urge her and the others to follow him and Rianna upwards. "You obviously have the object or those stupid things wouldn't be so persistent. It is up to Rianna and I to guide you toward using it. It will be drawn to its other part, but you will only be able to use both if you are out of this place."

A small feeling of protest rose up in Sara, reminding her that Shalsar was still aware and trying to find a way to make her feelings known. She quickly walled her off from the main part of her mind and did as Charlie asked, walking upward with her two companions close at her heels.

Chapter Thirty-Two

As soon as the beautiful dark-haired woman appeared in the doorway, Vincent moved forward and reached out to her. It was an instinct he couldn't resist. It was, after all, Marlaina, and they had come into the world together. A wall had been knocked down and memories so clear, he wondered how he could have ever forgotten any of them, came rushing to him. Secrets shared, moments of peaceful companionship, hit him with all the warmth of a summer day. She said she would always be there for him and he promised the same to her, and then in the blink of an eye, she had become a pleasant dream that faded to almost nothing. Maybe he should be mad and full of vengeance to those that had separated them, but now all Vincent could do was bury his face in her dark hair and cry with relief. At this moment, he was complete and so full of life, it was as if everything before now was just a nightmare that had nothing to do with reality.

I've missed you so much! he whispered in her head, realizing the emptiness he had always felt was gone. Her life at the orphanage as the strange girl everyone adored when they got to know her played in his head, along with images of all the people she cared for. The joy and pain associated with her gift were as familiar to him as his own triumph and sorrow over what he could do with his own.

Me too, only I didn't remember you until now. He could feel her smile as they continued to hold on tightly like one of them would disappear if contact were lost for a second. He knew words weren't really necessary between them, but he was anxious to sit with her and talk about how happy she made him. He was so overjoyed and anxious, he blurted out the first thing he thought of after they met in front of the portal.

"I'm so glad you didn't die when I touched you!" His voice echoed awkwardly in the cavern as relieved laughter came from the refugees who were thinking the same thing. Boy, where his social skills lacking! He was connected to her again; he should have been able to continue their relationship as if all that time had never gone by, but he was so nervous, and she was so beautiful.

He pulled away to give her an embarrassed smile and just look at her. She was so pretty, with her black hair, pale skin, and the darkest, most soulful eyes he had ever seen. She was the exact opposite of everything he was, right down to the gifts they had.

I think the two of you even out each other's gifts somehow. Eric's voice popped into his head and suddenly he knew this young man as well as he knew himself. He turned to see him standing a short distance away, having crossed through the doorway behind Marlaina.

Wow, you really did it! he spoke silently, glad to be able to get through to his Circle member so clearly and on such a personal level. Visions of Eric and Finola changing their age was visible in his head, like he was seeing and feeling it from Eric's perspective. *I just saw everything you two did, and it was amazing!* He was so excited at the change in his status with the others, the closeness he felt to all

254

of them, especially Marlaina, that he sounded like a big, deep-voiced kid.

Impressed by the more mature version of his Circle member, he reached out to take Eric's hand without giving it a second thought, and was, once again relieved to find him still smiling and perfectly not dead. *So glad you gave that a lot of thought,* Eric said, wiping sweat from his forehead.

Oh, come on, you knew I couldn't kill you. As soon as he said this, he knew it was true. It was a strange feeling to touch people so easily. After all the years of misery he had endured, it was almost overwhelming to feel this joy. All the good things he had ever imagined had come rushing in all at once and he almost couldn't believe it was happening to him.

You know this only works if she is right there with you, Eric cautioned, as happy as he was to finally know Vincent, he felt compelled to warn him of this fact. *You still have to be careful.*

Yes, and I am staying close to her from now on. Marlaina responded by squeezing his hand, showing how pleased she was to be with him.

"I thought you were only holding her hand so tightly because she was so pretty, " Randall spoke out loud, making his presence known as he moved forward with Alice close at his side. The sun mark on his hand glowed brightly as he clasped Vincent's hand, their closeness making the identical mark on his own just as visible. Conversation was easy and relaxed now that they were on the same level, and his powers were neutralized, making it safe to interact with him. Standing here holding Marlaina's hand filled him with so much love he thought his heart would burst. Vincent suddenly had a group of people who loved him like family.

He turned to Franklin and nodded, feeling the need to acknowledge this young man who had been his friend long before the true bond had been forged. Pulling Marlaina along with him in his haste to reach out to his companion of the past few weeks, he gripped Franklin in a one-handed hug, expressing his gratitude for all he had done for him. "Thank you," he said, choking up for a second with the impact of his emotion.

"Thank you," Marlaina echoed the sentiment. Vincent's memories were hers too and she liked Franklin the moment she picked up Vincent's feelings. Vincent felt her wince when her fingers were squished between him and his friends.

It's okay to let go of my hand, we don't have to hold on constantly for you to be safe.

Shocked by her statement, Vincent started to pull his hand back, only to have her grip his hand tighter, her dark eyes twinkling as she smiled. "I didn't say I didn't want to hold your hand, it's just that we don't have touch to make you a safe person, we just have to be close. It's okay."

Vincent nodded his head, experimentally letting go of her hand when the four other Keepers present greeted him with a newfound understanding of who he was. He shook their hands and hugged them, each time holding his breath as he waited for something bad to happen. To his great delight, everything remained fine and he allowed himself to enjoy their company. The moment was peaceful and lovely, and he wanted to bask in it for a little while, so they sat and talked about what was happening in the worlds. While he listened, his hand sought Marlaina's once again just because he could, and it felt so good.

"Finola has managed to feed the refugees as we went along, growing wonderful things. We have been to all the worlds, saving this for last because Marlaina had to bring the dead refugees back to life. We were not there when they needed us the most, but fortunately someone was," Eric paused, trying to suppress his smile as he made his statement. "We saw Olie,"

"But Olie's dead," Franklin said. "Sara told us so, and we haven't felt him since he left."

"Well, he was present in Relgar; we went there to help the few creatures left alive, which was strange because this was the place where Randall was held captive so many years ago. You know, where those ugly monsters kept him in a cage." The group nodded when a picture of the rubbery skinned beings with black holes where their eyes and mouths should be formed in their collective thoughts. Memories shared among every single member of the group of the gray skinned Gnafs or 'Uglies' as Alice had named them. Those beings had the uncanny ability to reassemble themselves when injured, body parts fitting back together randomly until they were facing a terrifying group with mismatched limbs pursuing them. Vincent was sharing the memory as they spoke, and it was both disturbing and wonderful to be able to see it all.

257

"They weren't all like that, though," Finola said softly. "When we went back, we found out there were kind and intelligent beings in that land. They looked nothing like the Gnafs. The residents of Relgar had long ago retreated to the underground, driven there by the Gnafs. Braccus had already corrupted that world, it was sort of practice for what he wanted to do to the rest of Iam's worlds. "The survivors we spoke to don't look anything like the creatures that roamed their lands. They were beautiful people with dark hair and pale skin, just like Marlaina's." Finola smiled at the subject of the conversation. They were sharing such pleasant memories of their recent trip. "You seemed to fit in quite well with them. I would love to go back with you and Vincent sometime after things return to normal."

There was an uncomfortable silence after Finola made her statement, none of them knew when, or if, things would ever return to normal. Maybe this life, down here, hidden from all the rotten things above was the new normal. They had no way of knowing when or if things would turn around for them. What was their next move anyway?

Olie and the other original Keepers are moving through the worlds. Your parents are among them, Robert said through their mutual connections. *Would you like to meet them?* A yearning spread through the collective group to meet the grand entities that had made their existence possible. A chorus of *yeses* broke out as each member embraced the possibility of seeing the parents they had never known. All except for the two Keepers who had never had parents, Marlaina and Vincent. But strangely enough, that knowledge didn't bother them in the least. They were completely fine as they were, they had each other and that's how they had always been, how it was supposed to be.

Vincent vaguely heard his companions express their joy at the news and Robert's reply that they should move to a remote area of the tunnels so as not to alarm the refugees with the presence of these powerful spirits. It was their one and only opportunity to meet them, to ask all they never been able to. It was understood that their forbearer's' time here was limited and only achieved through extreme stubborn determination and of course, could not last. They had arrived and helped when they were needed most, but they were also needed elsewhere. This was not the only level on which a battle was being fought and the Land of the Living was no longer meant for them. Olie, Ferd and Maggie were the only ones allowed to move between the worlds at random. They had been around the longest and in their last acts of sacrifice had bargained for the right to roam the worlds without rest.

It was amazing; all he could learn when he was a full partner to those around him. "You must go to them right now," Vincent said to each of his companions. Staying here with Marlaina was certainly not a sacrifice on his part. She was all the family connection he would ever need and her smile at reading this thought was all the reward necessary. Hand in hand, they settled down to enjoy each other's company while the others went to say hello and goodbye to their newly met family members. It was a bittersweet event; all this happiness and sadness was actually a welcome break from the fear and anger they had been experiencing on a daily basis. Taking advantage of their time together, Vincent sat and stared at his companion, having a silent conversation with her. The refugees finally finished giving their thanks and wandered off to do some chores, leaving them truly on their own.

I love you, he said to the woman who was as much a part of his life as she had ever been, the years having melted away, her beauty only having improved with age.

I love you, she answered, kissing him softly as they sat and talked like they had just left each other yesterday.

Chapter Thirty-Three

The climb upwards was long, and the air got thinner and cleaner as the group moved away from the stench and filth that would soon overwhelm the Afterworld if they did not succeed. Looking behind them only confirmed Thomas's suspicion about what was being rapidly lost to the change. He could see a wide area of the Dead World and noted with dismay that very little of it was now composed of light. In fact, a small section of the clean area was clearly visible as a bright dot in the center of a growing swamp of darkness.

Thomas walked beside Sara and slightly behind James and Rianna. Ahead of them all, Charlie led the way up the steep staircase. It wound upward without an end in sight until, after what seemed an eternity of climbing, it began to slant sideways at an impossible angle. Their feet stuck to the steps like they had been glued there and were walking almost completely sideways. Thomas looked to his right one more time and saw the small bright area flash brightly in the darkness. Several small bursts of light erupted upward into the inky air around it. Something important was going on and he wanted to bring this to his companion's attention, but he had a feeling they already knew. His theory was confirmed by the grim looks on Charlie and Rianna's faces when they glanced in his direction, and the way Sara gripped his elbow to keep him from turning back.

The activity below pulled at his soul, like something calling him to defend the area for the last of the good souls hidden there. "We can't help them," Sara said, as the staircase behind them crumbled away, giving them no point of return to the area below. A dread overtook Thomas when he gave further thought to trying a descent without it, without her. His heart couldn't stand a separation from her and he was surprised he'd even thought of it.

He looked into Sara's eyes and knew she had destroyed the staircase somehow; there was a slow-moving wave of clean raw energy rolling from her. She stared back at him with no regret; she had dug into her hidden pool of power out of instinct to carry them further toward their ultimate goal. Following Charlie was their only choice; their mission had to be completed. There could be no deviating from their course, they could not run back and solve a problem that was no longer theirs.

"My brothers and sisters are returning to defend their territory," said Rianna. "What is happening down there is no longer your problem, you can never return to that place. The best thing you can do for the original Keepers is to finish what you have started. It is all or nothing for all of us."

Thomas remained silent, his hand still firmly clasped in Sara's as they lost sight of the struggle occurring below them. The scene was no longer visible; all he could see was what was in front of them, a clean path far from the eternal nightmare. There was only one way to proceed and he knew that's what Sara was pushing them all towards. Charlie spoke to break the silence that followed the moment of no return. The horrific scene was gone, and they had only one direction to go in. "The item you hold is personal to Braccus and he is very upset at its loss. He will not suffer your victory in this situation."

There was a brief, troubled pause. "It is unusually quiet down there." After the strange sidestep in subject, Charlie pointed vaguely downward at where the solid living worlds existed side by side. "That isn't good." He made the statement without looking back or slowing his pace. Strands of pink hair floated in the air as he continued to move forward, his voice not registering any emotion at the seriousness of what he was saying.

"You realize he has not given up, he will just change his tactics. The challenges your fellow Keepers face will be even more extreme, but you are not part of that struggle any more. What you do from now on will increase their chance of survival." The sky around them was a soft buttery yellow, flowing warmly over them like a comfortable invisible blanket. All Thomas could see was the pale white staircase but safety here wasn't an issue; the air around them carried nothing but good feelings. The wind blew by his ear and he could swear he heard soft gentle laughter that reminded him of a youth spent among people he loved. His mind strayed back to a time before he knew the responsibility of his power and the enemies that came with it. Thomas knew it wouldn't last but he loved every second of it.

"What is this place?" he spoke to Charlie, unable to hide the smile the memories brought to his lips.

"This is the area of the Afterworld that is the closest to Iam that most will ever get and still be able to move back into the other places. If you got any closer to him, you would never want to leave. You wouldn't care about anything below you. All the people you loved and wanted to save would no longer have meaning for you, and it would be impossible for me to bring you where you need to be. The only entities that ever managed to leave here were the Originals."

At this point, Charlie's voice did have some emotion in it. Thomas heard a softness that indicated respect for the people he spoke of. "They were with him from the beginning and he was counting on their hearts being strong enough to do what he had intended from the start of it all, but he will never allow them back. He gave the best of his children a choice and they did not let him down."

Charlie moved further along the path.

"How do you know all this?" James asked, looking at the funny short guy still moving at an impossible angle directly in front of him.

"I have been able to talk to them from time to time. My duties have taken me in and out of this place a lot. It has been awhile though. Too long, or I would have expected some of what happened already. I am sorry to say I did not."

Thomas stopped and faced Sara who was openly crying. fighting the urge to move further upward on the staircase which began to twist and turn backward. Where it led was less bright and wonderful than where she was tempted to go. He and James felt it too, the aching void they knew could be filled if they just dared to move a little further off the path toward the blinding white light, a light that promised a happiness and peace they had never known in their short lives. Iam was somewhere close and if they could just find him, they wouldn't have to suffer any longer.

"You can't go there. It's not your time for that," Rianna addressed them all, stopping on the stairs. Her hair was flowing around her head, caught by the gentle breeze that carried a symphony of chirping birds and crickets. A sad smile passed her lips while she gazed longingly above her. Recovering her emotions, she quickly squared her shoulders and reached out her hand to squeeze first Sara's and then Thomas's, and patting James's shoulder in a sign of support for all of them.

"Let's go on now," Charlie's voice sounded out over the crickets and birds, stilling the beautiful sounds altogether, leaving only silence in its wake.

"Where does this lead?" Thomas was referring to the path in front of him. He was determined not to take another step until he knew what came next.

"She knows where it goes." Charlie's eyes sought out Sara, watching her intently. So intently, that Thomas glanced down at her to see what made him focus solely on her. She had stopped crying and was staring back at the Surren, but her expression was puzzled.

"No, not you," Charlie clarified. "The one who refuses to give up her spot inside you. You thought she'd left, and she let you believe it for a while, but she came back, didn't she? She started out as helpful but began to change, becoming more resistant, more helpful to him. I know part of you is still there, isn't it, Shalsar? Are you going to help at all?"

A screaming sound pierced Sara's skull and vibrated in Thomas's. It hurt him to hear this second-hand, so he was sure Sara was in pain. As for the other presence they both shared, Braccus's shadowy remains; other than a low growling sound, they heard nothing. Rather than be comforted by it, this troubled him. Internal eyes were watching them all. He felt James quietly listening to their thoughts and he suspected he was there as often as he could be without intruding on their new intimate relationship. He had pulled back as far as he could when Diandra was taken, not sharing even half of his grief and rage. Now he was letting down a few walls and reminding Thomas that he too had more beneath the surface than he might have guessed. He had known some of this was going to happen, not that Diandra would be taken like that, but he knew that he was being shut out and had been able to look past a few of the barriers.

When you know and love someone so well, it is easy to forget the grit and determination that had gotten them this far in such an evil place. James had a power to be respected and not underestimated. A nod from his brother spirit showed him he knew how much he had given away of his secret, and the understanding was there between the three of them. *Well, are you going to help, Shalsar?* It was James, getting as close to the separate area of her head as he ever had. He did it so easily, that Thomas was surprised at his growing talent. He knew James had the ability to see inside Sara to a certain extent and he had been so jealous of that in the past, but when he had pulled back, he had forgotten just how silently he could move around in people's minds, just about as well as he could control the lesser minds of those around him. When their eyes locked, Thomas could tell that James knew a lot more about their situation than he had ever let on. He also got the impression from their shared thought process that he was able to hide a few things of his own. It was also obvious that he had managed to find that faint path Diandra had used to connect with Sara, after the incident that took her from him, but the result was that he was a little calmer and more determined than ever to get this thing done. He was drawing his own conclusion about the possible outcome of Diandra's disappearance. So, he listened with the understanding hanging between them that James could do so much more now.

Answer me, please, James spoke on a level that moved beyond the blocks and connected with the person who might help them. Despite all of the energy his friend had put into blocking her guardian soul out, she was still having a difficult time taming her rebellion. The love she carried for this soul was getting in her way. Shalsar wouldn't cooperate with Sara, but she seemed to have a harder time with the young man who dug at her.

I can't let you get to it. He would be so angry with me and it matters so much where you go from here. He has ways of making the world even worse than it is now. Both he and James were taken aback by the tone of admiration that accompanied Shalsar's statement. Needing to know more but unwilling to ask Sara to remove the blocks between a more dangerous part of her mind and her rational and powerful self, James spoke again:

Show us the way out of this place and point us in the right direction to find it. The sharp tone he used rang in Sara and Thomas's heads. Silence followed until he pushed harder, determined to make her give him what he wanted. Sara seemed a bit distracted, torn between going back and moving forward, caught up in a moment of indecision. Unlike him or James, she was still reaching for the power just out of her grasp. They couldn't go back. But for a short time, despite her wish to go onward and find out how this affected their fate, she was feeling the pull from above and having a hard time resigning herself to moving on.

Thomas raised his head and caught her eyes in time to catch the slight red flare in the center of the blueness followed by a low wail and then a loud creaking that marked Sara's sudden decision to do the right thing, spurred on by James's direct approach to Shalsar. The stairs suddenly straightened out and led to a path downward. The sight that swam before their combined eyes was of clouds and mountains. They walked along a path that no longer existed in any world but was familiar to the person who had traveled it often. It led straight onward to an object that lay miles in the distance, the observer having driven toward it by an unending curiosity. Memories came to them of a kneeling form in the semi-darkness, a soft thumping sound and a cry of agony followed by sharp laughter.

Knowing this was as close to the truth as they were going to get from Shalsar, their unwilling assistant, they continued onward. Their destination now clear; it was once again necessary to move into the past, to the scene of the incident that started it all. The steps guided them forward; each footfall sent time back a day, ten days, a month, then finally hundreds and thousands of years. It was the first time they felt the passage of time in this area and it was all for one purpose, to take them to the time of the original incident. Much against her will, Shalsar was going to show them what this was all about.

Chapter Thirty-Four

The handsome young man stood on the surface of the lands enjoying the sights around him. His rage had destroyed all trace of beauty. Any natural object that had extended toward the heavens had been flattened and he laughed at his success.

When he had first landed back in the living place again, it had been as the meaty mass of skinless flesh he had left the dead worlds as. He'd hit the ground in a rage, ripping the few remaining living trees from the soil and spitting fire into the holes left behind. He had been so angry at the loss of his possession that he'd basically thrown a tantrum. Rocks and broken bones flew around and imbedded themselves into larger pieces of rock. Makeshift structures made of the remains of dead things and stones shook under his assault but stood nonetheless.

Braccus had always tried to keep himself calmly superior to his creations. When he got angry, he was imposing and swift in his action. Fear was what he craved, and he got it without trying very hard; it was easy with the dimwitted beasts he had made. Even now, the Ornose stood back, shivering, and blinking their three sets of eyes, while a few slimy, rat-faced creatures cowered behind broken rocks and stared at him respectfully. This, he was used to, and it made him feel better at being able to vent on Iam's favored ground. He had landed in the Land of the Keepers, knowing the last Original one was somewhere below him. The idea that he still existed at all was like a slap in his face; Robert should have been killed like all the others.

Ripping and tearing at anything within his reach, Braccus threw himself down on the ground like an animal. Screeching and frothing at the mouth, he replayed his last moments with Sara riding along under his skin. It had felt so good, so right, that everything should be going according to his will; then it had all changed. How had Thomas been able to get her away from him? After their playful encounter, he had hoped the young man understood enough to give in. Sadly, he never did.

He reached for the thread of control he had over Thomas in attempt to both punish him and influence the return of what was his, but was rebuffed quickly, which made him even angrier. That wasn't supposed to happen. Reaching down, he grabbed hold of a hairy mass that was his version of a rabbit, only more vicious and ten times uglier. With a quick flick of his wrist, he flung it at an Ornose. The dead creature bounced off the thick figure and skittered to a stop among smoldering stones, bringing the stench of burning hair to his nostrils. The creature's death was briefly satisfying but failed to bring him any measurable relief. He wanted to hurt something that mattered, to get hold of something that Iam held precious and use it against him. Having control up here wasn't enough; he had to have it all. It could all go against him again if Sara succeeded; he had to find a way to stop her. It had taken hundreds of years to get back where he needed to be, and he wasn't going to lose it.

With thoughts of regaining control, he sniffed out a power that hung tantalizingly close. *Robert,* he called out mockingly. Braccus felt him so strongly he could almost tell the exact spot where he was now standing. He remembered Olie's brother well; they had shared space above the worlds before they came down and walked the surface. Other than a vague acknowledgement on his part that Olie's brother was slightly greater than those puny living things they were supposed to look after, he had barely considered him for years. But now he was so close and would come in handy as a hostage if he could just get to him. Braccus stomped his foot, creating a big hole in the ground. So close, he could feel him. He stomped his foot again, hoping to bore his way downward and grab this one soul to use as a bargaining chip to get his object back.

There was no reply to his summons, though he could sense Robert's breathing and all the simple little animals that Iam called intelligent life forms that were gathered close to him. If he could just get his hands on any one of those lesser beings it would be so wonderful, but it would really be great to have Robert. His only regret at letting his creatures roam around and kill was that he hadn't specifically told them to save one for him. What he could do with one of Iam's people if he had half a chance. Having one of them would help him gain access to that refuge far below.

It enraged him that Iam retained enough power down here to keep him away from the few people left. For all he could do, he still couldn't get past the barrier he felt hovering below the ground. This could not be! He was the better one! There had to be a way for him to get down there.

 A screech of frustration tore through the air as he saw the ground fill up with dirt in a protective manner and he was unable to create enough damage to make it stay open. As much as he tore at the soil, it kept repairing itself at the lower level. He could just go a few feet below the surface before the earth was healed and access to the underground was denied.

Iam was still fighting him and it didn't help that he saw one of his Garren standing behind the Ornose watching him with impassive interest. This was behavior he was not used to. His creations looked away from him, afraid to meet his eyes; this one was staring at him openly. It was at this point that he changed his appearance once again, going from the skinless, bloody body to the handsome, tall, dark-haired form that had always captivated everyone who saw him.

Locking eyes with the Garren, Braccus straightened his body to a full six-feet in height and brushed a crumb of dirt off his immaculate dark suit. He needed something to help bring his mind back into focus. It must certainly be Sara's distraction that was causing him to appear so much lesser than he was. This was unacceptable. Cruelty, that was what he needed. It always made him feel better to hurt something. There was nothing quite like pain and humiliation to make him aware of just how powerful he was.

Looking directly at the Garren, he raised his hand and twisted it into a fist. The motion was intended to force the being to its knees. All he got for his action was a smile before the Garren turned, walked a couple of feet, and disappeared in a puff of dust. A whiff of subdued power blew over to him on a soft breeze that had nothing to do with his influence over this land, it felt too clean and was making him sick to his stomach. Iam's influence was behind this and it set Braccus off again, spurred on by the sound of soft laughter coming from a place he could never return to again.

Spitting out words that came from an ancient language few would remember, but would have made many blush, if they understood, Braccus let his displeasure fill the air. The spit that flew from his mouth burned holes in the ground, but no trace was left due to Iam's interference. He followed up his angry tirade by wiping out every Ornose and mutated being he had around him with a swipe of his hand. Now that there were no longer any witnesses to his moment of weakness, Braccus stopped and took a deep breath, calming a bit when a sudden thought made him smile. He was smiling because he remembered something he should have thought of quite some time ago. A creature he had created as an experiment in a time before all this began. A creation he had not used for some time but still dwelled beneath the earth, the Gargylon. This long-forgotten asset of his was about to become of use once again.

Chapter Thirty-Five

Moving downward once again, Sara felt a pull on her that came from deep inside, from a place where feelings and memories dwelled. There was something else happening here, in the ever-shifting universe where life could be one way for a second or two by Iam's clock, but hundreds of years in the experience of his creations. A new element was being introduced to her current adventure, and Sara tensed up in preparation for it. A soft mist fell upon the glowing stairs. As she looked down, she noted with interest that the worlds below were visible again beneath the clouds. This time, rather than starting with the pristine beginning they had seen before, it was the ugly burned-up mess the worlds had become as they had last seen them. With each step downward, the scenes changed, the damage was being erased as time went backward before their eyes. Back further still, Sara saw order restored. People, as they were seen from a distance, were at first terrified, then cautious, then happy as they basked in the blessings given to them by the Iam and the Keepers he sent for them.

Sara, Thomas, and James were puzzled by what they were seeing; knowing in their hearts it wasn't a true reflection of what was occurring below. Things were never that easy. What they were being shown were the experiences of several centuries being rewound in front of them. But the review didn't stop with the pastoral scene they remembered from months ago. They had landed in the Land of the Keepers at the beginning of all worldly settlement and encountered Braccus long before the struggle between him and Iam had ever affected its inhabitants. Slipping way beyond that time, they saw the solid orb below change into almost nothing. With interest, they watched the surface fade away until they were looking at a vast void of silver-tinged darkness. A few stars pushed it back just enough for them to see a small wavering disk occupying the same area the world had occupied just minutes ago. It was on that disk they saw a kneeling figure, hiding far away from spying eyes. There was a darkness surrounding the figure that, if they had existed then, an ordinary soul would never have seen beyond. In fact, Sara was sure, given the power signature the form was giving off, that none of the first Keepers would have followed. At first, her feeling was that none of them would have expected anything evil to exist and would not have been looking for it, certainly not from one of their own.

Within seconds of sighting the figure, the stairway adjusted itself, winding downward in its direction. The answer to what they must do was down there, and Sara was eager to get this all finished somehow. Her feet moved faster, eyes straining to see the person far below them. To her great surprise, her feet stopped moving and she found herself looking down at Charlie, who now stood where Thomas had been just seconds before. Thomas now stood next to Rianna and James, watching her curiously while Charlie spoke. He held his hand out and the box contained in James's shirt sleeve began to glow and float. Rising just about chest level, it sent out a steady hum of sound that made the figure below look up for a moment, giving Sara just enough of a glimpse to tell her who it was.

Startled. she tried to move back, not wanting to be seen yet. Hoping the element of surprise was not lost.

"He can't see you," said Charlie, looking downward toward the evil being. "We are in a different level of time then he is. It is not you he senses, it is that." He nodded toward the floating object on James's belt loop. "We are caught in a small window of time. You have to face him where it all started. It is a short but painful journey to where it began, and to get there, you will have to have your solid bodies. That is why I came here. We have to find our way back to the living world, to find your bodies. The actual contact between you and Braccus must be in the flesh in order for this to work. You will have to return the object to him and force him to take it back."

"How are we ever going to get back to our bodies?" Sara stared at the man in disbelief, not comprehending how this feat would even be possible. When they died, they had certainly not carried any knowledge of the shells they left behind. "I didn't realize he was serious." James stared in amazement at first Sara, Charlie and then Rianna. His expression was guarded when he met Sara's eyes. He had been listening to a lot more than he let on. She should have been angry, but what purpose would that serve? She had hidden far too much from him and it had cost him dearly.

"Your father told you it was possible, didn't he?" Charlie addressed Sara, who simply nodded and tried to convey her regret to James, who wasn't sharing his thoughts at the moment.

"He said this wasn't final, but I didn't know what he meant. I have no idea how to get back. How do we reverse death? I know I don't have the power to do that. Do you?" Sara looked expectantly at Charlie, who obviously knew a little bit about everything, both here and in the living world. He was able to move between the two so maybe he was the one to guide them and return their souls to their corpses.

"No, Sara, I can't do that. There is someone down there who can though, and if I can get you close enough to the barrier between the dimensions, maybe your fellow Keepers can pull you back through."

Rianna nodded at Sara when she looked at her guardian for reassurance that this man spoke the truth. Giving her adopted daughter the confirmation she sought, her eyes showed both joy and sorrow. "You all must go back, and this is the way to get there." Her hand gestured toward the stairs that wound downward to a point they could not see.

"What happened to our bodies?" Thomas squeezed Sara's hand. Visions of them starting their lives over together, alive and happy surrounded by their friends, passed from his mind to hers and James's, who simply nodded slightly, still not meeting Sara's eyes. She could tell by the look on James's face that he was thinking of something while not quite sure how to react to her keeping secrets. He didn't look angry, but the outcome would all depend on what conclusion he came to.

"Your bodies are still down there," Charlie informed them. "Olie told me this before I came here. I made contact with him and Ferd; they came to me to tell me where they were. The caves hide many things and your lifeless forms lie far below the surface in the land of Relgar. No one knows this but them. It was safer to do it that way. Iam made sure to transport them to a safe place after you died. They were the only two spirits to know. It was at this point that I knew it was my job to come and guide you back to them. Once we get you to the entrance, Alice will have to bring you through, and the newest Keeper, the giver of life, will have to call your spirits back to your corpses."

"Are we the only ones that can be brought back from death?" James spoke after a minute of stunned silence, in which they all considered the miraculous news.

"Do you mean: can Diandra be brought back to life?" Charlie's pink eyes focused on James, knowing the intention behind his enquiry. "I don't know." As soon as the answer was given, James's hopeful expression disappeared only to reappear seconds later by what Charlie said next. "It is possible. After all, she is a gifted woman, and she was brought here to help you. She is your soul mate and I don't believe Iam would let that connection die." He paused before adding, "It is the best answer I can give you for now. I have not been back in the living world since she was taken, and I don't know that I can cross over again."

Sara heard the sadness in Charlie's voice. The little man realized that his time on the surface lands was at an end. She was sad for him, for all of them; it was unfortunate that all the wonderful things Iam had given to the worlds were slowly being taken away.

"Not everything." Charlie pulled her thoughts out and offered her some reassurance. "There are still Keepers and other things that most beings have never seen for you to discover. For every ending, there are many beginnings. Iam adjusts for the needs of his creations. It is what helped keep the inhabitants of the worlds alive for centuries. It's up to you to find a way to help them make it through another of Braccus's assaults, to bring him to the time when he must pay for what he has done."

When he had finished speaking, Charlie's hand rose above his head and when it came back down there was a dark, finely carved stick in his hand. When she saw it, Sara revised her assessment of what it actually was. The pointy end was visible, and she recognized it as the spear she had held in her hand in what seemed an eternity ago.

"Now you have both parts of what you need, and it is time to put them to use." Rianna's voice broke the silence. Moving to join her and Thomas, her mother figure grasped her hand gently. It wasn't as if she needed to be guided down; Sara knew she just had to follow the path she was shown but the contact with her was exactly what she wanted, for it carried the right amount of love and support.

With their goal finally clear, the group moved along the trail set before them. Downward they went toward yet another inevitable confrontation with evil.

Chapter Thirty-Six

Eric sat in a circle where all the young Keepers were gathered to talk. They had all traveled to meet with Robert below the Land of the Keepers weeks after they had managed to get the seven worlds provided for. Each world now had numerous thriving gardens full of all kinds of food, plants, and trees. All the caves also had a small sun provided by Franklin. The suns rotated to a remote area of the caves at scheduled intervals, caught in an electrical current Randall had set in place to imitate the passage of time on the surface.

So the refugees were given a form of day and night. They had no moon, but they did have the marvelous light source provided by Charlie for the world of Marrik. A larger form of this material was used as moonlight. The doors were closed against any movement, except for the Keepers, whose powers allowed them to pass through. The portals no longer allowed access from or to the surface for anyone or anything else, and Eric felt secure that the refugees were safely settled. He was listening to Robert speak, but kept getting distracted by a different sound, amid the familiar noise of his companion's voices. A low and regular shuffling movement threaded throughout the conversation, and he fine-tuned his hearing to pinpoint its location.

One by one, he effectively eliminated the sounds put out by the refugees and the Keepers, eyes moving over the group as they spoke among themselves. He watched them talk, lips moving but no sound came out. The Keepers had been congratulating Robert and Maryann on the news of their baby. The pair had made the announcement shortly after the group had come together and the expressions of joy had been long and loud. It was another sign to them that life was going on; the unexpected birth of a living Keeper's child was miraculous, having never occurred before. It gave them all hope. But as he sat there among all his smiling friends, Eric felt uneasy. Finola held his hand, settling in his mind to hear what was causing him concern. She was talking to him and he could tell from reading her lips that she was asking what was wrong.

The noises puzzled but didn't necessarily alarm him; he knew there were several animals they still hadn't found wandering around in some remote areas of the caves. He didn't even know if what he was hearing was even in the caves with him. With the doors open for their travel, he could sense things in the other worlds, and didn't even know for sure what caught his attention in the first place. All he knew was that among the distant noises he could hear, something sounded a bit off, like a rough scraping against a hard surface, and then the clattering of falling rocks followed by silence. Shrugging his shoulders when Finola heard the noises through him and failed to be alarmed, he relaxed a bit. Eric also noted with interest that the other Keepers were watching him expectantly, giving him their full attention, while still listening to each other. The bonds were growing, especially since Vincent and Marlaina had completed his group and were tuned into the attention he was paying to something besides their conversation.

"Is everything alright, Eric?" asked Robert.

"I'm not sure, I thought I heard something a minute ago," he answered honestly.

"Do you still hear it?"

"No."

Robert looked expectantly at the others. "Do any of you sense anything?" A collective shaking of heads was his answer. As a group, they were able to use their combined powers and scan the air for anything that might be unnatural. They all now knew the feeling that surrounded the shadowy dead things thanks to Alice, but nothing felt like that.

Eric could tell Robert was exercising caution, after all that had happened he took nothing for granted, not even safety. "Are you sure?" He was trying to find Olie and Ferd wherever they might be, but they were nowhere near. After several minutes of careful consideration, Eric could tell that Robert had relaxed a little, but he could feel the inner caution staying in his head. This made sense to him and he vowed to be alert and watch for any sign of that sound again.

"What's next?" Finola asked what they were all thinking. "How can we find out what's going on with Sara, James and Thomas?"

"Yes, we need to find a way to get them to as soon as possible!" Diandra's voice sounded out from her spot next to Maryann. She had become quite attached to the older woman shortly after they met, a bond forged by having the same abilities. They were gifted people among ordinary ones, surrounded by even more powerful companions. Eric and the others had learned of the Seer's connection to James and his Circle. It still amazed him that she had been beyond the barrier of death, dwelling for quite some time in the Afterworld and had still been able to return with Marlaina's help. It was something he had never considered possible and he watched her with awe. He could feel how eager she was to see James again and his heart went out to her.

Though Eric didn't know the Circle of the Moon as well as the others, through them he felt the bond they shared. He wanted to bring them back as quickly as he could for all their sakes. Especially Finola, who loved Sara like a sister; he would do anything to bring that connection back to her. It seemed even more important now that she found out about Rianna's death in a conversation with Robert and Maryann. She had told herself that the loss of that zombie-like shell her guardian had become wouldn't mean too much to her. She knew that all the love and memories they shared had departed with her soul, but when life was taken from the body altogether, she felt pain all over again. He wished he could make it all better, but he couldn't. All he could do was hold her hand and hope that being there for her was enough. Maybe Robert could settle all their minds with what he said next. He, and the other Keepers, anxiously awaited an answer that would suddenly make their next move absolutely clear, allowing them to straighten out this terrible change of fate for the worlds. When Robert

288

spoke though, it wasn't to say what they had been expecting at all.

"We do nothing, except stay here and watch out for Iam's people. When the time comes for us to act, you will know."

Maryann comforted Diandra as she cried out in surprise and tears fell down her face. She held her close while Robert continued to explain, "When it is quiet like this danger becomes greater. Don't think for one second that Braccus is finished with us. The moon circle's bodies have been carefully hidden from the enemy and they have to remain that way for now."

"Can't we go to them and have Marlaina call them back to their bodies?" Finola's voice rang out sharply, anxious to solve what she considered a simple problem.

"No, you can't, I'm sorry," Robert tried to explain without sounding cruel. "I do not even know where they are. Sara, Thomas, and James have to show you where to find them. It is safer for them to remain hidden until everything is in place. They will find a way to communicate with you. You just have to wait and watch for them. The three lost souls have to find their way to the doorway between life and death. Then it's up to you to bring them back."

Eric squeezed Finola's hand when what they were told brought nothing but disappointment. As he looked into her eyes, he knew they could and would survive and thrive down here. A small doubt remained though: he kept remembering the elusive sound. In fact, it served as a reminder to the entire group that all was not as it seemed. The conversation ended with Robert issuing instructions as to how to move between the worlds now. They were to patrol constantly and provide support to the inhabitants of each area. They quickly worked out a schedule of travel that allowed them to spend some time in each world and gather now and then in the Land of the Keepers.

All the Keepers agreed with Robert, looking to him for guidance, giving him their absolute loyalty and respect as the only remaining original Keeper. He was their leader now and they would follow his directions. It was alright when they saw things coming together in a positive light but the importance of listening to all he said was brought back to them with the next sharp reminder.

"When they come back, it will also be time for you to separate into Circles again." Each couple present grimaced at that inconvenient reminder. Eric swallowed down his panic, the connection with Finola could never be broken, but he knew leaving her would be the hardest thing he ever had to do. The looks on his friend's faces told him they felt the same. Everyone except Franklin had something significant to lose. Separation was going to be terribly difficult.

"You have to understand that their return will be the beginning of a confrontation that will require your bonds to be the strongest. For now, we take our lives one step at a time with the knowledge that more will be asked of you before this is all over." Nodding solemnly, the couples moved on to an uncertain future together

Chapter Thirty-Seven

Casting his thoughts outward, Braccus smiled, a live connection had been made. He sent a warning to the creature to keep silent, the noise it had made earlier was enough to catch his attention. The other Keepers, lesser beings that they were, would surely have noticed, especially that pale one who could control sound and hear every little thing. He didn't want the enemy to be prepared in any way for what was coming next. They thought they were safe; let them continue to think that for a little longer. All he had to do now was wait for the time to use the Gargylon to his advantage. While he was gloating over his good fortune, something else happened that pleased him tremendously; an added bonus to his growing list of victories. At first, he couldn't hear everything that was being said below; Iam's protection had provided privacy for the Keepers and their refugees. Then he had received an unintended invitation, a wonderful opportunity he just couldn't ignore.

An angry old man sitting far below was quietly listening to the Keepers and his rage was strong enough to catch Braccus's attention, drawing him in like an addict to a drug. This man was not dead, physically, but that wasn't required for Braccus to find a way inside him. It was the darkness in the man's soul that made him an open vessel for Braccus to enter. He was able to hone in on the intense anger and grief of this man, after losing every member of his family to his wonderful killing machines.

291

Anger like this was the easiest trail to follow, and this one particular man had not been able to settle down into the routine of life below with Iam's other refugees. After the initial fear and general relief to be alive had worn off, the man had pulled his grief up around him and got comfortable with his misery. It took a day or two before it occurred to him that, while some had lost a family member or two, they still had someone to count on. While he was totally alone in his own eyes; his sons, wife, and daughter had all been killed on the surface. He had not been a bad man, but somewhere along the line, once he was sure he wasn't going to die, the thoughts of all he no longer had begun to fester like a bad infection and Braccus sniffed it out like a tracking dog. This man was so overwhelmed with everything that had happened, he had come to the conclusion that Iam was no longer to be believed in.

This man's thoughts reflected his inability to grasp how he and his loved ones had been made pawns in this game for control and he no longer felt a strong tie or allegiance to his creator. In fact, the resentment he felt was growing by the second. Braccus understood this and sent out his own suggestions to further ignite the man's ire. He may not be able to gain entry to the lower levels of the world but was still very capable of exploiting the most intense emotions for his own purpose. Sending the man visions of his family members, he played his regret about being the sole survivor while his loved ones had been butchered by the enemy.

The man wasn't just weak, Iam would have been able to help him overcome that, it was much deeper than an ordinary lapse in faith. It was rage. This bitterness had seeped into the man's soul, effectively distancing him from Iam. This person had all the ingredients that made him perfect for Braccus to use as a listening device. Evil always found a way to gain access where welcomed, and Braccus felt perfectly at home in this man's head without his knowledge. With this man's ears listening for him, Braccus became calmer and calmer. Control was returning. How could he have gotten so angry he let himself forget how wonderful he was?

Iam had quite the laugh at his expense and Braccus was eagerly awaiting his chance to get even for that, and here it was. Evil was lingering in the most delightfully advantageous place, right where Robert was hiding. So now he knew Iam's secret: Sara and her two little puppies still had bodies down there. It was just a matter of time before he found out exactly where. He had the good fortune to have once again found a way into the inner circle of his enemy and was going to quietly mingle with the crowd, getting as much information as he could till he found where those bodies were. If Sara didn't make it back to her body, then she couldn't possibly make use of the thing she had stolen from him. With a low chuckle, he sent a silent message to his recently awakened servant. His other secret weapon, the Gargylon scrambled up from its hiding-place deep in the caverns. The wondrous creature had hidden further in the shadows after losing the Healing Stone to Sara, James, and Thomas years before. The Healing Stone had brought Olie out of

the deep trance he had been in after the last battle
for control of the worlds.

The Gargylon had been trusted with keeping it away
from the Keepers but had failed, being buried under
broken rocks and other debris thrown at him by
Thomas. At the time, it angered Braccus, but look
how it had worked out for him now. His creation
was conveniently located in just the right place.
Once Braccus figured out where the Keeper's
bodies were, all he had to do was order their
destruction. If they had nothing to return to, the
confrontation couldn't take place and he would be
able to give all his attention to remaking the worlds
as he would have them, both on the surface and
below.

Once he was securely in his position of power,
without the threat of Sara's interference, Braccus
would be free to gain entrance to the underground
hiding-places. There could be no survivors; no
creations of Iam's would be allowed to occupy any
part of his worlds. Braccus would clean up all the
objectionable beings, including the last of the
pathetic Keepers. He would rebuild to suit his needs
and Iam would only be able to watch helplessly
from a distance.

With an inside source at his disposal, he was ready
to act when the time came. His angry listener would
eventually provide the location of the bodies. When
he did, the Gargylon would go there and destroy
them, leaving their souls trapped in the Afterworld
forever. All in all, he had to say, it would be worth
the wait. With a satisfied nod of his head, Braccus
ordered his creations to construct another hulking

structure of dead things on the broken earth. They quickly added the bodies of the Ornose he had just killed to the pile of rotting material that would form part of his private residence. Originally, he had used all of his enemy's corpses to build the three-story, mile-wide residence but had run out of material to work with after they had hidden underground. As it was, he might have to sacrifice a few dozen more of his own creations to finish the last wing of the structure. Those creatures he could always make more of just to see it complete. It was comforting to have all that death around him, it meant more than any other luxury he could have created for himself. Though it wasn't nearly as satisfying to kill his own things as it was to kill Iam's, he would just have to make do until he could get past the fortifications Iam had set up below.

The knowledge that he had the power to bring both life and death offered him even more comfort. The remains in the structure spoke to him as he absorbed the lingering misery and fear from the air around them. These feelings hung over the surface as a reminder of all he had accomplished. The annoying feelings of love and goodness had disappeared with the souls, leaving only the last emotions felt before death. It made sense to him; these were his worlds and he wouldn't have welcomed anything less than the ugliest of feelings.

Walking up on steps made from crushed bones compressed into square blocks the color of faded grayish-blue clay, Braccus scuffed his feet across a wide porch that gleamed dully with shards of broken glass and metal from objects destroyed

295

during his creature's rampages. Opening a door composed of pieces of wood and thin strips of a leathery substance stretched thinly across the front where one might find windows in an ordinary door, he ran his fingers over the rough material. He smiled at the sickly aura around the entry; it welcomed him in with its memories of misery and suffering. Once inside, he moved through the large entrance hall painted a dull red. The smell that accompanied the color was also pleasing to him as it was naturally, blood, his favorite scent. With a satisfied sigh, he surveyed the walls lined with broken pieces of devices created by Iam's people. Slashed tires, broken dishes, a water pump handle and pages torn from books were plastered on the walls. Trophies of all he had managed to destroy were displayed as a reminder of his success.

A baby doll with a cracked face and limp body with the stuffing hanging out, dangled from the high ceiling, glowing red, providing a dull light source for him to enjoy his new home. Opening a door at the end of the long garbage strewn hallway, Braccus moved into his office, circling behind a desk made of bones and boulders, and settling in a chair of broken sticks and more leathery material. He got comfortable, letting himself enjoy the thought that it was only a matter of time until all he hoped for would happen. He couldn't possibly have enough suffering to suit his tastes, and there was so much more to come. He might even let some of the good souls live on for a while, just to relish the hopelessness of their situation. What fun this could be!

Chapter Thirty-Eight

With each step downward, Sara felt a tingling from somewhere deep in her soul. The very idea she could once again be in her body, be able to feel her soul slip back into that familiar comfortable shell, was just too wonderful, especially since she had been convinced it would never happen.

Instinctively, she reached for James and Thomas's hands as they walked side by side on the steps. She knew they felt the same; the excitement ran through them like electricity. She also knew James was thinking not only of himself, but of the possibility of seeing Diandra again. He was sure she was back down there in her body somewhere. He knew from speaking to her what seemed like ages ago, that she had not known how she died, which sounded familiar to him.

The way Diandra had described it, one minute she was alive and the next, she found herself being escorted to meet him. Sara smiled as she heard his thoughts because it reminded her of their own painless passing and if their bodies were down there, then it must mean hers was too. Together they were overjoyed at the possibility of this very special woman being down there and very much alive. There was so much to look forward to; the group couldn't reach the end of these stairs fast enough. With hope restored, she was eager to face Braccus again, power was bubbling underneath her skin, yearning to come to the surface and burst free. The time to use her increased power was near, she could sense it, and yet, there didn't seem to be any foreseeable end to these steps. When Sara looked down, the worlds were no longer visible, all she could see were more stairs winding downward into a milky sky. She wondered when their journey would take them back to everything she held dear.

"Be patient," Rianna's voice broke into her thoughts, and she suddenly felt horrible in the midst of all the hope she held for the future, because she knew it would be a future without Rianna.

Without knowing how it happened, she felt herself holding tightly to her guardian's hand.

"I can't leave this place, I know that," Rianna acknowledged. "I'm okay with that. I won't be alone; the others will be back soon. We will reclaim this place. Your victory down there will help us do that. Live for me, your parents, and all those that sacrificed themselves to get you as far as they have. We will always be there for you." A soft hand touched, first her head, and then the empty place in the center of her chest where her heart had once beat so strongly.

The truth of what she was saying made Sara smile and nod, her resolve to move on stronger than ever. She found her hands in Thomas's and James's again, with Rianna standing in front of her next to Charlie, just as she had been an instant before. As the companions began to walk once again, Charlie glanced back at her.

"It's about time you made your presence known down there." He nodded vaguely in the direction of Iam's worlds. "They have to know what is expected of them too."

"How do we do that?" Thomas wanted to know.

298

Sara spoke to him next, "I'm not allowed to move back through to the living worlds. I tried a few times and was pulled back here very quickly. I got the message that Iam wanted me to stay here. Have things changed? Can I go back now that we got what we came for?" She anxiously awaited an answer, ready to try to contact Alice, even though she had closed off the connection they shared what seemed like ages ago.

"No, your gifts are for other things. Your connection to Shalsar and Braccus must be kept closed. If you try to get through the barrier, they will interfere. It is our intention to keep your return secret. This is something for you to do Thomas. Iam has broken the connection you share with Braccus. I have seen so much, and I know when evil is present. You fought so hard against the darkness that it has been removed from you. Iam did that for you,"

It was too good to be true. Thomas tentatively searched through his own mind, each barrier he had put up was let down slowly. Nerves on edge, he prepared to throw up his protective walls if any sign of Braccus even remotely became evident. To his surprise, he felt absolutely nothing. The presence he had feared would use his own lack of control against him was gone.

Charlie waited until he saw Thomas's relief. Sara watched them both as they shared their feelings with her, without intending to. It couldn't be helped at this point. She wasn't even sure if she could stop herself from eavesdropping. It was coming far too naturally to her even when she wasn't invited in. This little exchange was meant for Thomas only. He thought he was keeping her out to protect her from what he was sure was Braccus. He was terrified of involving her in this, throwing up a few evasive measures to keep her safe, and Charlie was helping him.

Afraid that the evil parasites that waited to invade her mind would combine themselves with the bad part of him, he did the one thing she never thought he would do again: separated himself from her. As for the little man Charlie, he was perceptive, but she didn't think he realized how far into his mind she had gone. It had taken a few minutes, but she had managed to see a lot of marvelous things through his eyes. He had seen and done so much, watching the passage of time, and fighting the darkness in ways that were far more violent than his innocent appearance might have suggested.

She stood still, no expression on her face, listening despite the tangled strings of memories that floated in her way. She rapidly followed twisted paths that led nowhere. Sweeping past them without appearing to, she found what she was looking for, discovering everything she wanted to know. She believed in his power, but also believed in what was happening inside her. What she had been waiting for was starting to materialize. She knew deep down inside that this is what she was destined to do.

Still, she had limits placed on her, but they would become fewer and harder to find the closer she got to the exit. It was all part of what had been planned in the beginning. When they were able to find a way through to the living world and make it back to their bodies, the souls that returned would be so different, even their friends might not recognize the three of them. But for the time being, she knew that getting out of here was not possible for her without help. She needed to back off and listen to what Charlie was saying, so she traveled out of his thoughts and listened to him speak as if she did not already know what he would say.

"You cannot pass through without help, but you can get the Keepers' attention in another way. You can affect things in the world, Thomas. Your gift will allow you to move objects. Use your mind to get a vision of the worlds and use your gift to send them a message. I will be able to guide you part of the way; you will have to find the rest on your own. You need to bring her to them." Charlie continued speaking even though he was no longer looking at them. His back was turned, and he was walking away. "I need you to concentrate on the flesh you used to occupy. All three of you need to join Thomas and help him."

"How am I supposed to know what to focus on? I don't know where we are down there. How can I take them to us when I don't have the slightest clue where we are?"

"You don't have to know." Purple hair continued to float freely above Charlie's retreating figure. He and Rianna were moving so fast now the Moon Circle members had to pick up their pace to keep them in sight.

"All you have to do is remember yourselves as you were before you died, and your energy will transmit to the Keepers as soon as they realize you are present. As soon as the newest Keeper becomes aware of you, and trust me, she will; you will be found."

"How will she find us exactly?" James wanted to know.

"As you get closer to the entrance, your souls will automatically seek out their former homes, and it is your souls that will call to her."

His statement was continued by Rianna, who walked further down the stairs, "Marlaina will lead the other Keepers to you. It won't be long before she feels you and asks for Alice's help to travel around in the in-between place located close to the exit."

"Her name is Marlaina." Sara played the name over in her head and decided she liked it. She wished she could put a face to the name but, since she had never met her and couldn't get through to the living worlds, it just wasn't happening. Her feet stopped moving just seconds before her guides did. She knew this was going to happen and just what Charlie was going to say but still managed to look puzzled when the ancient being spoke his last words to them.

"This is where we part ways. I can't get you any closer to the exit. I am no longer allowed. My time down there is at an end. You will have to proceed on your own from here."

Rianna nodded as Charlie said his goodbyes, wishing each Keeper a safe journey back to life and success in the mission, but she appeared too choked up to speak. Tears were streaming down her face, followed by a sad smile for the group as both she and Charlie faded out of sight where they stood.

The intense feelings of love and loss lingered in the air around the group for just a second and then it was gone.

The trio stood in stunned silence for a moment, processing yet another significant loss before Sara turned to Thomas and James. She was so tired, yet there was no rest to be had, not even in death and, based on all they had seen, that condition wouldn't last much longer. The time she had shared with her parents, in parody of a life she had never lived, stayed in her mind. She stored them in a special place for later. Heartbreaking as it was, she left them where they were, they couldn't help her now. Her thoughts then moved back to a time when they still moved through the solid, physical atmosphere, fighting the enemy with her fellow Keepers.

Thomas and James focused in on it all, sharing memories of their own, seeing themselves as they had been, envisioning the skin-clad forms they needed to find.

Wishing she could do this herself, Sara still had the satisfaction of being with Thomas as he used his power to get them back down where they could do the most good. She smiled when, far below, she could sense things shifting in the caverns and best of all, the feeling of living beings close-by to witness it. She just hoped they were the right witnesses, those who would know what to do and where to go to help them.

Chapter Thirty-Nine

Sitting down after a long day of traveling, Alice rested her head on Randall's shoulder and closed her eyes. It was good to be at home, in the large central room of a complex they all shared when they were in the Land of the Keepers. She had learned so much about Iam's creations and she was in awe of all the wonderful life forms occupying the worlds. As a Keeper, she was humbled to find all the good beings that lived and depended on her and the others. With each passing day, her affection and commitment to keeping them safe grew. The caverns were shaping up very nicely due to the combined efforts of the Circle members. They had each used their gifts to improve the lives of their charges, in an organized and civilized manner. Society had been reformed with rules of conduct and tasks assigned to everyone based on their talents or abilities.

While the Keepers were relied upon to provide for the refugees, they were not truly part of the crowd. Seers had been chosen as leaders, acting as representatives for the people with the Keepers. It made sense they had these positions because they had gifts too, not as great as the Keepers, but gifts that made them different from the others. These gifts made them perfect spokespersons; they were able to identify with the Keeper's visions, keeping up quite easily with their ever-changing abilities. While all the current Keepers had been raised as humans, they were changing in so many ways, their powers having matured due to the loss of the

Originals. Though still identifying with the human forms they grew up among, they became a little bit more distanced from them each day. It was all part of their evolving role in caring for Iam's non-gifted people.

The underground areas were now fully functional, with food crops and supplies made with wood from trees Finola grew. Clothing was made from the wool of a few rescued sheep who, strangely enough, Vincent had been tending carefully. The Keeper who could kill with a touch was very good at nurturing living things and appeared to be enjoying every minute of it. Alice now knew and liked him and was happy to see him doing something he enjoyed. Not killing everything he touched was a wonderful change for Vincent and Alice noticed he was becoming quite the touchy-feely kind of guy. The young man was constantly patting people's arms as he passed, shaking the hand of everyone that helped him, even hugging Maryann, Finola, and herself a few times for just being his friends. He had been unable to touch anyone before, so he was making up for lost time by being as close to normal as he would ever get. Of course, most of his attention was centered on Marlaina. He kissed her so often she was surprised they didn't have permanently chapped lips. Oh well, he deserved to be happy.

Franklin was also around Vincent quite a bit, both young men talked a lot, checking in often to make sure each was alright. The bond those two had developed while traveling together was a strong one, and she could tell Vincent felt bad for Franklin, who, other than his brotherly relationship with the Keepers, was still without his true soul mate. She didn't know if it was possible for him to date an ordinary human, but after all this was straightened out, she would really like to see him happy with someone.

"That's what happens when you have too much time to think. You get a little silly," Randall teased her.

"I know," she whispered back, "It's just that sometimes I wish this was all different."

"It's not, though." She was comforted by the vibration of his voice as her head rested near his throat. "We are not normal at all, we were never meant to be; we couldn't help them if we were." Nodding in agreement Alice focused only on the warmth of his shoulder, trying not to listen too closely to the mocking voices from the Afterworld telling her they would soon find a way in to the living world and that she was the first one they would seek out. When she heard the words 'seek out' she knew it meant hurt her in every way imaginable before killing her and taking over her dead body. Wincing slightly, she backed out of the in-between place and focused solely on Randall. She had kept in touch with the Afterworld from time to time hoping the shadowy forces there would give her some information. So far, all she had been able to force from them was that there was an intense struggle taking place on that side too, and that they hated her almost as much as they hated the ugly things moving around their personal areas.

307

Latching onto the reference to three light-filled intruders wandering around, Alice had pushed for more answers. This had to be Sara, James, and Thomas. Excited by this news, she had pulled out all the stops, almost completely losing herself in the efforts she was putting forth to get more information. Pushing herself to the point where her nose bled, and she got very dizzy. Randall had forced her to stop digging any further, as she had just barely recovered from overextending herself weeks before. The inky, foul creatures she was hearing weren't helping anymore anyway; she had managed to learn all they knew about her friends, that they had gotten something they wanted and moved beyond their area.

 This was good, but she really wished they could tell her where the Moon Circle had gone. All the pressure she had exerted on the ugliness had made them shrink back from her and answer all she asked, but they could not answer what they didn't know. The Keepers had moved on and she was left wondering where. Alice backed off enough to make those things feel comfortable, throwing out empty threats which she soon tired of. She knew she was stronger than them but listening to all the garbage they spewed out did take its toll on her after a while. She had initially refused the assistance of the combined group of Keepers in helping her recover from her exhausted state, believing a lot of sleep would help, but now she kinda wished she'd let them in. It was still taking longer to recover, and she knew she needed to be stronger than she currently was and so, she finally allowed the warmth from Randall's skin to seep into her own and she felt the others join him. Strength surged through her, pushing back all the bad things, and making her light shine even brighter than before. She felt great! The voices of the dead things screamed loudly in the background where she had left them, and she was snuggling up to her boyfriend. It couldn't get any better.

"The others will be coming here soon," Randall 's voice hummed against her ear again. "I think we have all earned a day of rest. Eric suggested we gather at the Crystal ponds and enjoy each other's company," Raising her head from his chest, she smiled at him. Besides Robert, they were the only other Keepers currently in the Land of the Keepers. They had only just returned from their travels in the land of Relgar and Farlan where all was going well for the refugees.

Beings of all kinds were beginning to trade and conduct business on a primitive level. Labor was performed in return for items made by those skilled in making baked goods and crafting items like beds and other furniture. There was no form of currency yet and so each party agreed on a reasonable exchange, one thing given for another based on their needs and wants.

It was working well because no one here really owned anything that was being used anyway; it was easy to share because no one was going without. All necessities were made from salvaged items from the surface and Finola had promised to make a small amount of wood available later for building material to help all the refugees have comfortable living areas. Most of the houses were carved into the stone around them, a technique taught to the various worlds by the Marrikans who had perfected it, bringing a wonderful light source with them that could easily be moved to where it was needed. The bluish light could be touched and carried from one place to another without burning hands and could grow according to the area it was situated. It didn't give off the much-needed heat and intense light of Franklin's mini-suns, but it was helpful for lighting the houses.

Quite some time ago, the refugees had begun to use a few special underground doorways opened by Finola. They mingled freely among the worlds, developing friendships and business relationships. It was working well for all, but Alice knew that Iam's beings needed to get back to a more realistic way of life. There was no telling how long these caves would be called home. Robert couldn't even tell them when this would all change.

More jobs were being created and everyone was expected to contribute in their own way. As Robert explained it, everything was too easy. There would be no value in anything received for free, and Iam never intended his people to sit back and take without giving something in return. So common wisdom had them devise a form of coin made from metal mined in the caves. Each coin would vary in size and value to be circulated among the worlds' soon. Whatever could not be traded for would be purchased honestly so that all could benefit regardless of what they were capable of doing, or the amount of coin they possessed.

"Evil gains ground when things are not earned honestly," Robert had told them, and plans were made to begin using the money after all housing was finished and supplies divided equally. It was a fair and fresh start for all the refugees; what each living being did after that time would be a matter of choice. Success or failure from then on would depend on the effort extended for it. Robert had explained that he was acting on instructions he had been given when the worlds had first been created. It had worked well the first time around and Iam was sure it would again.

Alice held Randall's hand as they sat waiting for the others to arrive. Weeks had passed many times over, and with each day she watched life become more routine down below the earth. With the passage of time, she felt more guilt over the things she couldn't remember about her long-departed friends. Accepting things as they were was a necessity, but she ached to set things right for both her friends and those she was charged with protecting.

"Stop doing that, it's not going to help." Randall smiled as he said this, offering his hand to help her up. "Let's go meet the others." She felt her friends approaching and she was excited to see them again, even though they hadn't been gone that long. They had all been through so much that the connection they shared brought comfort and stability to balance out their constant state of watchful dread.

Randall's beautiful smile was infectious, and her lips turn upward in response. She was drawn toward him, wishing only to give him a kiss before they joined their friends. A shifting in the air made her pause just inches from his face and both their heads turned in the direction of a disturbance that could only be felt by someone who had enough power to sense the slightest change in the atmosphere. Rocks of different sizes were scattered on the cave floor to their left and she was sure they had not been there when they first sat down.

"Where did those come from?" Randall put her thoughts into words. Experience had taught them any slight difference in their surroundings could be followed by a sudden enemy attack. Alice's senses flared up, restlessly searching every dark area for any sign of the filthy black presence only she could see. With her strength restored, she should have been able to see them and get rid of them easily but, to her surprise, there was nothing remotely like them anywhere in the whole cave system. She sent her thoughts outward, past the barriers, and was pleased to find the doorways to the surface still sealed and the barrier between them and the Afterworld secure too.

She felt nothing evil in the area, neither did Randall, but something was here. Turning her head to the

312

spot that had caught their attention just minutes before, Alice was startled to find the stones now piled neatly to form a skinny tower that stayed upright despite the uneven stack of pebbles that formed it. Heart pounding with excitement, her mind sought the source of this disturbance in the atmosphere but couldn't sense a thing. Whatever had made the stones move, was no longer in the area.

While she stood still, exchanging puzzled looks with Randall, trying to figure out what had just happened, her thoughts were interrupted by excited messages from many places at once. Finola entered her head, speaking so fast, she had to ask her to slow down and repeat what she said.

A bunch of berries just flew off a bush and hit Eric! Alice heard amazement and surprise but there was no fear. *Do you know what it was? We can't sense a thing here and believe me, we are really looking.* Franklin spoke to her next. *Pieces of furniture just moved themselves from one side of the room to the other. I almost got knocked over by a large dresser. It's true; Marlaina and I were sitting in here with him. We all had to get off the benches we were on because they were sliding and tipping sideways.* Vincent's piped up, he and Marlaina had been traveling with Franklin for quite some time. The bond Franklin had shared with Vincent seemed to have been inherited by Marlaina, who was an extension of him.

There is no evil here, Alice answered them, *And I can't find any that would have been able to make it through to you. I don't understand. It's like something is reaching out but I can't get a grasp on the power signature. When I look for it, it's gone too quickly.* She hoped she was correct in her assumption that whatever was doing this was good. All the bad things were accounted for, throwing insults at her freely from the safety of their distant location.

It's them! Marlaina broke in excitedly. The way she said this made them understand that she was talking about the three important souls they had been missing. *That stuff was moved by a soul more powerful than any I ever felt before.* The new Keeper was so anxious to get her point across she was practically breathless in her head. *It came from the Afterworld and I think I can call it back, but I usually have a body to bring it back to. If that soul can make contact again, just for a little while longer, maybe I can bring them back. I've never done this before, but if we can get them to the entryway between life and death, maybe they will find their own bodies. Alice, you can look around in there, can you find out where they are?*

I'm not sure, Alice admitted to her. *Sara made a point to block me out of her activities. I know she wanted to protect me, but it also prevents me from helping them.* She thought for a minute before sending another message to Marlaina. *Maybe if I concentrate on Thomas or James, I can get through. You bring them toward you and I will be able to speak to them.*

While part of her rejoiced at the prospect of seeing her friends return, another part faced a sobering reality. Contact had been made. If Marlaina was

314

right and she did manage to latch on to whichever soul that had reached out, that meant it was time. Something she had been expecting with a certainty would soon happen. This special fantasy life she had been living with Randall would have to come to an end. She would have to gather with her own Circle and watch Randall return to his. As close as they were, this was going to hurt badly, like having a limb ripped from her body, but she couldn't avoid it.

It won't be forever, Randall whispered in her head. *I know* she answered softly *It'll just feel like it.*

They moved toward Robert's house for the meeting that would happen shortly.

Chapter Forty

Thomas was concentrating so hard, he was sweating. He knew it wasn't real, but his dead form was still feeling the strain of his efforts. He didn't know why he thought it would require less effort to get the attention of the Keepers on the other side. He had been working at this for quite some time as both James and Sara watched with thoughtful expressions. They didn't look as stressed as he was sure he did. He got the impression that, unlike him, they expected this to take a while and were happy to wait for the inevitable result of his hard work. One of the things he had come to learn about getting things done for Iam was that just because you were capable of doing it, didn't mean that it would be easy.

Since time had no meaning here, he couldn't be sure how long he had been working at this, but Thomas knew the moment he broke through the barrier. It was just like when he died and arrived here in the blink of an eye, alive then suddenly not. Only difference was, he hadn't fully passed back into the living worlds, he was still dead.

He felt a tugging sensation deep inside, as if his soul was split; part of him was here, the other part raced through the worlds in a hazy confused way. It was such a strange feeling. He couldn't see much, but he could make out what he thought were living forms as he zipped around in unfamiliar dark places. Shadowy and unformed, he slipped past blurry black walls that occasionally gave way to soft grey patches of light. Not having the slightest idea which of the worlds he was passing through, as there wasn't enough of anything visible for him to identify, he continued in this aimless fashion for what seemed an eternity.

Thomas was new at this, but he knew his time here was short and that he needed to make an impression while he could. Question was: how was he supposed to know the Keepers from ordinary people? When he was alive, it would have been quite easy, but he was weaker and not so sure what was possible.

There were too many variables here and he didn't need to waste his energy on the wrong beings. It would only scare them, and they wouldn't know what to do anyway. The Keepers would be looking for something more to happen. If he successfully made contact with his friends, they would be guided back to their bodies. These pale imitations of themselves would be left behind and their experiences would be real again. James would be with Diandra, and he with Sara - always with Sara. Together they could start to set things right down there. As good as their experiences had been together here; he wanted life and purpose, and he wanted it with his friends.

After passing many wavering forms, his attention was drawn to a few distinctly shiny human shapes. The colors surrounding them were bright, beautiful and oh so familiar; much like the supernatural strings that bound the Keepers together. While they were alive, they had used these strings to find each other and he was happy to discover that he still had the ability to see them. He was close to those he needed to contact; now it was time to find out if he truly was able to do what Charlie had sounded so convinced he could. Taking a deep breath, he concentrated his energy on moving something solid. Sweeping his eyes from side to side, he saw a few loose objects that, after intense concentration, he was able to see as more than blurry blobs, they looked like stones. Finally, something he could work on!

It seemed to take forever, but with a great deal of effort he was able to throw some of his essence into the solid matter, first scooting the stones across the floor, and eventually stacking them in an organized pattern. Thomas would have done more, but before he could, his spirit shot around again like a firecracker in a small room. Thankfully, his wild flight through this strange place was stopped when he spotted several other shiny blobs. Zooming in closer to the forms, he put everything he had into moving all things close to what he now knew to be Keepers. Thick, wide shapes slid and toppled, and he was satisfied that an impression had been made on those he needed to contact. But before he could see the result of his labors, he found himself fully present in the Afterworld again.

The two halves of his soul snapped back together and, looking down at his hand, he found Sara's fingers entwined in his own. *Keep trying,* she said softly. *You will get us back where we need to be.* As she said this, he knew she was telling him what was meant to happen. He felt James's complete conviction in this also and so he tried once again.

To his great surprise, it was easier to move back into the living worlds this time.

After a minute or two, by his estimation, he was able to zig-zag through narrow openings until something caught his attention, pulling him up short like a puppy who had reached the end of its leash. His soul latched onto a maroon colored string hanging just ahead of him. As he burst back in, it was easily visible against that messy mixture of grey and black blobs dominating this strange area. Thomas's wispy hand slapped at the string in a clumsy attempt to catch it, but without form, all he could accomplish was to make it sway around in the wind. Try as he might, he could still not manipulate the connecting material like he had the other solid objects. A grunt of frustration broke through his lips as he made one more pass at the magical object. As he did, a voice sounded loudly in his head.

Who are you? Soft, feminine, and totally unfamiliar, the voice called to him from the living world. He had someone's attention; a powerful someone. Momentarily, he was distracted by the unfamiliarity of her essence, but the connection she had with the others was undeniable. He felt them through her, she had an intimate knowledge of them, and that could only be because she was a Keeper too. A scan of the confusing nearby blobs revealed only that there were no bodies around him, not even a Keeper. She was using the private path of communication shared by the Keepers and he knew this was the one Charlie had spoken of.

Trying to stay calm, he spoke to the voice, her name tumbling from his lips when she made herself her

320

known to him. *Marlaina, my name is Thomas. My companions and I would like to find our way back home.*

He caught the impression of a smile as he heard the words he had hoped for. *Well, hello, Thomas, I can guide you back. I can't feel you strongly, can you move closer to the entrance, so I can bring you in?* After that message was relayed, the conversation ended, the string faded from sight quickly and he was sucked back through into the dead place. He came back to himself, finding Sara and James close at his side with bright smiles on their faces. They couldn't do what he did, due to the limitations placed on them, but they knew what he had accomplished. Looking downward, he saw a bright green blob flare up and twinkle merrily like a beacon. It called to them, welcoming them toward it. With the thought of returning to their bodies first and foremost in his mind, Thomas pulled his friends downward, tumbling toward freedom and the chance to live again.

The End

www.ingramcontent.com/pod-product-compliance
Lightning Source LLC
Chambersburg PA
CBHW051408170626
46809CB00006B/2064